WHITE CLIFFS OF
DOVER...

ALSO, BY THE AUTHOR...

BLESS ME FATHER... For I have sinned

ONE SQUARE MILE OF MEMORIES

WHEN THE HEATHER IS KNEE HIGH

THE SKY IS NOT THE LIMIT

WE ARE NOT LETTING GO...EVER!

A THANK YOU NOTE TO GOD

THE WHITE CLIFFS OF DOVER...
A story of Irish Immigrants

WHITE CLIFFS OF
DOVER...

A story of Irish immigrants

James E. Woolam

authorHOUSE®

AuthorHouse™
1663 Liberty Drive
Bloomington, IN 47403
www.authorhouse.com
Phone: 1 (800) 839-8640

This is a work of fiction. All of the characters, names, incidents,
organizations, and dialogue in this novel are either the products
of the author's imagination or are used fictitiously.

Published by AuthorHouse 10/25/2019

ISBN: 978-1-7283-3075-4 (sc)
ISBN: 978-1-7283-3076-1 (hc)
ISBN: 978-1-7283-3074-7 (e)

Print information available on the last page.

Art By: Joan Woolam

This book is printed on acid-free paper.

DEDICATION PAGE

To Diane Cleary Woll, for her inspiration, and
support to continue the story of Delanie.

A special thank you to our Niece

THE WHITE CLIFFS OF DOVER... The story of Irish Immigrants

THE SETTING-Ireland, England, Dover (and the
world-famous White Cliffs of Dover)
The English Channel, The Normandy Coast of France, Europe during
World War II

THE CENTRAL LOCATION-Folkestone,
an English seaside community
and the White Cliffs of Dover

THE PRINCIPAL CHARACTERS-Michael Matthew
Magee and his wife, Catherine Colleen
Kelly, known to everyone simply as CC

THE STORY-The lives of a young couple and their
journey through a long marriage and life.
A life filled with success and failure, highs
and lows, great adventures and
mundane daily life. Disappointments and
wonderful surprises. In other words
The Circle of Life that we all experience.

THE TIME FRAME-The story begins in Ireland in
the 1840's, through the Great Depression,
World War II, and into the early part of the 21st Century.

CONTENTS

PART ONE

The Great Potato Famine In Ireland 1

PART TWO

The Growing Up Years And Their Marriage World War II 13

PART THREE

The Beginning Of Their Family And His Ship Building Career 34

PART FOUR

His Election To Parliament 157

PART FIVE

Michael And The "The Chunnel" Project 213

PART SIX

The Autumn Of Their Years 218

Epilogue 229

PART ONE

THE GREAT POTATO
FAMINE IN IRELAND

Michael was on a ten day leave from his duties while serving in the Battle of the Atlantic. His ship was in dry dock for repairs that would take approximately 60 days. They had been at sea for an entire year. So, this short break was a welcome gift from the drudgery of war. When he entered the Royal Navy in April 1940 the plan was that they would marry during his first leave. The timing could not have been better. CC wanted to be married on her birthday-November 19. War, and all the hell and horrific events that it brought, was not about to deliver a dark cloud on this very special day.

The wedding, and a long life together that would span many decades was about to begin. A life filled with success, failure, children, a great career, and at times some real heartache. But in the end a grateful, and purposeful lives with fond memories. A marriage and lives, well and fully lived. They truly were soulmates.

So, we look back to the beginning... Where the story begins...

The wedding day. November 19, 1941. Michael Matthew Magee and Catherine Colleen Kelly grew up together in the Irish neighborhood of Folkestone known as Little Dublin. They were both twenty-one years old. As kids they attended Stella Maris Roman Catholic Elementary School in the Parish of Our Lady, Help of Christians. They fell in love

1

in high school and now they were at the altar of the Parish Church that has been at the center of their life since being baptized as babies. The Mass and marriage ceremony were being performed by their good friend Father Francis O'Rourke. The O'Rourke family lived in Little Dublin as well and were good friends.

Father Francis, better known as Franny, was a few years older and recently ordained. When he was growing up, he was very much a part of the games and mischief that boys will do. But there was never any question where his future would take him. From his days as an altar boy it was clear that one day, he would become a Roman Catholic priest. Never any doubt.

Following the ceremony, a reception was held in the Parish Hall. A combination of lively Irish and English music provided the background for a wonderful evening. Young girls dancing the Irish jig. The Irish tenors of the church choir singing all the favorites such as When Irish Eyes are Smiling. The plan was to spend the night at CC's home and then a short honeymoon in London.

Up early they had a hearty breakfast prepared by CC's mother, and then the entire family was escorted to the train station. The 9:04 am Silver Liner pulled into the Folkestone Station right on time. They entered their compartment in the first-class section compliments of family members. The two-hour trip to the Charing Cross station would give Michael the chance to reflect not only the events of the past 24 hours, but on his family and how this Irish family from County Cork ever ended up in Folkestone, England on the English Channel.

CC was excited and busy reading the many cards that they received from their friends and neighbors. Both of them were well liked and respected in their community. Michael glanced over at her and smiled. It was obvious that she was engrossed and lost in her thoughts. He noticed a tear on her cheek. He squeezed her hand, settled back in his seat, closed his eyes, and listened to the rhythm of the train on the tracks and reflected on his ancestors. He heard the story many times from his parents and grandparents. They would go into great detail how they found their way to this beautiful seaside community tucked below the world-famous White Cliffs of Dover and the beaches of the English Channel.

Michael believed there was an order to the universe. It was not simply a big blue ball spinning aimlessly through space. Life unfolds as part of God's plan. As his thoughts came together, he could see clearly, two major events involving England and Ireland came together in the 1840's. The Irish Potato Famine and the building of the London, Chatham, and Dover Railway. The English and the Irish-two extremely unlikely partners.

The Irish Potato Famine was a period of mass starvation, disease, and emigration from the mid 1840's and lasted into the 1850's. It was given this title due to the fact approximately one-third of the population depended on this cheap crop for numerous reasons. In the Irish language it is referred to as Gorta Mor (the Great Hunger) or Drochshaol (the Bad Life.)

During the famine one million people died and another million emigrated from Ireland to places all over the world. A decrease in population of twenty-five percent. This was all attributed to a disease to the potato crop. The common use of the word "famine" is not exactly right. Indeed, the potato crop did fail; but Ireland was still producing and exporting more than enough grain to feed the country. The famine combined with a number of other factors such as land acquisitions, absentee landlords, and penal laws is considered by many as a form of genocide,

The famine is, without question, the most dramatic event in the history of this great country. It had a major and permanent impact on culture, political, and demographics of the island nation... The relationship between Ireland and Great Britain became more strained-if that was possible. Many believed that this period in history led to the fight for independence from the United KIngdom.

People had to make decisions to save their family. Emigration seemed to be the answer. Once that decision was made the question was where to go. A key factor in making the decision was of course money. Finances always factored into any decision for these people of extremely modest income. Word of building the London, Chatham, and Dover Railway reached the shores of Ireland.

An exodus across the Irish Sea to Wales and Great Britain was a much greater possibility than trying to cross the Atlantic Ocean halfway around the world to Canada and America. The Irish people loved their country and did not want leave; but survival was on everyone's mind. There was reason other than money that made the possibility of crossing the Atlantic Ocean a risky venture. Death. Malnutrition and disease were a real possibility. Mortality rates of thirty percent were common aboard the so-called "coffin ships."

The belief was that if they could make it to the east coast of England the European Continent was but a twenty-six-mile ferry ride to the French town of Calais. All of Europe would then be in their reach. They were indeed strong people that had vision. They were willing to take any risk if it meant the possibility of a better life for the future generations of their families.

The Industrial Revolution was expanding from Great Britain to Continental Europe. Technology was purchased from British engineers and entrepreneurs were moving to the Continent to search for new opportunities. It only followed that as the engineers and entrepreneurs created new products and methods, they were going to need workers. Lots of workers. Workers that could hone their skills and good paying jobs in a number of industries. The Ruhr Valley was referred to as a "Miniature England" because of its similarities to the Industrial sections of England.

Belgium was the first country on the continent to move into the Industrial Revolution. Beginning in the 1830's numerous ventures comprising blast furnaces and rolling mills were built in the coal mining regions around Liege and Charleroi. The driving force behind this movement was an ambitious and visionary Englishman by the name of John Cockerill. His factories integrated all stages of production from engineering to the supply of raw materials. Needless to say these operations needed workers. Workers with a variety of skills that were willing to take part of this great experiment.

Clearly, relocating to the English Channel region seemed to be a wise decision. Not only opportunities with the building of the London to Dover Railway but the Industrial Revolution occurring on the other side of the English Channel. The Industrial Revolution played a major role in the area of politics. The two major forces were the owners and the workers. The birth of trade unions and the Socialist Party. Down through history change and development provided opportunities for the masses, but tension and stress were sure to follow. Having said that, progress may present pain, but we must remember nothing of value comes easy. No one understood that better than the pathfinders of their ancestors from Ireland.

Michael and CC's ancestors were faced with this difficult decision. They believed that leaving this intolerable situation would be difficult for them; however, future generations would be the real benefactors. Life would be better for them-much better. Like thousands of others, leaving their homeland and going to Great Britain, the very country they held responsible for the problem, was a painful but necessary decision. Today everyone is grateful that they made the difficult choice. It was clearly the correct one. Generations of both of their families have enjoyed a wonderful quality of life. They love their community and the people of England.

The decision to leave Ireland was made. Now action would be required. How to get from Ireland to Wales. Once they made it to Wales how would they go about finding employment regarding the building of the railroad. Getting to Folkestone was not in their thoughts at all. Once they made it to Wales, and hopefully hired, Folkestone would follow.

Families held group meetings to determine how the logistics and financing of the journey would happen. The groups were as small as maybe ten and as large fifty. Hopefully, the outcome of these meetings would be a plan outlining how all of this would happen. A plan that would lay out the strategy of who would be the first to go-the true pathfinders.

The members of the group would be composed of the younger family members not tied down by marriage and children. Then they focused on how each family member would contribute financially to make all of this happen. Finally, what means of communications would follow once they were established with a job and a place to live. Indeed, an ambitious plan to deal with all of these issues. A plan fraught with all kinds of potential problems. The chances of failure were great. The entire concept required an enormous amount of trust and faith. The cooperation, faith, and trust of every family involved was incredible.

Of course, some disagreement and anxiety was displayed, but absolutely no distrust. The strength and sense of family was amazing. The hallmark of all Irish families. Nothing, absolutely nothing more important than family.

After a few weeks the financing was coming together, members were selected, and the process was set in motion. Among the members of the first group selected to be a part of the original journey were the great-great-grandfather of both Michael and Catherine Colleen. Both of these young men were single, in their early 20's, strong hard workers, who were more than up to the challenge.

As fate would have it a small group of 25 young men gathered at the foot of the Dublin Bay for the four-hour crossing of the Irish Sea. In the hope of bringing some good luck to the venture the decision was made to embark on St. Patrick's Day, March 17, 1860. The prayer was that the luck of the Irish would be with them. And it was. A beautiful morning filled with plenty of sunshine and calm seas. A rarity, especially at this time of the year.

Final goodbyes, lots of hugs, laughing, smiles, and a few tears. The young men boarded the ship with duffel bags containing their few belongings of clothing, religious items, Celtic cross, and photos of their loved ones. Some of them had small gifts from parents and sweethearts.

Once they were all aboard and the cargo was loaded the ship was ready to sail. And sail it did. The men all went to the bow of the ship to watch as the sea unfolded in front of them. Occasionally they looked back to watch as Ireland disappeared. The scene was actually a metaphor for what had been and what was to come. Most felt that they would most likely never return to their homeland. Feelings were a mixture of sadness and excitement for the life about to unfold. They were full of hope and the belief that one day they would have their families join them and a better life for everyone.

What seemed like an eternity, but in reality, some four hours later the ferry approached the port city of Holyhead, Wales. Anxiety increased as the ferry was in the process of being moored securely on the west side of the harbor. Last minute instructions were given and the young men began to disembark. Once on the dock they were met by the Superintendent and several foremen of the LCD Railway (London, Chatham, and Dover.)

The Superintendent instructed the men to gather their possessions and proceed to the warehouse at the end of the pier. Once there he would explain what would happen next and answer their questions. He then went on to encourage them. His hope was that they would join him on this history making project. When completed there would be rail transportation from Holyhead, Wales, to Dover, England. A distance of more than 500 kilometers. The railroad would open the country to movement of commerce and citizens. The seacoast of the English Channel would be developed and crossing the channel would open the Continent to everyone.

He went on to say the project would be historic and would change England forever. The work would be hard, hazardous, and long hours. But once completed a source of tremendous pride-and you will have been part of the project that changed England. With that said he concluded his remarks by saying that they should reconvene in the warehouse to answer questions after they collected their personal possessions and the commercial cargo was unloaded.

To the surprise of the young men as they entered the warehouse they were met by probably 200 other men of all ages. They represented various parts of the United Kingdom and some from as far away as the European Continent. No one from their small group anticipated anything approaching this size and scope. They became a bit tentative and concerned that the possibility might exist that they would not be hired. That fear was soon put to rest.

The next part of the process were remarks made by a senior official from the LCD. He explained that there would be jobs for everyone that wanted to work. Then he outlined the ground rules. Railroads were becoming a major force worldwide. America was endeavoring to build a transcontinental railroad connecting the east coast to the west coast. A distance of some 3,000 miles. Nevertheless, what was being attempted in the United Kingdom was of equal, if indeed, not more important. Once completed there would be easy access to Europe and beyond.

First, he went on to explain about the work force and the rules of employment. They would work six days a week. The hours would be six o'clock in the morning until six in the evening. There would be a thirty-minute break mid-morning and the same mid-afternoon. No whiskey drinking during the work day. Showing up late or absenteeism would not be tolerated. He went on to say that they suspect some of you will not meet, or accept, these rules. Noncompliance will result in immediate termination. The company will provide food and shelter. They began to understand why there was such a large pool of men. Obviously, the company anticipated that there would be terminations along the way for a variety of reasons. They were also beginning to see the size and magnitude of the project. They also began to realize that they were going to be a part of a history making event and this small band of brother from Ireland were going to be a part of it.

The senior official introduced the next speaker who was going to talk about the American project. The Central Pacific Railway in America was having serious labor problems. A significant number of workers were from Ireland. Drinking and gambling was a major issue. At the same time a major immigration to the United States was taking place from China. Race fights were breaking out constantly. The Chinese were being paid twenty-seven dollars per month, minus food and shelter. The Irish were paid thirty-five dollars-food and shelter was provided. The American project was months behind schedule. Fights were a daily occurrence. The Irish had dysentery issues due to their unwillingness to eat a reasonable diet.

The owners of the LCD were determined not to make the same mistakes. They outlined to the workers the plight of the Central Pacific Railway in America and how they intended to learn from the situation. The workers were informed that they would be paid forty dollars per month and would be provided with housing and a well-balanced diet. Their plan was to treat the workers fairly. They expected the workers to reciprocate-treat the company fairly. Thus, the necessity for the ground rules. With the rules in place there should be no misunderstanding. All of the Irish young men agreed the arrangements were definitely fair and they liked the idea of being part of this historical project.

They were determined to not let their families back home down. They wanted their families to proud of them.

The Central Pacific in America had a plan to lay down ten miles of track per day. They were failing miserably at this goal. The LCD had a similar plan and had no intention of failing. With that said the speaker concluded his remarks by saying that he hoped the workers would agree and become an integral part of this ambitious endeavor. He closed his remarks by saying if any of the workers felt the plan and rules were unreasonable now was the time to leave. No questions would be asked. They would receive passage on the ferry back to Ireland. The speech was delivered in an inspirational tone. The men reacted with spontaneous applause and cheering. Everyone-management and workers were anxious to begin the project and change the face of England forever.

The men were given information about the various positions and a description in some detail. A foreman would be there to assist and help find the right fit based on their interest and any skills that they may have. The list, included a variety of railroad positions such as-Platform car operator, Straighteners, Spikers, Levelers, and Fillers. Of course, the all-encompassing position of General Laborer-the only requirement-a strong back and good attitude. All of the young Irish lads met those requirements and then some. The positions came under the slang expression of "Gandy Dancer." The title given railroad laborers as the result of a tool used in laying railroad tracks. Other positions would be Cooks, Dishwashers, helping to establish sleeping facilities. Basically, huge tents for sleeping and others for cooking and eating. The tents went up for a few days and were torn down and put back up every few days as the railroad progressed. Building bridges across rivers, going around mountains, and bad weather were just a few of the hazards to be dealt with. Everyone was quickly realizing the magnitude of the project.

Literally overnight the process was completed, jobs were assigned and the railroad building was about to begin. Time was of the essence. Excitement was at a fever pitch. The workers were given one day to get acquainted with their fellow workers and living arrangements.

Boom! The work began. Noise everywhere. Horse drawn wagons dropping railroad ties along the bedside. Sledge hammers, picks, and shovels in constant motion. Everyone seemed excited and pleased to get started. Lots of laughing. Smiles everywhere. A fantastic beginning. It seemed a bit unrealistic to expect that this situation would continue for the entire project. Not to worry. It did not. As the weeks became months much changed. Tensions mounted. Accidents happened. Even deaths were happening. Bad weather. Fights breaking out almost daily. Alcohol and gambling nightly. Prostitutes following along the way. The list goes on.

The problems, difficulties, and setbacks aside, the railroad was progressing along. Actually, albeit slightly, the project was ahead of schedule. Thanks to some ingenious innovation that enabled the engineers to connect parts of existing track in small towns to the LCD project.

To the amazement of all parties some ten days ahead of schedule the last spikes were driven into the rails situated less than one kilometer from the landmark White Cliffs Hotel. Incredibly, a passenger could board a train at the Charing Cross Station in London and ride nonstop to the English seaside. From that point one could board a ferry across the English Channel and arrive in Calais, in the Normandy Region of France. From there onto Paris and the other major cities on the European Continent.

A word about the White Cliffs Hotel in the center of Dover. The hotel was built in 1841 and has survived for more than a century. World War I, World War II, and natural disasters has not been able to destroy this beautiful grand lady. She still stands, an elegant hotel, which serves both society and citizens of the community with great distinction. In the future the hotel and the seaside community were favorites stops for Sir Winston Churchill during most of the 20th century. With the beautiful White Cliffs stretching to the blue sky above and the green waters of the English Channel mere meters to the front was an incredible sight to see. Sitting on one of the large rocking chairs on the vast verandah was both relaxing and exhilarating at the same time.

The Dover area was a nice area and excited many of the Irish workers. Several decided to settle there. Others, including the ancestors of Michael and CC, felt more comfortable in the seaside community of Folkestone, some 20 kilometers south. The established Parish of Our Lady and the tightly knit community of small row homes with tree lined streets conjured up thoughts and comparison to Ireland. The decision was made and roots were planted for future generations of both families.

Next on the of challenges was to find housing. After a few weeks of looking for a home and enjoying the good life it was time to settle down. Michael's great-great-grandfather decided on a modest home near The Leas. A two-mile long road on the top of the White Cliffs overlooking the Channel. The house was on the corner of Harbor Road and High Street. Situated on two acres with a spectacular view.

Land prices in Folkestone were extremely low in the mid 1800's. The upper class wanted Victorian homes in Dover near the White Cliff Hotel neighborhood and the Railway Train Station. They felt that the shanty Irish could settle in Folkestone. That was fine with these new immigrants. The property has been in the family four generations. Following their marriage, Michael and CC, built a larger house to accommodate their family. The modest house of their ancestors was maintained and continues as a residence for friends and family.

Once the housing situation was resolved a job was next. The railroad was the logical choice. When the final spikes were driven the President of LCD made a speech on the railroad station platform in Dover. He thanked many people-bankers, politicians, engineers, and the leading citizens of the communities that helped make his dream possible. He went on to say most of all a huge thanks goes out to the Gandy Dancers. They did the hard work tirelessly under hazardous conditions, bad weather, and near impossible time constraints. They made it happen. They are the people who built this railroad. Without them it would not have happened. They made his dream a reality.

And then to the surprise of everyone in attendance he made an offer. They could all have a job with the railroad. He went on to say that yes, the railroad was built and now completed, however, workers will be needed to operate the railway across England. Who better to fill these jobs than the very men who built the railroad. Conductors, brakemen, repairmen, engineers to name a few. The list goes on. A rousing round of applause, hooting, and hollering went up. Decision made. The Magee and Kelly family would be part of the LCD Railway for generations to come.

The people who built the railroad focused on the next giant project-The English Channel Tunnel Project. With the advent of steam trains and the completion of the rail network across England ingenuity was being challenged. Entrepreneurs s, Pioneers, Dreamers, and Laborers were all part of the dream-build a tunnel across the English Channel.

The idea of a tunnel across the channel began when Albert Mathieu, Napoleon's engineer, first proposed the idea in 1802. Before the attempt to move on to the next step it took another 75 years. The first excavation began in 1880. What followed was mostly failure. Undaunted the dreamers never gave up. It took more than another 100 years to see the dream become a reality. The Magee family was involved over the generations. Michael Matthew Magee, the politician, worked tirelessly to make certain that it happened. He felt a strong commitment to the family generations before him to see that this happened. His ancestors built the railroad in the late 1800's and the generations that followed would commit to what was to become known "The Chunnel Project".

PART TWO

THE GROWING UP YEARS AND THEIR MARRIAGE WORLD WAR II

Michael Matthew Magee and Catherine Colleen, or CC as everyone calls her, grew up in the same neighborhood known as Little Dublin. Most all of their friends and neighbors are lifelong friends. One of their special friends is Franny O'Rourke, or more formally known as Father Francis J. O'Rourke, catholic priest and Pastor of The Parish of Our Lady, Help of Christians, or simply "Our Lady." Father O'Rourke performed their marriage ceremony.

The children of the neighborhood attended the Parish school, Stella Maris Elementary School. Times were different back then. Simple and idyllic. The center of all activities in the neighborhood, especially for the children was the beach. Fishing, swimming, and sailing. Family picnics and bonfires on the beach on a Sunday evening with the entire family was enjoyed by everyone. Climbing the white cliffs was a specialty of the boys. Although some of the tomboys, including CC, were as good at climbing as the boys.

From the time Michael was a young boy sailing was his passion. At the young age of 12 he managed to convince one of the local boat builders, Sean Fitzpatrick, to hire him. Every day after school he hustled down to the shipyard. When the summer break from school arrived, he spent his days at the shipyard watching, learning, and asking questions. He performed a variety of menial tasks. This did not bother him in the least. To be around the men who were building world class sailboats was an incredible opportunity. This exposure combined with a natural ability and his passion was an opportunity he was not about to miss. He did receive a small paycheck, but that mattered not. Truth is he would have handled his responsibilities without compensation.

When he was sixteen, he decided that he wanted to try and build his own sailboat. He approached The owner, Cap'n Fitz, as he was known to everyone, asked permission to use the various scraps to work on his project. The owner not only gave Michael the scraps he provided a fair amount of lumber, sails, and hardware. Several of the workers agreed to help Michael in their spare time. You could not help but to be impressed with his passion and ambition.

Less than a year later the project was completed a sleek twenty-foot sloop from bow to stern. As the jib (a triangular sail set prominently forward of the forward most mast) billowed in the wind a large green shamrock was prominently displayed. Michael was one proud young man. The good Cap'n and the workers gathered to be a part of the christening and launching of Michael's new boat. The name simply-SERENITY.

A perfect day for sailing. Plenty of sunshine. A gentle, but steady breeze. With the wind at his back in a matter of minutes he was out to sea. As he looked back to the shore line the small group began to disappear on the horizon. To say that he felt a bit overwhelmed would be putting it mildly. A powerful sense of gratitude came over him. He realized this dream would have never happened without the help and gifts from the good Cap'n and the workers. The patience and support from his parents and friends. The list went on. He choked up a bit and said to himself this is what I want to do with my life-build boats!

Following high school graduation, a decision had to be made. On to university or enter the boat building business as a career. His parents were definitely hoping for university. He would be the first in their family history to attend university. After thoughtful reflection and meditation Michael announced his decision. He sat down with his parents to explain his feelings. He opened by saying he did not want to disappoint them-but his passion was simply too strong. He wanted to build boats. Specifically, sailboats. He assured them that he would continue to pursue education in the area of business and finance as well the technical points of boat building.

He went on to say that he did not want to simply be an employee and work in a boatyard. He had a vision that one day he would be the owner of a boat building business. By doing so he would create jobs for his friends and members of the community. Good paying jobs that would strengthen Little Dublin. Most importantly he planned to be on the cutting edge of new developments. New and innovative ideas for the modern sailing vessel. His parents had trust and confidence in their son. Michael's parents gave their wholehearted support and unconditional love. A sense of relief came over everyone involved.

This was become an exciting time in Michael's young life. The relationship with his high school sweetheart, CC, Catherine Colleen was moving to another level. They both believed that marriage would soon follow. Michael explained to CC that a decision would have to be put on hold. At least for a while. First things first. He wanted to immerse himself in his work and develop some real skill and comprehending the business end of the operation. Also, Hitler was making a great deal of noise in Europe. It was not clear what his agenda was-other than it was not good.

He approached Cap'n Fitz and explained what he was hoping for the future. He went on to retell the conversation with his parents about college-or more accurately not college. His commitment to the boat business. And finally, his hope that the good Cap'n would agree to help him. Cap'n Fitz liked young Michael-a lot. He assured Michael that he would help him in any way that he could. They shook hands and hugged. The contract was complete and the deal closed.

The next few years he was consumed with work. Working days had no boundaries. He was constantly questioning the skilled artisans that were his teachers. They were more than willing to give their time and talents to him. He was a quick study. Always asking questions. Constantly drawing blue prints of a new sailing vessel. Sharing the drawings with his mentors. Asking them... What did they think... What changes have to be made... Are the sails in proper positions... How about the keel... Occasionally they would laugh and then put their arm around him with a big smile. It was easy to see his passion and enthusiasm. They did not want to dim his interest or discourage him. From time to time they would remind him of the fact that he was a young man with a sweetheart that needed some of attention.

Whenever that happened, he would smile and thank them for this important, and accurate, advice. He would then turn his attention to CC-the love of his life, however; ship building came in a close second. He did his best to explain how strongly he was committed to the business. He definitely wanted to get married. Soon. But he also wanted to be successful. He wanted the two of them to have a good life. A family. He wanted to help his family. He felt a strong obligation to his ancestors that came from Ireland and built the railroad. Their risky trailblazing gave him the opportunity to build a life in Folkestone and the English Channel.

When he finished talking CC spoke of her dreams as well. She wanted to marry Michael, have children, build a family and home. Work to make the Irish community one they all could be proud of. Whenever they were together these were the two topics. The other topic that would creep into the conversation was Hitler and what appeared to be an inevitable war in Europe. It appeared to no longer be "if" but "when" it will happen. Their walks and conversations usually took place on the beach at the end of the day. CC would usually pack sandwiches and drinks and meet Michael as his work day came to a close.

On more than one occasion she was left waiting. In the middle of some project he felt that he had to finish before the end of the day. She came to understand and accept the situation. It was a pattern that continued through their married life. Michael always offering an explanation. CC accepting. It carried over into his political career as well. He simply got lost in the task and challenge at hand. Trying to make the company stronger. Concern for his employees. Helping the constituents that he represented in Little Dublin. A responsibility he felt extremely committed to. He never wanted to disappoint any one of them.

The rumblings in Europe continued to grow and the noise on all sides were growing louder. Finally, on March 1, 1939, Hitler and his thugs seized Czechoslovakia. His tanks rolled into Poland on September 1, 1939 and World War II began. September 1, 1939 Great Britain and France declared war on Germany. December 7, 1941 the Japanese bombed Pearl Harbor and the United States declared war with Japan. Germany and Italy responded by declaring war on the United States on December 11, 1941. Almost immediately more than 50 Allied nations joined in the fight. A literal world war was underway. For the next six years, until the spring and summer of 1945, global events were in turmoil. Fortunately, freedom and democracy prevailed. But an enormous toll was taken in human life and resources.

Michael was about to get himself into the middle of the fight. A fight that he was eager to be a part of. Protecting his country, community, friends, and family was of paramount importance to him. And there was never any question which branch of service he would become involved with. The Royal Navy of Great Britain. An organization that built the British Empire worldwide. Without a doubt there was not any navy in the world that remotely approached its size and power.

Historians have longed disagreed on the exact date of the beginning of the war. But they offer three events as the cause-The problems left unresolved by World War I, the rise of dictatorships, and the desire of Germany, Italy, and Japan for more territory.

While they could not agree on the exact date many consider the Germans invading Poland as the beginning. Some say that it started when Japan invaded Manchuria on September 18, 1931. Others even regard World War I and II as part of the same conflict with only a breathing spell between.

Whatever history will have to say time will tell; however, make no mistake it was indeed a horrific time in the history of the world. Michael was about to become a part of this war. An event that will have a profound impact on the rest of his life.

During on of their famous walks Michael announced to CC that he planned to join the Royal Navy one April 17, 1940, his great-grandfather's birthday. He decided on that date as a means of paying tribute to his ancestors and the struggles they went through so future generations of the family could have a better life. April 17 was only three weeks away. CC was frightened, but certainly understood.

Next on his agenda was marriage. He did not want to get married until the war was over. He went on to say that no one could know how the events of the war would unfold. He did not want her to be a young war widow. She replied in typical CC style. Her strong personality came out loud and clear. Nothing was going to happen to him and she had no intention of becoming a young war widow. This was the beginning of how decisions were made during their long marriage. Michael was the public out front person of the two. But behind the scenes CC was the strong woman who guided him in all major life decisions.

She was willing to wait until he entered the Royal Navy and got his so called "sea legs"-but no longer. Michael smiled and agreed. As usual her logic was hard to argue with. He removed his high school ring from his finger, put it on her finger, and gave her a kiss on the cheek. The engagement was now official and the wedding would take place on November 19 (her birthday) some 18 months in the future. They left the beach and headed home to announce their engagement and wedding plans to both families.

The next few weeks were both busy and exciting times. Finally, the morning of April 17th arrived. Michael was up early and after a quick breakfast-headed out and arrived at the local recruiting station a few minutes before they were open. He waited patiently-or more accurately impatiently. After a series of examinations and a thorough physical examination he was sworn. A new member of the Royal Navy of Great Britain. He was assigned the rank of Able Body Seaman. He experienced a wide range of emotion-excitement, adrenalin rush, pride, and, quite naturally, some fear. Some six years later, with the war coming to an end, he was discharged with the rank of CPO-Chief Petty Officer, The top rank for enlisted men.

But we are getting a bit ahead of our story. Following taking their oath and being sworn in all of the young men were given a seventy two hour liberty to take care of their personal affairs and say their goodbyes to family and friends. They were given orders to arrive at the recruiting station at 0700 hours the morning of April 20. From there they would board a bus for the five-hour ride to Southampton. Indoctrination, basic training, and assignment would follow. Then the war. Reality.

There was not any question Michael was growing up fast-real fast. One night while having a difficult time sleeping the thought entered his mind that less than two years earlier both he and CC were high-school sweethearts. He was learning the boat building business. They were taking long walks on the beach. Dreaming about their future. As the result of a madman named Adolf Hitler all of that has changed. His life, and the life of millions of other young men, have been turned upside down.

The weeks flew by and before he realized it basic training was coming to an end.

Assignments were being made. Michael and his fellow sailors hurried down to headquarters to read the bulletin board and find their new duty station. He scanned the posted orders and quickly found his name. Wow! He was assigned to HMS Vivien, a destroyer under the command of Sir Percy Noble. The ship would see action in The Battle of the Atlantic. A battle that became the longest continuous military campaign of World War II. The battle began in 1939 and came to a close in 1945 with the defeat of Germany. Michael's naval career was spent entirely in this battle.

At its core was the Allied naval blockade of Germany and their counter-blockade. The battle pitted U-boats (submarines) and other warships of the Kreigsmarine (German Navy) and the Luftwaffe (German Air Force) against the Royal Canadian Navy, British Royal Navy, and Allied Merchant ships. The convoys, coming mainly from North America, British, and Canadian navies and air forces.

As an island nation, the United Kingdom was highly dependent on imported goods. Britain required more than a million tons of imported material per week in order to be able to survive and fight. In essence it was a struggle by the Allied Forces to supply Britain and by the Axis to try and stop the flow.

From 1942 on the Germans sought to prevent the buildup of Allied supplies and equipment in the British Isles in preparation for the invasion of occupied Europe. Winston Churchill stated the defeat of the U-boat threat was mandatory if the Germans were going to be pushed back.

The Battle of the Atlantic was the dominating factor throughout the war. However, never for one moment could we forget that the success of everything happening elsewhere, land sea or air, depended on the successful outcome of this battle.

The outcome of the battle was a strategic victory for the Allied Forces. The German Blockade failed. But the victory came at a great loss of life and resources-36,000 sailors, 36,000 merchant seamen, 3,500 merchant ships, and 175 warships. Germany lost 30,000 sailors and 783 U-boats (submarines.) Michael was one of the tens of thousands of sailors who made this victory possible.

While Michael was engaged in the war CC was busy at home. She was determined to do her part to help her country and the war effort in any way possible. She volunteered with the Red Cross and participated in several different activities. One of her favorites was the USO. Giving a big smile and warm welcome to servicemen from all over the world. Coffee and donuts. Providing a listening ear. Help with writing a letter to a sweetheart back home. Share a dance when the band played Glenn Miller, and the Andrew Sisters singing "Don't Sit Under the apple tree, With Anyone Else but Me." Bing Crosby singing "White Christmas." She tried to give them a few hours of normalcy before heading off to their new assignment and the rigors and stress of war. She was very good at making that happen-very good. Simply being engaged gave her the feeling of "being a part of."

She also volunteered at the local Naval Hospital. Several of her former high school classmates joined her. Her duties were mostly visiting with the patients, helping with their therapy. Writing letters and reading to them. Basically, similar to her involvement with the USO. Some of the veterans would fully recover from their injuries, while others would have issues that will challenge them for the rest of their life. They were just kids. Out of high school a year or two. (like Michael.) It was truly heartbreaking. Her efforts gave a sense of connection to Michael.

At times when she was alone with her thoughts, usually when she went to bed at nights, tears would stream down her cheeks-she would say to herself, "Whoever came up with the idea of war to settle a difference." Old men start these wars then send boys and young men to fight them. They are the ones who pay the price-with their life, limbs and their minds. Simply horrible. And these wars have been going on since the beginning of time.

Her other passion was developing her artistic gifts in both painting and sculpting. When she was involved in these endeavors, she was able to escape the horrors of war. If only for a few hours. She attended the Folkestone School of Art. An institution that began its long history in the early 1800's. Several prominent artists and former students of the school now offer their time and talent. The school is funded through philanthropy and the voluntary teaching efforts of successful former students.

The war raged on months which turned into years. Words, phrases, and battles that would become part of world history became all too familiar while Michael was a part of the battles taking place on the sea, the defeat of Hitler on land was moving on in an extremely aggressive way. D-Day, June 6, 1944 was the beginning of the end for the Axis. Bastogne, the Battle of the Bulge, are just a few of the bloody battles. Dunkerque off the coast of France on the English Channel was fought with every type seafaring vessel from Battleships to rowboats. Michael was very much involved in this event.

Hitler was on the run. Investigators had learned that Hitler and his wife Eva Braun had committed suicide on April 30, 1945. Unconditional surrender occurred on May 8, 1945. The free world celebrated V-E day. After five years, eight months, and seven days the European phase of World War II had ended. On October 24, 1945 the United Nations was born. The world prayed for peace-wars no more. Sadly, civilization would not see that happen.

War has been part of the world for all of its past history and continues on today. Why man cannot "live and let live" is a mystery for the ages.

Michael was anxious to get back home to Folkestone, his wife, CC, and get started on his ship building career. He left for the war almost four years ago and was at sea for just about all of that time. Yes, they had exchanged letters and a few telephone calls, but no other contact. They were married on her birthday, November 19, and five short months later, April 17, boarded a bus and was shipped off for basic training.

During his absence he spent all of his free time, (which was at a minimum) at sea, he thought about their future, hopes of a family, and starting his career in the shipbuilding business. He also kept every letter from CC and reread whenever the moment allowed. Their letters shared the same hopes and dreams.

Occasionally, he would reflect on the way the motion picture industry portrayed war. One of romance, heroes, and flag waving. Wrong! War is none of these things. The truth is killing, bodies mangled, families destroyed, careers ruined to name just a few. He made a commitment and resolution that once home and in recognition to friends and shipmates that would not be coming home, he would devote his life working against issues that were part of war.

His ship was coming to port in Southampton and in less than 48 hours he would receive his discharge and be free to take the train for a short two-hour ride to Folkestone and CC and his family and loving friends.

He was consumed with mixed emotions. First, and foremost he was extremely excited about returning to his loved ones. Secondly, he would be leaving his shipmates. Friends that he had bonded with strongly over the past four years, including some that were not returning and others that had parts of their bodies mangled. This would be emotional and not easy. They agreed to stay in touch and to have reunions. Somehow, they knew that most likely that would not be happening. Maybe occasionally, but they all knew it was time to put this part of their lives behind them and move own.

As the hours ticked away the sailors exchanged mailing information, hugs, and promises to stay in touch. The ship arrived early on what would be the last time this group would be together. It was a bright sunny morning as the moorings were securing the ship and disembarkation would take place. Sunny mornings were not that common, especially this time of year, on the south coast of England. Perhaps a sign that better times lay ahead for this group of young men. A group a few years ago that were not much more than teenage kids. Now, battle hardened veterans of a devastating war. Devastating not only for the vanquished but the victors as well. It is often said there are not any true winners in war with all of its countless consequences. A Chinese proverb states "In war you kill 1,000 of the enemy. Unfortunately, at the cost of 1,100 of your own.

All of the necessary processing and paperwork took place below deck. Discharge papers, mustering out pay, and copies of their service time furnished each sailor. A very solemn and official event. Lots of saluting, aye, aye, sirs, standing at attention, and formality. Once completed you were free to go topside. Once there the scene was entirely different. Cheering, laughing, hugging, and yes even a bit of "bubbly" compliments of the good Captain. Yes, the war was over and it was time to go home.

At the foot of the gangplank busses were waiting to take them to the train station a short five kilometers to the center of this seaside town. Local residents were out in huge crowds cheering and waving the Union Jack flag. Lots of excitement, collecting your train ticket which was arranged by the railroad. One whirlwind of an event. In a matter of minutes Michael was aboard the London Chatham and Dover (LCD) Chatham for short, along with a number of his shipmates from the Folkestone area. They were indeed on their way home. Finally. A day he often wondered if it would ever happen. Indeed, it has. As he settled back in his seat, he closed his eyes as the train pulled out from the station. Again, amid cheers of pride and thanks from the citizens of his homeland-England.

As the train made its way inland for the two-hour journey to Folkestone, his hometown he reflected on the history of his country and how his family and ancestors fit into the many pieces of the puzzle. Of course, they were a part of the puzzle of the war, World War I, the Great Depression of the 1930's and other events of the 20th Century. But what came to mind was his ancestors during the middle of the 19th century. They risked everything when they left Ireland to find a better life not only for themselves but future family generations to come. He now felt by serving to defend the freedom his ancestors risked everything for he had made his contribution.

He then smiled to himself as thoughts entered his mind about the very rails this train was riding on. Maybe my great grandfather was one of the "Gandy dancers" who laid these very tracks. With those thoughts and others in his mind and the anticipation he drifted off into a deep sleep. It was indeed an emotional and adrenalin filled last couple days.

He began hearing noise and some commotion as the train was slowing down. Still in a bit of a fog he rubbed his eyes and looked around. Many of his fellow passengers were on their feet, gathering luggage, and moving toward the exits. Wow! They were pulling into the Folkestone Station. He could not believe he had fallen into such a deep sleep. He jumped to his feet and pulled down his duffel bag and lined up for the exit.

As the train groaned to a stop, he looked out the window at the large crowd on the platforms to welcome home their returning heroes and loved ones. Try as he may he could not identify CC, the love of his life, in the crowd. As he stepped off the train on to the platform it was total bedlam. Lots of hugs, kissing, crying, and of course-screaming.

After what seemed an eternity, and in reality, was a matter of minutes there she was. Waving furiously, she spotted Michael, and yes, she too, was screaming. Screaming his name. Their eyes connected and he pushed and shoved his way. An emotional embrace. Not a word exchanged. Hugs. Kisses. Tears. Finally, the war was over. He was home. They were together again. Ready to put the past behind and build a life together. A beautiful and heartwarming event. As they walked along the platform, they saw the scene repeated over and over again. Thank God. We pray peace will hold around the world and people and families will be able to build a life and future.

First thing on the agenda for the young couple was a few days of rest and relaxation and making plans for their future. A family gathering at their home on The Leas overlooking the sea. Several neighbors and fellow veterans attended. Lots of hugs as well tears-tears of joy and tears of sadness and pain for friends that came home seriously and permanently injured, and of course those that did not make it home.

One of the top priorities on Michael's list was to create a memorial for those who paid the ultimate price. This would give his neighbors a peek at where much of his energy would be committed in the future-remembering and working for those people who gave much for their community. The average hard-working citizen. A commitment that would only grow with the passing of time.

Following a few days at home they decided to take a ferry across the channel and spend time on the Normandy Beaches. The same beaches that were the scene for D-Day, June 6, 1944. The costliest of life for the entire war. A total of 425,000 casualties, both Allied and enemy forces. Over the years many versions of what the "D" meant in the term D-Day-"departure" "doomsday" and "decision" day. The fact is none are correct. The "D" simply identifies the letter as the "day" of invasion. It was commonly used in military jargon. It is now used exclusively to identify the historic D-Day invasion.

The plan was to spend two weeks touring the Normandy region and places like Mont-Saint-Michel, an island commune located at the mouth of the Couesnon River. The Abbey was built in the 8th Century and has withstood an endless list of attacks and disasters both, natural and man-made.

After several days it was apparent to CC-loud and clear that Michael was getting itchy and restless. Over breakfast one morning in the beach village of Calais she decided it was time to approach him. She insisted that he be honest. He said he would. The question-are you ready to go home and move on. His reply-"I thought you would never ask! Yes, I am ready for us to go home and start our life and start a family." She gave him a big smile, hug, and kiss. They went back to seaside hotel, packed, and were on the afternoon ferry for the 26-mile cruise across the channel. Later that night they were safely home in their beds for a good night's sleep.

A pattern that would follow the rest of their lives. She knew instinctively when some-thing was not right with him. He was always reluctant to be honest with her. Whenever the situation would develop, they both would smile, hug, and then openly discuss the issue. Their system worked well and both agreed not to ever make any change.

Michael was up early and ready to swing into action. He told CC he was ready to go to his old employer in the boat building business and see if he could have his old job explaining to her he wanted to build boats and make a living on the sea. CC responded that it was no surprise of course and she was 100 percent in favor of his plan.

As he walked the few blocks along the waterfront to marina area, he felt great. A deep breath as he thought how great it was to be home. Forever grateful that the horrendous war was finally is over. Grateful that he made it home safely to CC and his family. Then a feeling of guilt-why did he survive and so many others lose their life fighting for freedom. Once again, he vowed to do something in the community to remember not only the individuals but their families. They did not make the ultimate sacrifice in vain.

He then focused on his mission. To meet with his old employer-Sean Fitzpatrick-known to not only waterfront people but the entire community simply as "Cap'n Fitz." He was a successful builder of all type boats. His specialty was sailboats. The type that Michael loved the most. Cap'n Fitz was a fixture on the waterfront for many years. Always there to help anyone. Involved with the parish. Sharing the financial successes he was blessed with. Whenever Father O'Rourke had a situation that needed help-financial, job, rent, a place for someone to live Cap'n Fitz was the first person he turned to. He always responded. This was one of the many character traits that Michael admired about his friend. He hoped Cap'n Fitz would be his mentor.

When he walked into the ship-yard he saw Cap'n Fitz on one of the docks talking to a client and one of his employees. He definitely was a hands-on type of guy. No front office executive was he. With his hands in his blue jean pockets, a smile on his face with the rugged weather-beaten face of someone who has spent a lifetime on the waterfront. They made eye contact and the Cap'n rushed to hug his young friend. They had a long embrace and a few tears.

They then went off to a quiet spot on the pier to reunite. Cap'n Fitz said of course he could have his old job back. The conversation went on for more than one hour. Michael said we need to move on. He thanked the Cap'n and said you need to get back to your clients. He responded by saying don't worry. The least we can do for a veteran who put his life on the line for the rest of us is to spend a little time with them. A fantastic visit as Michael left with his new boss telling him to enjoy the rest of the week and report bright and early Monday morning ready to build boats. They embraced and the meeting of two close friends came to a close. Michael became a bit emotional as he hugged the Cap'n. In his typical fashion the Cap'n low keyed the event. Whenever he did something nice or helpful his manner was to downplay. This was no different. When Michael began to tear up the Cap'n said in his soft voice, "I'm just delighted to have an excellent boat builder back on the job." With a new job Michael could not wait to get back home and share the results of his visit with CC. He was thrilled to be part of the Cap'n Fitz operation.

As he began walking the few blocks home, he could no longer contain himself. He broke into a quick step walk that turned into a run in a matter of minutes. Arriving home, excited, out of breath, and almost in tears he opened the front door and began shouting, "CC, CC, where are you?"

CC returned with, "Why are you shouting? Is there a problem?"

"No, to the contrary. I have wonderful news." With that said he told her of his visit with Cap'n Fitz and again choked up and the tears began flowing. CC knew quite well how emotional he became with either good news or not so good news. Truth be told he probably became more emotional with good news.

They sat down and CC prepared a cup of tea and a biscuit for both of them. They took a seat, she took hold of his hand and stroked it gently. In her typical soft voice and warm smile, whenever he was excited, she said settle down and share the good news. "Okay, Okay," was about all he could get out. He then took a deep breath and told her all the details from the meeting. He was so excited he could hardly contain himself. CC smiled and sat back in her chair and smiled.

Michael looked at her and asked, "what is that wry smile all about."

"Well it sounds fantastic. A great job. A mentor to teach all aspects of the boat building business. Right in our little town. A wonderful man in Cap'n Fitz. The list just goes on. Just one question"

"What have I left out or not told you."

"You failed to tell me what type of a princely salary are you going to be paid for all these benefits."

They both broke into spontaneous and loud laughter. "Oh well, that's a minor detail," replied Michael. The fact was both them knew that the good-Cap'n would be more than fair.

Michael then began a conversation with CC about the fellow veterans from the neighborhood that would not be returning from the war and the ones that were wounded or lost body parts and were now severely handicapped. He asked the question that has no answer-Why them and not me. Every returning veteran down through the ages has asked the same question. The question that leads to a weird sense of guilt. The only answer is Faith and only God knows.

He told CC about the promise that he had to himself not to let those men be forgotten. About his commitment to build a memorial in the town square. He would to talk to their friend and spiritual advisor-Father O'Rourke. Maybe he will be able to help in both areas. The building of a memorial and the interminable question of "why them and not me." He told CC of his intention to go visit their good friend first thing in the morning. She agreed. Off they went to bed, hugging, they both slipped into a deep sleep after an emotional and fruitful first day at home.

Up early he was ready to rush off and try to make contact with their old friend, Franny O'Rourke. Or more appropriately the title Father O'Rourke, Pastor of Parish of Our Lady, Help of Christians. The oldest Roman Catholic church in this part of England. A quick cup of tea, biscuit, and a bowl of porridge and he was ready to go. CC wished him good luck, a kiss on the cheek and off he went. Just a few blocks to the rectory at 42 Guildhall Street in the heart of Little Dublin. A neighborhood all too familiar to him. All the kids in the neighborhood, including CC, attended the parochial school, including Father O'Rourke himself.

The walk was literally a walk down memory lane. Past the fire department, one block of the small shops, the neighborhood grocery store that let the residents by groceries "on the book." On Payday the women of the house would come in cash her husband's paycheck and settle her account. Many were the day when Michael was but a young boy, he was sent with a list of items for his mother to prepare meals. He would hand over the list and the book where the item and cost were listed. Back home with the groceries and the book he would give both to his mother. She put the groceries away and the book in safe place in the kitchen cabinet. Neither the mother or the grocer ever questioned the bill. Integrity of either was never questioned.

Lost in his memories he almost walked right past the rectory. Up the three steps of the front porch, rang the bell, and waited. He was hoping to surprise his friend. The front door opened and there he was. An old classmate and now the Pastor of this important part of the Irish fabric in the town of Folkestone.

Surprised, stunned, and overwhelmed Father O'Rourke could not contain himself, "Michael, Michael how are you, what are you doing here, when did you get home,"

"Whoa, Whoa, my friend, give me a chance," he replied with a big smile.

With that they settled in for a long conversation to catch up on the past and what the future holds. Michael was very proud of his old friend and what he was doing with his life. There was never any question where and what Francis O'Rourke would do with his life. An altar boy from the day the church would permit him. He spent time at the rectory helping wherever and whenever he could. He loved the church. He was also a typical young boy loving fishing, playing soccer, and even smiling at the girls. But first and foremost, in his life was always the church.

He loved the church. The church was first. Did then. Does now. Always will. He told Michael during their visit how much he enjoyed his youthful growing up days in this very neighborhood. Attending Stella Maris School. The direction he was given. Now he wanted to give back. Certainly, helping with the memorial, he felt grateful that he was asked. And help he did.

Michael brought up his idea of a memorial for the young men who served in the cause of freedom. Father O'Rourke agreed wholeheartedly and said he would help in every possible way. He suggested the park across from the church would be a great location. Michael left with the feeling that they were on the right path and things would happen. Franny, as he was known to his old school buddies, was a mover and a shaker. The other parishioners referred to him as Father Francis. Everyone in the parish loved. him. Men. Children. Women. Especially the women. He was a big man physically, and his personality was even larger. Always giving hugs and big smiles. Always calling people by their name. He simply seemed to know everyone. Michael smiled and thought to himself Franny would have made a great politician. After a couple hours visit it was time to move on. They hugged and said goodbye. More, much more to follow.

Walking home he reflected on the history of the parish-What we know today as Parish of Our Lady, Help of Christians. Or more commonly referred to simply as "Our Lady."

A history that was drilled into him, indeed, all the children, when they were attending Stella Maris School. The church and the community were a vital part of life for everyone in Little Dublin. The parish dated back to the 1840's:

As the population of Folkestone grew, mainly as the result of the influx of Catholic workers who arrived from Ireland to build the London to Dover Railway Line it became clear that there was a need for a Catholic place of worship. During the earlier days the Mass was celebrated in private homes.

Around 1860 a building, which had earlier served as an office for Mr. Hart, a lawyer, was purchased and converted into a chapel. The building stood on the south side of Martello Street and the tiny chapel was dedicated to St. John the Evangelist.

The chapel was indeed small, accommodating about 60 people, half had to stand. The little building also served as the first Catholic

School in Folkestone. The sanctuary was screened off from the body of the chapel for school activities. Education was extremely important to the Irish immigrants and they were determined that their children would receive a good education-in both education of their religion and in the field of academics.

As the size of the Catholic community was rapidly outgrowing the capacity of the tiny chapel plans were made to construct a new chapel. In 1869 construction began and the opening service took place on Sunday January 31, 1870. Once again, an extension was screened off and used as a schoolroom.

This was the beginning of the parish. There was a great deal more history of this integral part of Little Dublin. The young school children would learn more as their education progressed. It would come in stages.

Michael arrived home excited and anxious to share with CC about his visit with their friend, Franny. He suggested that they take a walk on the beach explaining that he was simply to overwhelmed to sit still. Walking on the beach was always his way to deal with an adrenaline rush. Whenever anything important was going on in his life that was the way he tried to sort out the details and find a solution. CC knew that quite well. The two of them had many such walks dating back to their high school days.

As they strolled the warm sand with their shoes off and the tide washing over their feet the conversation began. To the surprise of CC, he brought up an entirely different topic. Her. She looked at him with a quizzical expression.

"I thought this walk was going to be about you and Franny, she said.

"No, not right now. We have plenty of time to talk about my visit with Franny. Seems all we have done since I arrived home from the war was talk about me and my future. I want to talk about you and your future."

CC was not too surprised. This was typical of him. He would tend to get all wrapped up in some project and then suddenly realize that he forgot about her. He didn't like that about himself. Once he was aware of what he was doing he would refocus-refocus on her.

They were holding hands at this point. She stopped, turned toward him, a big smile, hugged him, and they embraced. In the passion of the moment Michael got more than excited.

CC said, "Whoa, slow down cowboy. Wait till we get home."

That he did. He began to ask her questions. What about your art. When do you want to start a family (something they both wanted)? Are you going to continue volunteering at the hospital with the veterans? Do you want to be involved with the memorial project?

Again, she replied with a smile and laughed, "Whoa! Too many questions at once. All of what you mentioned are important to me, us, and our lives together. But we need to deal with them one day at a time. CC with always the sensible and logical one in the relationship. He had no doubt that she would be the glue to hold their family together. And that she did for many years.

Art, in any form, was her first love. The Folkestone School of Art was where she wanted to put her energy. Thanks to some of the professional artists that gave freely of their time when she was a little girl at Stella Maris School her talent was clear. She loved plein air painting atop of the white cliffs. Painting seascapes, children playing on the beaches below, the beautiful sailboats on the sea with their sails billowing. She would spend hours lost in her paintings. The other art form that was becoming more important was sculptor. The art school provided lessons and direction from the professionals who came down from London on a monthly basis.

Michael with his job with Cap'n Fitz and CC with a full schedule they were ready to move on and begin a life together. They would set up housekeeping in the modest home located in the Leas area. A modest home on the corner of Harbor Road and High Street overlooking the sea. The property sat on two acres of land that his great-great-grandfather purchased when he was a young man in the 1800's and remained in the family for generations.

The property was of great value today. Probably could not be purchased by the family in today's real estate market. But back in the 1800's this was not a problem. The upper class had no interest in living in the area. Therefore, buying real estate in that area was easy if you had just a bit of money. As a matter of fact the people that sold them the land believed that they were taking advantage of the poor uneducated Irish population. It is interesting to see how events develop over time.

Folkestone in general, and Little Dublin specifically, was not considered a very nice neighborhood. The aristocrats of that day lived 25 kilometers to the north in the affluent town of Dover. Large Victorian homes were situated on the White Cliffs and had panoramic views of the sea.

The occupants of the home were wealthy merchants that conducted their business in London and on the Continent. The "itinerant Irish men and women in Little Dublin" were hired to tend their grounds and gardens, the women became their cooks and housekeepers. Definitely an "upper" and "lower" class system. The "haves" and the "have nots." A system similar to the one in America. No, it was not slavery as it was in America, but not far removed.

Of course, the system began back in the mid 1800's and a great deal of progress developed over the generations.

PART THREE

THE BEGINNING OF THEIR FAMILY AND HIS SHIP BUILDING CAREER

The war was over. Michael was back home. He was able to return to the business of building boats with his mentor, Cap'n Fitz. He had met with his friend Father Franny. Plans were being made for a memorial.

CC was more than busy herself making their house a warm and comfortable home. She was active with her volunteer efforts at the Naval Hospital and the returning veterans. Of course, the Folkestone Art School was high on her list of priorities. She continued, as always, with her involvement in the Parish and the Stella Maris School.

Life was fulfilling and the future looked bright with a great deal of promise. They spent the next couple years working hard, saving their money, and were looking to the next part of their life-and at the top of the list was a family. They both were ready for an addition to the family.

Michael got up one morning, went through his usual early morning routine followed by a few minutes of prayer, meditation, and a thank you to God for bringing him home safely from the war. He always closed his prayer with-" Thy will, not my will be done in all matters. Please free me from the bondage of self so that I might be of maximum service to my fellow man. A quick breakfast of porridge, tea, and a biscuit then the short walk to work. The same routine he had been following for some time.

When he arrived the good Cap'n was already there hard at work. Nothing new here. The Cap'n was always the first one in. He greeted Michael, as usual, however; something seemed different.

"Michael, please come into the office for a few minutes," he said, with a smile.

Michael responded with a rather weak, "Okay." This office visit was definitely a bit out of the norm.

They both took a seat in the crowded space that served as an office. Papers, blueprints, hand tools, pictures of boats to be built scattered everywhere. This was definitely not the office of an executive. This was a space for hands on work to be done.

Michael looked at the Cap'n with both a nervous and anxious expression. What is going on he thought to himself. With that the Cap'n smiled, told Michael to relax and expressed the thought that he was certain the news he was going to deliver would be good news. Michael took a deep breath and indeed felt a bit more relaxed. He had total trust in the Cap'n.

The Cap'n began by saying he was getting to be a bit older. That we had been working on this waterfront all of his life and realized that he was slowing down. It was time for a younger man to take over. Handling all the building permits, drawing blueprints, negotiating with vendors, and a million other details that had little, if anything, to do with actually building a boat was wearing him out.

He talked for at least another half hour before Michael finally interrupted with a question, "What are you telling me. Sounds like you are going to retire or sell the business. Neither of those options sounds like good news to me."

The Cap'n responded with, "Let me finish. Yes, I am planning to retire and yes sell the business. I am hoping that you will be pleased with the new owner. He is a much younger man. He has been building boats since he was a young boy. I have known him much of his life. His character, integrity, and reliability are unquestionable. I believe you will be pleased."

"Okay, who is this new owner and when will this happen. I am hoping that I will still have a job," replied Michael,

The good Cap'n smiled and said, "You! You will be the new owner and I assume that means that you will have a job. Indeed, a big job."

Michael was flabbergasted. He mumbled, stumbled, was at a loss of words, and began to spout a million and one questions.

"Easy does it. One question at a time. We will get them all answered. First let's have a cup of tea," was the Cap'n response.

They had their tea and rehashed some of the details. Michael seemed to be over the shock. At least a bit. The Cap'n had already talked to Tommy Doyle, President, of the local bank and he has agreed to provide the financing. Michael asked the obvious question. When is this going to happen? The, answer-as soon as we finish this cup of tea we will walk over to the bank and get the details.

Michael went on to say that this was a fantastic opportunity and that he could not believe it was happening. He had one question-would it be alright if he went home and discussed it with CC first.

The Cap'n replied with a big smile, "Of course. I have known CC her whole life and feel as strongly about her as I do you." He suggested that Michael go home, have lunch, share the details with CC, and they would meet at the bank at one o'clock.

Michael stood up gave the Cap'n a big hug and said that he would be at the bank exactly at one o'clock. With that he started on the fifteen-minute walk to home. Thoughts were flooding his mind. The reality still had not registered. He felt like he was floating home. In a matter of minutes, he was opening and calling her name-CC! Michael coming home for lunch was a rare event. Her first thoughts were one of concern.

In a nervous voice she asked, "Why are you home. Is something wrong. Did something happen at work."

Michael responded with a big smile, "No nothing is wrong. Relax. I have something incredible to share with you. Then I have a big appointment at one o'clock with Tommy Doyle at the bank."

"At the bank." CC knew Tommy from their school days. He was a good businessman and friendly with both of them. They were not especially close and CC could not imagine why Michael would be meeting with him in the middle of the day.

He put his arm around her and held her hand. He then went on to share what transpired with the Cap'n. If possible, she was in more of a state of shock. How was he possibly going to buy the business? They had saved a little money, but certainly not enough to buy a prosperous business like Cap'n Fitzpatrick's. He assured her that he would not make any commitment without discussing the details with her first.

They both agreed that they had complete trust and confidence in the good Cap'n. After the meeting with Tommy Doyle he will bring the proposition home for her review and input. Michael explained that is exactly the way the Cap'n wants it handled.

They finished lunch, CC gave him a kiss, and wished him good luck. She squeezed his hand and with a big smile sent him off to the most important meeting of his, indeed, their young life.

Walking to the bank he reflected on the events of the day. Wow! God has certainly blessed them with good people in their lives. He walked into the bank and was greeted by the receptionist, Bridgid. Another friend and neighbor. His thoughts about this neighborhood and how everyone knew one another. Of course, it was not perfect-but pretty damn close to it.

Bridgid smiled and asked him to have a seat. She said the Cap'n telephoned and advised that he was on his way. Tommy was ready for them. A few minutes later the Cap'n arrived and the two of them were ushered into the office of Tommy Doyle, President, of the bank. A warm greeting was exchanged and then they settled down for a business and finance meeting. This was pretty heady stuff for young Michael.

The opening remarks were made by Tommy. He asked what were apparently perfunctory questions in this type transaction. Basically, did Michael understand and agree to the transaction. Did the good Cap'n agree. His reply, "Absolutely." How about you Michael. A nervous response of yes. All three of them chuckled. That certainly broke any tension in the room. Michael explained that transactions of this type may well be routine to Tommy and the Cap'n but a first for him. They assured him that all was fine and that this may be his first business transaction, but it will be the first of many to come.

Tommy asked Michael if he had any questions before the ceremony of signing loan papers and the other endless forms that the bank and the government required.

Michael said, "I have basically one question. Why are you and the bank willing to take this risk? I have very little money and no experience as an owner of a business."

Tommy went on to explain the logic behind the decision. Captain Sean Fitzpatrick, or Cap'n Fitz if you prefer, has built a successful shipyard over the past 25 years. The bank has made countless business loans to him over these many years. Everyone was repaid, with interest, on time and usually finalized the loan before the due date. His character, integrity, and trustworthiness is beyond reproach.

He is ready to retire from world of business and move on to the many other projects that he has in mind for the second half of his life. About a year ago he told us of his intentions and that he wanted to turn the business over to you Michael. I have known you pretty much your entire life and you have always exhibited the same qualities of character as the Cap'n. And everyone on the waterfront is well aware of your skill and talent as a builder of top-quality sailing vessels.

The decision by the bank to make this business loan was truly a no brainer. We are confident that you will be a successful owner of the company and will continue to produce and sell top quality vessels both here and on the continent. Also, who knows how far the company will expand and grow, not only here but around the world.

Oh, one other extremely important factor went into our decision. Captain Fitzpatrick is going to co-sign your note, Tommy added with a chuckle, and made the remark, "This loan is as solid as gold." There is absolutely nothing at risk on our behalf and the Cap'n has complete confidence in you. We have a solid company, a note co-signed by a wealthy individual, a new young owner of impeccable character and honesty. And if any of these assets went wrong a company we could repossess and sell tomorrow at a profit. Looks to me like we have made a solid decision and a great loan to help develop and reassure employment for an entire generation of new boat builders.

Michael was speechless. On the verge of tears, he embraced the Cap'n and told him he would never let him down and that he would work tirelessly to validate the confidence that he had shown. He then embraced and shook hands with Tommy and repeated his comments. Michael expressed his gratefulness to both of the men and had a feeling of being overwhelmed.

God had certainly showered him with so much. First and fore-most he returned home from the war without an injury of any type. Maybe a bit of mental anxiety, however, that seemed to be fading slowly. A beautiful wife. Good friends. An opportunity to own a business doing what he loved to do-building sailboats.

They all left the bank and Michael headed directly to Our Lady to light a candle for those that did not make it home from the war. A tradition that he would continue for the rest of his life. Kneeling at the rail he made a solemn promise to work on the memorial and make that a reality. He also made a covenant to help and pass on to the young people of the community the same gifts that was given to him by God. He had no question that all the Glory goes to God. None of this would have happened without His help.

He left the church following an emotional fifteen minutes of prayer, an attempt at a few minutes of meditation, but simply could not stop the racing in his mind. The next stop was home and announcing the incredible news to CC.

CC met him at the door with a combination of smiles and an expression of anxiety in her beautiful blue eyes.

"Relax, it is all great news. You are not going to believe what transpired during the last two hours," he blurted out.

"Try me," she replied.

They walked to the kitchen and CC put the kettle on the stove. Michael then relayed the details of the meeting. He explained how nervous he was in a big financial meeting with the president of the bank and his good friend and employer, Captain Sean Fitzpatrick, the owner of his highly successful boat business.

How he would now be the owner of this business with all the rewards and sense of satisfaction plus the high anxiety that goes along with the obligation and responsibility. CC was extremely proud of him and the hard work that he had been doing since he was a young teenager. How he was almost always late for their date because he was wrapped up on some project that he felt needed to be finished. She was well aware of the character traits that both Cap'n Fitz and Tommy Doyle mentioned.

After a couple hours of give and take conversation they both concluded it was time for a break and do one of their favorite things. Down to the beach, off with their shoes, and a long walk and watch the sun go down. As the sun began to set the sky lit up like a light show. The scene was a foreshadow of what would be. A metaphor of what would come in their young future.

The close of an incredible day. They were both somewhat exhausted in a pleasing way. They were now the owners of an amazingly successful ship building business that had been a part of their lives since their teenage years. Wow! Off to bed for a good night's sleep.

Most of the focus of their lives since Michael came home from the war was on his career, getting settled into married life, their new home, and reconnecting with old friends. Life was indeed good. Michael was concerned about CC. She willingly put her ambitions aside to help him. He wanted to see her pursue her painting and sculpting talents. He told her in simple terms, "That is going to happen. Period. No questions. You need to pursue your God given gifts."

She didn't argue. Her involvement at the Folkestone School of Art was still there, but on a more limited basis. That was about to change. In a big way.

CC was extremely pleased to see how determined Michael was to be certain that she pursued her artistic gifts. Following their morning breakfast together and the usual discussion of the schedule of activities for the two of them CC headed for the Folkestone Art School and Michael was off to work.

When she arrived at the school, she was introduced to a new member of the teaching staff, Annie Ackley, a sculptor from London. CC new of her work and was surprised to see her at their little school.

Even more surprising that she would be here on a regular basis and providing her expertise and talent free of any charge.

The two of them seemed to hit it off immediately. The chemistry was there and CC felt perfectly comfortable. They ordered a cup of tea and biscuit and went to the front patio to visit and get to know one another other better.

Annie explained why she was becoming a part of the School. She had recently purchased a seaside cottage near The Leas. The cottage had a marvelous view of the seascape and lots of window that brought light and sunshine. An ideal place to paint, sculpt and any artistic endeavor. Said another way the cottage was simply beautiful with a beautiful view. Period.

CC went on to say that she loved art in any form and sculptor particularly. She hoped that Annie would serve as both mentor and teacher. Annie assured her that she would be delighted to do so and trusts their relationship will become more than simply student teacher.

To say that CC was excited was more than putting it mild.

Annie said that her plan was to be at the school one week per month. That would give her the opportunity to spend time away from the pressure of London and the art world of cocktail parties, art shows, business and stress of the big city. Coming to this beautiful seaside community and the cottage would be a huge change of pace.

One of the big things that she liked about the cottage was its size. Or more accurately the lack of size. And windows. Lots of windows and light coming in from every angle. An artist's dream. A couple rooms, kitchen, a spare bedroom, and a wraparound porch. Large enough to have a guest, and much too small to entertain on a large scale. Something that she didn't like to do but her business required it in London.

Annie told CC that she hoped they would get together in London. CC assured her that would happen and that coming to London would not be a problem. CC loved the train ride through the English countryside with its rolling hills and beautiful farmlands. It always seemed to her that no sooner the train left Folkestone they were arriving at the Charing Cross Station in the heart of London.

That was welcome news to Annie. She went on to explain an easy taxi ride or the underground tube (subway) would get her to Piccadilly Circus, the art center of London and where she lived, in a matter of minutes. Trafalgar Square, The National Art Gallery, and all of the energy and excitement it generates is part of the neighborhood. The Saint Martin in the Fields Church is also there and a wonderful place for lunch. The church dates back to medieval times and is a major tourist attraction. CC told Annie that sounds so exciting. She was well aware of the history of that part of the city put never had the opportunity to visit.

After more than an hour visiting Annie thought the two of them should go inside and get to work. CC laughed and agreed. She was thrilled with the visit and would be willing to go on forever. They spent the rest of the day working. Annie worked with the other students as well.

The day did come to a close and it was time to head home. CC gave Annie a hugged, smiled, and said she was looking forward to building a professional and personal relationship together. Annie agreed. They exchanged their goodbyes and headed home.

CC could hardly contain herself and was anxious to get home and share the news and events of the day with Michael. She thought he would be pleased for her, but had no idea just how excited and supportive that he would be.

He listened intently as CC went into detail about the events of the day. She told him that she was actually going to receive guidance and instructions from a bonafide professional and successful artist. Michael asked a great deal of questions and told her that he would support her in any way that he could. CC supported him from the day that they were married. Actually, before they were married. Now it was time to return the support and that he would do. CC thanked him, they hugged and he kissed her on the cheek. Time to call it a day. And what a day it had been.

The next few years were busy ones indeed. They had both begun what would become highly successful independent careers. Michael had begun the developmental stages of the memorial largely through the support and efforts of their friend Father Francis. Expansion plans for his boat business were about to become a reality. CC's friendship with Annie, both professional and personal, was getting stronger by the day.

But no question the biggest and most important event in their life was the birth of their two children. A son, James-known to everyone as Jimmy Magee. Not just Jimmy. He was always referred to as Jimmy Magee. As in "Jimmy Magee you need to serve mass tomorrow." "Jimmy Magee get moving or you will be late for school." He was born on April 17. Their daughter, Molly Magee, was born on August 19. An absolutely delightful little girl. Big smile. Flaming red hair. Lots of personality. A friendlier Irish girl could not be found in all of Little Dublin. Everyone loved her. She responded in like manner. Always helping someone in the community. The little old ladies with their groceries. Helping Miss Nolan, the housekeeper, at the Rectory. Giving pencils from her pencil box to the kids in school that needed one. Wherever and whenever someone needed help you could always count on Molly. Simply stated they were two great kids and a credit to their parents and the neighborhood.

CC began to see that there was a bit of an issue to be dealt with. While they were two great kids, but if CC and Michael were to continue to work on their career arrangements would have to be made for their care after school.

She had what she thought was the solution but would need help from Michael. Following dinner one night while they were having their nightly cup of tea and discussing the events of the day, she broached him with her idea. She knew it would be difficult, but something that was difficult to bring up never stopped her.

They had finished their review of the day and Michael began to get up from his favorite chair. With that as a sign she said that there was one more item to discuss. He dropped back into his chair and said fine. Of course, he had no idea what she was about to bring up. He smiled, sensed that she was going to ask some small favor and asked, "Okay, what is it. Paint the living room. New curtains."

"No, a bit more than that. I want to start an after-school program for school kids at the Art School," she blurted out.

"What!" was his response, "How in the world would that happen."

In her typical low key, charming self, she suggested that he sit back, relax, and listen to her plan. She explained that she began thinking about it sometime ago when she realized that Jimmy Magee and Molly needed someone to watch over them after school. Right now they were using a hodgepodge of when and where they could go to have someone take care of them.

She went on to say that they were not alone. Any number of kids have to find someone to take care of them after school. There are a number of women in the community that have to work. Some lost their husband during the war. Others need to work to supplement the family income. The family simply can't make ends with one paycheck. Michael was well aware of those situations. But how would this care center work and operate. Do you expect the government to fund this endeavor? In the event that the government gets involved there will be a million and one regulations. If not, the government how will it function? Where would the funds come from?

CC explained that no she would not want the government involved. She has discussed the idea with Father Francis and some of the mothers and they are supportive. It will operate by volunteers. Many of the working mothers are available on various days. Some work nights. Others work on weekends. There will definitely be enough women to provide a staff. Father Francis offered to help in any way that the Parish can. CC offered to be the non-paid Coordinator and scheduling individual for the endeavor.

Michael listened intently. Then he spoke, "A project of this nature is way ahead of its time for the 1940's. But if anyone can pull it off you are the person. It sounds crazy, but I know better than to say no. You have my 100 percent support."

"I love you, she said with a big smile.

"Yea, Yea, I know you do. I must be crazy. But knowing you it will be successful," he said with a smile.

They both thought it would be great. A safe place for kids to go after school. Art classes. Organized sport programs. Volunteers coming into teach fun subjects. The opportunities for women to find employment and earn an income. The Parish involved from a spiritual position.

CC got working on the project the following day. She was definitely not a woman that would let "grass grow under her feet." A woman of action in all aspects of her life. Michael was indeed extremely proud of her.

A bit more of the history of "Our Lady"-The Parish of Our Lady, Help of Christians. More about the significance and importance of the church to the people of the parish and community of Little Dublin in general:

In 1874, Bishop Danell purchased a plot of land in Folkestone and 1883 his successor, Bishop Coffin, visited Father Cahill to discuss the possibility of building a new church on the site. Between 1880 and 1884 different sites were considered, including one which was to become Kingsworth in 1927. Proposals were put forth to Lord Radnor by the Diocesan authorities to exchange the plot for another in West Folkestone. Lord Radnor did not appear to have been very enthusiastic and the matter was dropped. In 1885 firm plans were made to construct a church in the site at Townsend.

In the 1880's Townsend was a rapidly developing area. The local authorities were anxious to improve the width of what had by then become Guildhall Street. At a meeting of the General Purposes Committee on August 9, 1886 it was enquired of Mr. Pledge what his clients, the Trustees of the Roman Catholic Church, intended to do about the three old cottages which stood there. He replied that they were ready to pull them down when the necessity arose, and that they would be willing to give up a portion of the land for widening the street,

However, things were not destined to run smoothly for a number of reasons. Father Dennan had wanted to employ Mr. Walters as architect but the Diocesan authorities ruled otherwise and Mr Aloysius Scott Stokes was finally engaged. In August 1888 the work of constructing the new church had begun. By the summer of 1889 all was ready. The outside of the building presented an imposing appearance.

It was said of it in the Kentish Gazette, "The church is a substantial building in the early Gothic style. It is built of local red bricks with Bath-stone dressings and has two towers. In the space between the towers is a very handsome Gothic window, one of the main features of the building. The wall above, like the towers, has a parapet in stone and is surmounted by a gable with a stone cross at the apex. On the left, and recessed from the church, is the Presbytery in the same style of the architecture, and glazed in leaded lights. The doors, external and internal, are of oak."

There were some assertions that the new church opened on June 21, 1889 but no evidence supports this. All recorded reports agree on one date-July 17, 1889.

CC was totally committed to the opening of the after-school program at the Folkestone Art School. After talking with the President and several Directors she was ready to move forward. And move she did. Her first contact was her old school chum and life time friend-Father Francis O'Rourke. He was an individual with a larger than life personality and a true mover and shaker.

He began his efforts by promoting the project from the pulpit. He explained that he was personally completely committed and determined to see that it succeeded. He then went on to say that the members of the community and parish need to pledge the support-both financially, and even more importantly their time. He went on to repeat that for the program to succeed full support was required. They will need to commit their-time-talent-and treasure. His gifts of leadership and compassion came through loud and clear.

CC could not have been any more grateful. Following Mass, she met with him in the rectory. Gave him a big hug, shed a few tears, and said simply there was not any way she could put into words what his endorsement meant to her personally as well as the project. With his blessing she just knew the program would be a success. He replied saying that he was delighted to be a part of the project. Everything he said he felt strongly about. And that he planned to show up on a regular basis. This was more to him than one sales pitch and walk away. He believed in what CC was going to do. He assured her to remember the famous one liner-"With God all things are possible." And this was important not only to the parish but the entire community of Little Dublin.

With the meetings behind she began what would prove to be the real hard work-lining up volunteers, providing the necessary art supplies, finding several individuals with an art background to work on the executive committee, and of course funding. As the result of her total commitment everything was taking shape, funds were coming in, and program was off and running. Of course, her good friend, Annie Ackley, was at the head of the line of the volunteer artists willing to give of her time and talent. And quietly always providing financial help. Nothing pleased her more than helping young people hone their artistic skills.

Michael offered his support and encouragement by listening, making suggestions when asked, and most importantly when CC got frustrated or disappointed, a big hug. But he always stayed in the background. This was her project and he did not want to interfere or deflect any attention his way. His project was the memorial he had discussed with his friend Franny.

The two of them had several meetings to discuss the possibilities. The parish owned some five acres of land directly across the street from the church. Father O'Rourke had some thoughts of his own on how to best use this parcel of land. Maybe try to build a few houses for the less fortunate of the parish-sell it for commercial development-perhaps the school could put it to good use. These, and a few other ideas, seemed to be good use of this precious piece of land that had been owned by the parish for many years. The original parishioners had great vision when they acquired it. The cost of a piece of property of that size would be cost prohibitive in today's world.

But, perhaps the idea he liked best of all was the idea of creating a permanent open space. A place that not only parishioners would enjoy, but a place the entire community could be a part of. A playground for the children. A place where young mothers could meet and walk their babies in carriages. Older men could sit and play checkers. Small flowering gardens. He was always thinking of ways to bring the entire community together-not just Our Lady parishioners. Now with Michael suggesting the memorial he was very excited about including this possibility. The park would be dedicated to the pathfinders who had the vision and fortitude to indeed make this parish a reality. Michael and Father O'Rourke knew what they had to do next. Bring the idea to the Parish Council for their thoughts, and hopefully, for their approval to move forward.

They put together a plan with some drawings and a proposal. The following month they were on the schedule for the regular monthly meeting. The big night finally arrived. Nervously, they held hands, said a short prayer, took a deep breath, and entered the Council meeting room. Following a few minutes of formality and small talk everyone settled down for business. The meeting lasted more than two hours-lots of questions, a bit of anxiety, tempers, and finally some smiles.

The council asked the two of them to leave the room for short time. Council wanted to convene themselves and make a decision. That they did. Less than one hour later they were asked to return. The Council President smiled and said the decision was unanimous-the plan is approved. Michael and Father O'Rourke hugged each other and then hugged the Council members. Now the hard work would begin. They hit the ground running. As in all matters Father O'Rourke offered his favorite quote "With God all things are possible."

Back in the Rectory Michael and his friend, Franny, had a cup of tea and talked about recent events. After an hour or so of conversation Michael asked to share a thought that has been on his mind.

Franny smiled and said, "Shoot!"

Michael then went on to talk about an idea that has been on his mind for some time. The thought of entering politics. Taking on this project and watching CC with her school involvement convinced him that they have an obligation to the community. To try to help make the community a better place for everyone. Try to become a member of Parliament. Go to London and represent the constituency of the district.

Father O'Rourke's immediate response was he was not surprised. Followed up with he thought it was a great idea. Michael had generations of family from the district. They both were well liked and committed. A military veteran. Parish member. Businessman. A wife involved in many projects. Michael thanked him and said the next move was to discuss the matter with CC.

They finished their tea and Michael was ready for the short walk home. They hugged and said good night. A powerful and intense day filled with two major decisions. He reflected on the events of the day and how proud he was of his ancestors and family heritage and the generations that made the community a great place to live and raise a family. Perhaps it was time for him to step up and make his contribution for his generation and the future generations to come.

When he arrived home, CC was anxiously waiting for his report on the Council meeting. Michael gave her the good news and then said that he wanted to shift gears and talk about his conversation with Franny and his thoughts of running for Parliament. She was both delighted and excited for him, for both of them. CC felt that they were blessed in so many ways. Michael was building a career. CC was moving forward with the after-school program and her own art career. They were blessed with two healthy and great kids who were moving into their teenage years.

With the thought of the children she began talking to Michael about them. CC went on to say how different they were. Molly seemed to have "sand in her shoes," an expression Michael used often. In a word-travel. She was anxious to travel and see the world. Experience different cultures and people. Live among them. Molly also wanted to help the marginalized people of the world. CC reminded Michael of the time she came home from school without her pencil case. When asked where it was. She told her mother, "I gave it to one of the kids who did not have any pencils." Molly was in second grade at the time and it was a foreshadowing of what was to come.

While Jimmy was a good kid. Thoughtful of his friends and their families. Active in the church and an altar boy. More than willing to share whatever he had with others. He loved the Folkestone area and especially the sea. Always the sea. He had no desire to leave the area. No desire to leave his family and friends. Most of them would most likely live their lives in the area. He was fine with that.

Michael agreed. They had two wonderful children. Two different individuals. Both would travel down two different paths. As it should be. Michael then told CC about a book that one of his shipmates gave him when they were discharged. A spiritual book that they read together aboard the ship. They found solace, hope, and spiritual direction.

With that said he took the book off the shelve. The title of the book is The Prophet, written by Kahill Gibran, a poet, philosopher, theologian, and artist born in the 1800's.

The Prophet was published in 1923, is still in publication, and has sold millions of copies. He told CC that he wanted to read her one of the poems:

ON CHILDREN

And a woman who held a babe against her bosom said, Speak to us of Children.

And He said:

Your children are not your children.

They are the sons and daughters of Life's longing for itself.

They come through you but not from you.

And though they are with you yet they belong not to you.

You may give them your love but not your thoughts for they have their own thoughts.

You may house their bodies but not their souls.

For their souls, dwell in the house of tomorrow, which you cannot visit,

not even in your dreams.

You may strive to be like them, but seek not to make them like you.

For life goes not backward nor tarries with yesterday.

You are the bows from which your children as living arrows are sent forth.

The archer sees the mark upon the path of the infinite,

And He bends you with His might that His arrows may go swift and far.

Let your bending in the Archer's hand be for gladness.

For even as He loves the arrow that flies so He loves also the bow that is stable.

Wow! As he was reading the last-line he looked over at CC to see tears flowing down her cheeks. He put the book down, got up, and gave her a huge hug and gentle kiss on the cheek. The message had a powerful impact on both of them. Over the years to come, whenever they questioned a life decision that either Jimmy or Molly made, they would read ON CHILDREN. As always, the reading provided faith and peace in their "CHILDREN."

It was definitely time for bed. Quite a day.

They were both up early and down in the kitchen by 7 0'clock. Guess all the excitement was a bit much. Especially for sleeping. The first thing CC wanted to know when was he going to take action about running for Parliament. She was disappointed with his response. He went on to say that it would not happen for a couple years. He explained timing is everything. The current member lived in Dover and indicated that he would be retiring after one more term. He held the seat for 18 years, was conservative, and tended to focus on the more affluent constituency of the Dover area and was not too interested in Little Dublin. The district covered the greater Dover/Folkestone area. He sensed the residents just might be ready for a change in their choice of a representative and direction as well. Michael's politics tended to be left of center. He was not a believer in the Nanny state, where the government acts as big brother. On the other hand he saw a void in the lives of many that could be changed with a hand up and not a hand out,

The other issues involved CC and her after school project and his ambitious plans with the shipyard and the Memorial Park. Also, they both agreed to stay focused on the last couple of years high school for Molly and Jimmy. After hearing his logic and plans CC agreed. She definitely agreed with the part about the children. As usual Michael was a bit more deliberate and CC was a bit more adventurous, and ready to "jump into swimming pools with no water." Of course, she was delighted that they had a plan. She did not like it when they were operating like "jelly out of the jar." She had a million of these theatrical metaphors.

With a loosely laid out plan they went about the business of executing it. Michael went to work only to find Cap'n Fitz already there. That was not something new. He was always the first person to be on the job. Michael realized that he was, as CC would say, "Like jelly out of the jar."

He was about to approach the Cap'n with an idea he had in his mind for some time. He asked the good Cap'n to have a seat and listen to a plan that he had in mind.

The Cap'n replied, "Okay, I can't wait to hear it."

Michael started by saying that this role reversal was not something he felt comfortable with, but the Cap'n is such an important part of his life he was going to make a suggestion. He reminded the Cap'n that anything Michael knew about boat building came from the Cap'n. That the Cap'n had an enormous amount of knowledge and skill. It seemed almost scandalous to let that talent go to waste.

How would the Cap'n feel about working with some of the young students, both boys and girls, from the Stella Maris School. Especially, getting some of the girls interested. That was very important. Perhaps, one day a week after school at the Folkestone Art School where CC was getting her program underway. And one day a week at the shipyard that was an important part of his life for countless years.

Michael went on to say that he had not worked out all of the details and he was definitely open to suggestions. His belief was that these young people could learn a real skill, and earn an excellent income, get married raise a family, and make a real contribution to the community.

The Cap'n would be an incredible mentor to these young people and put all of his talent and skills to a good cause. So, what do you think?

He looked over to the Cap'n and saw his eyes tearing up. The Cap'n responded with an overwhelming, "I love the idea! This retirement and sitting around building ships in a bottle and whittling all day is not for me. When do we start?"

Michael got up from behind his desk and gave the Cap'n a huge hug. He promised to work out the details with the school and they should be ready to start in a couple of weeks.

This type idea was exactly what he was talking about in giving the community a hand up and not a hand out. Teaching the young a skill and the ability to earn a good living and raise a family was something that he felt was extremely rewarding. No government involvement with endless rules and regulation. A volunteer program created by members of the community. There were few good paying jobs for young people that did not go on to university. Michael also believed that university was not for everyone. He felt that he was a prime example of that.

More history on "Our Lady"...

The opening of the Church of Our Lady, Help of Christians and St. Aloysius, was held on July 17, 1889. The morning of Wednesday July 17 dawned with clear blue skies and bright sunshine. There had been fears of rain and indeed the weather was to break later in the day. At one o'clock, the appointed hour for the playing of a game of cricket between the Corporation and Folkestone Cricket Club, a thunderstorm broke. The rain fell in torrents, "said The Folkestone Express." However, the prayers of the Catholic community were answered and as they gathered outside the new church there was an atmosphere of "gladness and delight."

Admission was to be by ticket only-such tickets being obtained from the Presbytery or from the offices of "Holbein's Visitor List" in George Lane. This was a local newspaper run and owned by Mr. Ambrose Hans Holbein. Despite being a Protestant, he would appear to have been sympathetic to the Catholics, and his newspaper was at the forefront of the publicity for the opening. Large notices appeared throughout July, giving full details of the important event.

At 10:45 the doors were opened to admit the congregation and all were in their places before the stated deadline of 11:15. What a sight the interior must have presented to them on the first day.

"In the interior of the Church a gallery is placed between the two towers, this is approached by a stone staircase in the turret on the right side of the building. The building, which is 138 feet long and 36 feet wide between the piers, is spanned by a steel roof, with the Principals of Gothic design, and is boarded and paneled on the underside. The Pulpit is of oak. The font, which is underneath the gallery at the east end of the Church, is of Hopton wood stone.

This description, from the "Kentish Gazette" July 23, 1889 continued, "The main altar is a magnificent piece of workmanship, carved in oak by Meyer of Munich. Above is a large crucifix and statue of the Virgin and St. John and below in an arcading are paintings representing St. Augustine, St Andrew, St. Patrick, St. Lawrence, and St Francis of Assisi. On the front of the altar table is a beautiful reproduction of Da Vinci's great painting, The Last Supper, and on the table is a very massive and elegant tabernacle."

However, there was one thing that was not ready for the opening- the organ, which should have graced the chamber-so for the occasion, music was to be provided by a large harmonium. The sacristy was approached under the organ gallery. As an addition to the main altar, the Church had two side altars.

At 11:30 the service started. The seating accommodations proved hardly adequate and all 750 places had been taken. The Opening Ceremony included a procession, blessing from the Bishop of Southwark, High Mass and the performance by a number of choirs. This was followed by an afternoon reception in the old schoolrooms."

Ancestors from both CC's and Michael's family were fortunate and blessed to be there for this extremely important event. The importance of this Church to their families could never be overestimated. They both took their commitment to "Our Lady" very seriously.

Michael continued to work on the growth and further development of his shipbuilding operation. The past few years he was able to diversify and develop sources of new contacts and expand the operation. But he was not content. If not anything Michael was a dreamer and a man with vision. He told CC of his latest dream. One-night following dinner he said he wanted to talk a bit about a grand idea he had been mulling over for several months. Whenever he talked like this she would get a bit nervous. He always had something going on in his head. For example-The War Memorial-Getting into politics-Helping with CC and her after school project-getting Cap'n Fitz involved teaching the kids of Little Dublin. He simply was never content to stay the course and relax. She smiled and said, "Okay, let's go out on the porch, have our tea, and I will sit and listen and you can outline your latest dream." He clearly was a visionary.

With their tea and biscuits in hand they sat down on the hard maple rocking chairs that they both loved. The porch was large and wrapped around the entire house. Cool breezes were always coming in off the sea. They both enjoyed sitting and rocking. They used this special place to discuss and resolve all the issues that a family is confronted with. Whenever they were there the correct answers always came. Michael was convinced the answer would be there for his latest idea.

He looked over at CC and smiled. "Okay, here goes. Relax. Remember these thoughts and ideas are still very much just a dream." He went on to explain that the company had developed and grown. Yes-there has been expansion. We have clients all the way south close to Southampton and north we are above Dover. The economy is booming following the war. Both in the UK and the Continent.

Bingo! CC immediately realized what was coming next. This crazy husband of hers wants to expand to the Continent. He responded with a smile, "You know me so well. Didn't take you long to figure that out. Yes, that's my thought. The English Channel is but 30 nautical miles across to the French coast of Calais. Once there the entire Continent is open for potential business. The Mediterranean. The coast of Spain. French Riviera. The island of Mallorca-sailboat capital of the world. The potential is limitless. He reminded CC of his former Navy friend, Eddie Boyle, who gave him the Kahill Gibran book of poetry and philosophy. He lives on Mallorca, is in the boat business and has many contacts.

It was clear to CC that Michael was more than just a bit excited. His passion was quite obvious. She had no doubt that he would pursue this the way he does any project once he makes a commitment. He went on to explain that the first step was to contact Eddie Boyle in

Mallorca. CC gave her blessing for Michael to make the trip to Mallorca. She realized that anything short of agreeing would be a waste of time. Once Michael had an idea a plan would surely follow soon.

CC then asked what other plans he was dreaming about. He quickly added that he wanted to take the Ferry from Folkestone to Calais and the major yacht basins in the Normandy Region. Contact the major Sailing Magazines on the Continent and put together an advertising campaign with the help of a major advertising agency in London.

With all of that said CC was a bit overwhelmed. She always knew that Michael was a big thinker, but never imagined anything of this magnitude. They talked for a few more minutes and CC finally announced that she was exhausted simply from listening. It was time for bed. She smiled and said we can talk more tomorrow. Michael got up from his rocking chair, walked over and placed a gentle kiss on her cheek. He was excited and eager to get moving on with the project, but he knew when it was time to stop. At least for a while. Tomorrow is another day.

Early the next morning he asked if she still felt it would be okay for him to contact his friend Eddie.

She replied, "Absolutely, make your phone call."

He thanked her said he would wait until he got to the office. He hurried through his breakfast and walked briskly to the office. As usual Cap'n Fitz was already there working on one of his many projects for the school kids. The Cap'n could see that Michael was a man on a mission, and said so. Michael said he had an important long-distance phone call to make and would fill him after he finalized the phone call.

As he was placing the call thoughts rushed through his mind-Hopefully, Eddie will be there, what will Eddie think of his plan-how soon can they get together-where will they meet. The list of questions seemed endless. The phone rang for what seemed to be forever. In the next instant he heard the voice of his old friend-Eddie. They spoke for a few minutes getting caught up with the recent events of their lives. Marriage. Children. Work. Health.

Finally, Eddie asked the important question, "Michael, what is the real purpose of the call. I have known you far too long and far too well that you are not calling to check on my health."

They both broke into laughter. Michael replied, "You are so right. You do know me. I want to share a vision and future plan for my boat building business"

With that said he spent the next thirty minutes outlining the details and responding to questions that Eddie brought up-legal, logistical, practical, financial, and many others.

To which Michael replied, "They are all details. With your help I know that we can solve all of them."

Eddie responded as always when dealing with his friend, "Of course they are details. You never look at issues as a problem. Always believing they are details and they will be resolved. And you are almost always right."

They both agreed it was time to get off the phone. The long-distance bill would be a whopper. Eddie suggested that Michael get a flight to Barcelona and meet at the airport. Michael was concerned how they would get from the airport to Mallorca.

"Don't worry that will be my job. You just bring all of your plans and programs on how in the hell you are going to pull this project off," Eddie laughingly said.

Michael immediately realized that he could not hold telling CC how the conversation went. He told the Cap'n he needed to go home and tell her the details of the phone call. He promised that he would return and fill Fitz in also. He did mention to tell him that the good Cap'n would be a part of, and included in, his exciting idea. Hustling home and thinking all of the way how and when he would leave for Spain it was difficult to contain himself. Once in he hugged CC and explained that Eddie would be more than willing to help

"Okay, next question. When do you want to leave, CC asked?"

"Wow, I got so caught up in the whole notion I never really thought about that," was Michael's response.

CC smiled and said, "That's kind of an important detail. No?"

"Ah, yea, I guess so," he laughingly said.

After a bit more conversation the decision was made. The sooner the better. Neither one of them were much on delaying whatever it was that had to be done. Today was Monday. How about Wednesday. Both agreed. Decision was made. A phone call was made to the airport and reservations made. A flight was booked from London's Heathrow Airport to the Barcelona El Prat Airport-a relatively short flight of some two hours.

A quick phone call to Eddie, his old Navy buddy, and the adventure was in place. He gave Eddie the details of the flight and now the plan was about to begin. A short 48 hours from now. Michael sat back in his chair and took a deep breath.

"CC can you believe this. We just talked about the idea last night and in 48 hours I am going to be on an airplane heading for a final destination of the island nation of Mallorca."

"Of course, I can believe it. You never cease to amaze me. You are definitely a man on a mission. Always," was her answer.

He kept busy for the next couple of days and before he knew it he was on his way. Up early and ready to go CC drove him to the Folkestone train station and the ninety-minute train ride to Heathrow Airport. As he boarded the plane, he became excited. Excited about a number of things. The flight to Barcelona. His first visit to Spain. Meeting up with his old Navy buddy. Spending time in Mallorca. Discussing his new plan. Eddie being a part of the plan. Lots to think and talk about. But for now, he needed to simply connect his seat belt, take a deep breath, sit back relax, and enjoy the flight.

And that he did. He drifted into a deep sleep. The next thing he heard was the flight attendant giving landing instructions. A bit groggy he slowly got himself together and looked out the window and saw the beautiful Mediterranean Sea below. He could feel himself getting excited in anticipation of what was to follow.

Bump! He felt the wheels touching the runway. Wow! He was in Barcelona, Spain! He could hardly believe that he was on his way to chase his dream. He checked through security, went to baggage pick up and collected his suitcase, and the short walk to their agreed meeting place in the airport. Just a few minutes of a walk, and there he was. His old friend, Eddie Boyle. They gave each other a big hug. Stepped back and looked only to see both of them were a bit choked up. Another hug and then off to the parking area.

Michael asked, "How are we going to get to Mallorca."

"Not to worry. Everything is under control. I have a rental car to the port and we will take a water taxi out to the island," Eddie replied.

Eddie headed in a northerly direction some 14 kilometers to the center of Barcelona. Once in the city he told Michael that he would take the scenic drive through the center of the city. He explained that they were on the Boulevard La Rambla. A wide pavilion lined with beautiful trees and flowers every color of the rainbow. Michael was overwhelmed. Shops of every size were everywhere. Nothing like this in Folkestone, England. Eddie explained that La Rumba is often compared to 5th Avenue in New York and the Champs Elysees in Paris.

As they approached the Parc de la Ciutadella Eddie pulled to the side of the road and parked. He explained to Michael that the park was the crown jewel of the city. The park was designed by Antoni Gaudi, a Spanish architect, who designed many of the Cities most beautiful parks and structures. A legendary figure in the history and culture of Barcelona. Born in 1852, he died tragically after being struck by a trolley car in 1926. However, he left a great history-a sampling-Park Guell, Casa de las Batives. It seemed that there was a Gaudi building on almost every corner. He truly is a revered member of Barcelona history. Even the young people of today know who Antoni Gaudi is and his place in the culture of this city.

The Parc de la Ciutadella was begun inn in 1900 and completed in 1914. Like the La Rambla, the park is compared to some of the famous parks of the world-Central Park in New York and Hyde Park in London. Michael was delighted that Eddie stopped and they were able to tour this beautiful place. Among the sights. A lake with young lovers rowing on a sunlit afternoon. A zoo. Trails for walking and hiking. Restaurants. Young mothers pushing strollers with their babies. A gorgeous piece of real estate carved right in the heart of a bustling city of millions.

Following lunch at a lakeside restaurant in the park it was time to move on. They had a pleasant conversation but decided to hold off a serious conversation about any business plans until they reached their final destination. Back in the car and a fifteen-kilometer drive to the harbor where they would turn in the rental automobile and board the water taxi for the one-hour trip out to Mallorca.

The drive was a pleasant one and the views fantastic. The roadway hugged the coastline, with the Mediterranean off to the right. The only thing unusual to Michael was that he was sitting on that side and Eddie was driving. He smiled when he finally realized why he felt a bit uncomfortable. In Spain you drive on the right side of the road and the driver is on the left side of the auto. Unlike England where the reverse happens. They both had a chuckle when Michael burst out laughing and said this really has been an adventure.

They pulled into the auto rental facility and returned the vehicle and purchased passage for the water taxi. A very easy transaction. Eddie explained that the harbor is always very busy and that this was the way you got out to Mallorca so the merchants try to make the whole process as simple as possible.

The water taxi was a power boat handling as many as 150 passengers and made a few stops once it arrived in Palma Mallorca. The trip was delightful. This was Michael's first trip. Little did he know at the time it would be the first of many. Before long he would be an old hand at getting from Folkestone to Mallorca.

Their stop was second on the schedule. Port de Solier was located on the northwest part of the island. As they pulled in Eddie gave Michael some of the details-A very popular vacation spot. Sport fishing for blue fin tuna. Commercial fishing. Gorgeous beaches. Home to many of the rich and famous from around the world. Sailboats of every size-Catboat, Sloop, Yawl, Ketch, and the biggest of them all-Schooner.

Michael was overwhelmed. He could not help but thinking the boats that he built were small potatoes compared to what he was looking at. His first reaction was that he was in over his head with the bright idea that he had. He would never be able to pull off his dream of building and selling boats over here. And just as quickly a second thought popped into his mind. I can do this! There is clearly a market here. And with the help of Eddie and Cap'n Fitz and CC back home we will do it. If Michael was one thing, he was a positive thinker and a man of vision.

The water taxi pulled into the harbor and they disembarked. Michael carrying his luggage and Eddie taking care of the briefcase that Michael brought with the details of his plan. Eddie's sailboat, and home, was docked a short 100 meter walk down the harbor. Everyone seemed to know him. Hi Eddie. Where you been Eddie. Who is your friend. The harbor has not been safe since you left, they teased. All could natured fun. Eddie would smile with a wave and kidding remark.

He stopped at the slip where his boat was moored. A beautiful fifty-foot Ketch. Wow! What a gorgeous vessel. As Michael stepped onto the gun-whale and into the ship Eddie gave him a helping hand. Once on deck Michael dropped his luggage and looked at the sights. "What a place, what a boat, what a view. No wonder you don't want to leave," He said with a big grin.

Michael could not help but see the name of the boat emblazoned in large bold letters-**JUST FOR TODAY.** He asked Eddie about the name and its meaning.

"We can talk about that a little later. Right now, why don't you unpack and take a nap," was his response.

He did not argue about a suggested nap. He was ready. A long day. As he prepared to lay down, he took a few minutes to reflect on the events of the day. Starting with CC driving him to the train station in Folkestone. Followed by a flight to Barcelona. Met by his friend Eddie at the airport. Their trip into Barcelona and their visit through Antoni Gaudi's parks and seeing some of his many structures. The drive to the harbor and returning the rental car. Finally, a water taxi ride out to Mallorca. Final thought on the day-Automobile-train-airplane-tour of Barcelona-automobile-water taxi! Wow! No wonder I am exhausted.

With that he drifted off into a deep sleep. Eddie walked down to the dock to get some seafood and vegetables for dinner. Stopping along the way to visit with friends and let them know who Michael was-simply an old Navy buddy who is visiting for a few days. The harbor is a close-knit group and if any stranger appears the gossip network goes in full mode. Eddie had absolutely no intention of talking about Michael trying to begin business in Mallorca. That would not be productive to anyone. If nothing else, no one was more-savvy about the boat business then Eddie. The boat business in Mallorca is THE business. Nothing even comes close. His plan was to hear from Michael first. Then give his input and suggestions on how he could be successful.

When he arrived back to the boat Michael was in the process of waking up and getting his act together. As they began talking Eddie started preparing dinner of two large lobster out of the sea two brief hours ago. A variety of fresh vegetables. Bread freshly baked at the harbor bakery. Topped off with homemade ice cream. Among any list of Eddie's many talents cooking would definitely, be near the top.

As they sat down to consume this fantastic meal Michael asked Eddie to tell a bit of history of this fabulous sailboat. He was very proud of JUST FOR TODAY. So talking about the boat and its history was a real pleasure for this old salt.

He told Michael to tell the story he would have to go back to the beginning and how he found himself in Mallorca several years ago. It all began during the war when they served together in the Navy. He explained how he made friends with a couple of their shipmates who were from the same small seaside community of Hastings on the coast of the Strait of Dover-some 50 kilometers south of Folkestone.

Michael spoke up, "I know all of that history. But what the hell does that have to do with the boat."

"Patience my friend. Patience. You always were in a hurry. We aren't going anywhere," Smiled Eddie.

"Okay, I'll try."

Eddie explained that these friends from his hometown had visited Mallorca prior to the war and fell in love with place. It seems once a sailor always a sailor. They wanted to live out there and find a way to make a living on this slice of paradise. They encouraged Eddie to join them. Being young, single, and a war survivor it sounded like an interesting proposition. So not long after they were discharged the three of them began the journey.

Not long after they arrived, he discovered that the owner of the boat was looking for someone to sail and be the captain of the ship. Eddie had the skill and jumped at the opportunity.

The owners of the ship that one day would be renamed JUST FOR TODAY by Eddie were from London. Ralph and Marion Wilkinson. Mr. Wilkinson was President of a large publishing company in England-Wilkinson Publishing Ltd. The company dated back to the 19th Century. They published fiction and nonfiction books. But the real source of revenue were the textbooks furnished to Universities and Elementary Schools throughout the United Kingdom.

They were a wonderful couple. Extremely wealthy and extremely generous. A trend he found to be quite common among the many wealthy members of the sailing community. They were kind and over the next several years a strong relationship and bond developed. Eddie captained the ship as they sailed the Mediterranean and Atlantic waters.

On one of the trips Mr. Wilkinson sat Eddie down and went on to explain that he had made arrangements with his lawyer to change the title, registration, and ownership to Eddie!

Mr. Wilkinson said that he was in good health and had no reason to believ anything was going to happen to him; however, there are no guarantees in life. He realized how much the two of them loved the boat. He went on to say that if he did not do something about the ownership the situation would not end well. The children would never appreciate the boat the way Eddie did. They rarely came to visit. They were self-centered and would most likely sell it for the cash. Eddie was stunned. He could not believe what he heard. He assured Mr. Wilkinson that he would never consider himself the owner. Merely the custodian, and of course never consider selling it. He told Mr. Wilkinson it was much more than a boat to him. The boat was his home and it was truly a privilege to be the Captain and work for Mr. Wilkinson.

Now a few words about this spectacular boat. It was built in the early days of the 20th Century by teakwood from Burma and mahogany from Brazil. If properly maintained it will last several more generations. It is a Two Mast Ketch, some fifty feet in length. Below there are sleeping quarters and a head both fore and aft. Living and dining quarters in the center. Top side what Eddie considered an open air 50 foot "living room." He went on to explain that is where he spent most of his time. Relaxing on a recliner chair, feel the breezes, watch the billowing clouds change forms, the dolphins playing on the horizon.

Michael could clearly see just how proud Eddie was of this gorgeous sailing vessel. He looked at Eddie with a big grin and said, "This is the kind of sailboats I want to build!"

They both had a big chuckle and sat down to enjoy the gourmet meal Eddie prepared for the two of them.

The next few days flew by. Eddie took Michael around "the Harbor"-(the locals refer to the dock, the small village, shipyard, the entire area as the Harbor.) They talked to several commercial fishermen, merchants in the village, boat owners, and friends. People that could be a big help in seeing Michael accomplish his business plan. He was quite impressed with "the Harbor" and the people. They all loved the sea and this special piece of paradise.

One day late in the afternoon they were relaxing on the "living room." Eddie changed his expression and appeared a bit on the serious side. He told Michael that he wanted to share some information of a personal nature.

Nervously Michael looked at Eddie and said, "Okay. You look so serious. What can it be. I am your good friend. We went through a war together."

"I know that. But I don't want you to be disappointed in me." He then went on to talk about the time when he first arrived on Mallorca after the war. His war injuries were causing pain and discomfort. He had not settled in to a level of security in his new position of captain. He noticed if he took a couple shots of whiskey at bedtime he slept better. When confronted with a business type appointment a couple of shots relaxed him. He began to walk down to the Harbor and join in for Happy Hour.

Michael began to see where the conversation might be going.

Eddie found himself getting drunk on a regular basis. A few of his friends confronted him. They pointed out that he did not drink that much before. Now he was drinking on a daily basis. His first reaction was one of resentment-"who are you to tell me that I drink too much." However, on reflection when he was alone he agreed. He was indeed drinking too much. He then began to control or not drink at all. Unfortunately, he could not control or not drink at all for more than a couple of days.

On one of his trips to Barcelona he looked up an organization that offered help with people having an alcohol problem-AA-Alcoholics Anonymous. Since that date he has not had a drink. As a matter of fact, he started an AA meeting in the little catholic church in the village. That all happened several years ago. He has committed his life helping people that suffer from the disease of alcoholism. He has made it common knowledge on the Harbor. Over the years he has seen many of friends and their friends find sobriety. AA is a major part of his life.

He concluded his comments by explaining why he named the sailboat JUST FOR TODAY. The statement is the guiding philosophy of Alcoholics Anonymous. He then gave a copy of the pamphlet to Michael with the comment-alcoholic or nonalcoholic it is an excellent roadmap for a life worth living:

JUST FOR TODAY

Just for today I will try to live through this day only-the next 24 hours. I will not try to tackle my whole life problem at once. I can do something for twelve hours that would appall me if I felt that I had to keep it up for a lifetime.

Just for today I will be happy. This assumes to be true what Abraham Lincoln said-"Most folks are as happy as they make up their minds to be."

Just for today I will adjust myself to what is and not try to adjust everything to my own desires. I will take my luck as it comes and fit myself to it.

Just for today I will try to strengthen my mind. I will study. I will learn something useful. I will not be a mental loafer. I will read something that requires effort, thoughtful, and concentration.

Just for today I will exercise my soul in three ways. I will do somebody a good turn and not get found out. I will do at least two things I don't want to do-exercise and not show anyone that my feelings are hurt.

Just for today I will be agreeable. I will look as well as I can. I will dress becomingly, act courteously, criticize not one bit, not find fault with anything, and not try to improve or regulate anybody except myself.

Just for today I will have a program to live by. I may not follow it exactly every day-but I will have one. I will save myself from two pests-hurry and indecision.

Just for today I will have a quiet half hour all by myself to relax and meditate. I will try to get a better perspective of my life.

Just for today I will be unafraid. Especially I will not be afraid to enjoy what is beautiful, and to believe that as I give to the world so will the world give me.

Michael got up, walked over to his friend, and with a tear in his eye he choked up, gave his friend a huge hug and said, "What a wonderful spiritual way of life to live by. Disappointed. Are you kidding me! I could not be prouder of you. You not only saved your own life you have helped save the lives of many others. There cannot be a bigger cause than saving the life of another human being. You not only saved them, but the other members of their family. The disease not only affects the individual but the family as a whole. I have had a limited exposure to the devastation. A couple of my employees and a few members of our parish. Unfortunately, not with any success. I tried, but had no idea what I was doing and I never heard of your organization. What is it – AA?"

Eddie thanked Michael for his support and kind words. He then went on to explain why he felt the way he did. They had many conversations during their time together during the war. Discussing their future after the war. Eddie listened with great interest as Michael talked about having a family. Building his own shipbuilding business. Providing employment for the young people of Little Dublin. His involvement with the Parish. The thought of maybe getting into politics. His list went on.

Eddie, while a spiritual person, mentioning the book THE PROPHET by Kahill Gibran that he gave Michael during the war, had no such plan or vision. He loved the sea and hoped that somehow, he could make a living from it. Beyond that he had not given the future much thought.

Michael interrupted him, "Whoa! Whoa! Think about what you are saying. You say not much thought for the future. You have committed your life to helping people and their families in the grip of the horrible disease of alcoholism. You took in Jose Perez a young boy without a family. You raised him to be a young man that is contributing to society. He now works building ships on the Dock and delivers newly constructed sailboats to the wealthy around the continent.

He then went on to say that they both had the same objective. To make the world a better place by helping their fellow man. They are taking two different roads to accomplish their goal. Different roads with the same result.

Eddie smiled and thought to himself, "This is why I love this guy. Always optimistic and positive." He also thought-maybe he is right.

Their time together was coming to a close. Michael would leave in the morning for his journey back to CC and Folkestone. A successful trip to put it mildly. His plan was beginning to take shape and Eddie would be a part of it.

Early the next morning they began the trip for Michael's return to Folkestone. Eddie made arrangements for the auto rental when they got off the water taxi. He explained to Michael that he makes regular trips to Barcelona and the main AA office on Boulevard La Rumba. A place he visited on a regular basis. He wanted Michael to realize that this was not a problem taking him to the airport.

A beautiful morning. Plenty of blue sky. Calm seas made for a pleasant trip on the water taxi. They picked up the auto rental and drove straight to the airport. There was not any time for sightseeing. A big hug for the two of them. Excitement about the business plan. Definite plans to stay in contact. Michael boarded the plane. The plane left right on schedule.

He settled back in his seat and reflected on the week. A great deal was accomplished. Several important contacts were made. Contacts that would have never happened were it not for Eddie. He was quite confident that this project would become a reality. Maybe slowly, but for sure it will happen. The market potential for the sale of sailboats on Mallorca had fantastic potential. He was anxious to get home and share the events of the week with CC and Cap'n Fitz.

He no sooner drifted off to sleep when he heard the stewardess announcing to prepare for landing.

Once in the airport he picked up his luggage, phoned CC and told her he would be getting the 2:20 pm train arriving in Folkestone at 4:40 pm. The train arrived right on schedule. Michael thought to himself how nice it was to depend on the rail service in England. The very rails his ancestors laid. He smiled to himself. CC could sense the excitement as Michael rushed to the car. After a brief hug and a few kisses Michael began talking. And talking. And talking. Nonstop all the way home. It was clear to her that the immediate future was going to be an exciting time.

They were sitting in the kitchen having tea and a biscuit and Michael was giving her details. Mallorca is a beautiful. Eddie is indeed a special friend. He introduced to me to some special people with contacts in the boat business. They have a framework for a business plan. He met some wealthy boat owners. They confirmed that there is definitely a market for quality upscale sailboats. Eddie has remarkable credibility with not only these people, but all over the Harbor. CC finally got him to calm down and take a deep breath. Tomorrow is another day.

Following a good night sleep, he was ready to get to the shipyard and bring Cap'n Fittz up to date. He suddenly realized that the only thing he has talked about since he got home was-HIMSELF! As he sat down to breakfast, he gave CC a sheepish look and said, "I apologize."

"For what," was her response.

He then went on to say that all he talked about was his trip and the challenges and opportunities. CC had an agenda of her own. Her relationship with the school program and working with her friend, Annie Ackley, on her artistic endeavors.

As usual, she told him not to feel bad. She realized how important the project was to him and, of course, to the business and their family. She brought him up to date with the school program and the progress Cap'n Fitz has made with the school children and their enrollment in his boating classes. Twelve children were enrolled and to the surprise and delight three were young girls. Annie Ackley was becoming more involved with the school program as well as mentoring CC with both her painting and sculpting talents. Annie invited her to London and some exposure to the art community and her art gallery.

Michael was extremely pleased to hear all of this. He thought to himself what a great wife and partner I have. She clearly is the glue that holds the family together. The rock of the family. He goes off on these adventures and dreams and she keeps it all together.

This led to another topic. The children. Due to the timing of their birth the children were able to enroll in school in the same year. As difficult as it was to believe that they were going to be graduating together in a few months.

Molly was an adventurer. She had been that way since she was a little girl. Always wanting to go to a camp. Some adventure with the church. Going into the poor neighborhoods to help. Much of this activity came as the result of her strong relationship with Father O'Rourke.

Through his efforts and contacts at Catholic University (and help from the Maryknoll Nuns) he arranged for Molly to be accepted at the Catholic University of America in Washington, DC. Father O'Rourke attended there for some graduate work. So, at the end of summer she would be heading to America! Molly could hardly wait.

On the other hand, Jimmy Magee was more of a local boy. He loved the sea and the English Channel. He loved working at the shipyard. The White Cliffs were special. His boyhood friends were important. He was quite content to stay in Folkestone, Little Dublin, and Our Lady.

Michael was somewhat emphatic that he go on for more education. The lack of his own education was part of why he felt so strongly. He also told Jimmy that the world was changing and being educated was part of the change. Their business was growing and professional skills in all facets of business were vital. Reluctantly, Jimmy agreed and would be going to The London School of Economics in the fall.

Michael and CC could not believe that their two little kids were all grown up. And of all things both were going off to college! The notion of going to college when they were children would not even be a dream much less a reality.

They were very grateful for the many blessings in their lives. Our Lady and the Parish school gave their children the necessary skills-both academic and life skills-to make this possible.

⸙

THE GREAT WAR

King Edward died and was succeeded by King George V, and a new era began. On August 4, 1914, war was declared between Great Britain and Germany. The town almost immediately became a "prohibited area." The situation naturally curtailed the normal life of the town. The first little fleet of fishing boats, motorboats and almost anything that would float arrived at the harbour. The refugees from Belgium had begun to descend upon the town.

Every available space was taken up to house the refugees including church halls, schools, lodging houses and an extensive block of buildings in the Sandgate Road. It is estimated that 64,000 refugees passed through Folkestone. Some 15,000 were provided with food and shelter during the first few weeks of hostilities.

On May 25, 1917, at a time when people were still doing their shopping and Tontine Street was a scene of bustle and activity, a squadron of Gothas arrived from westward, releasing about four dozen bombs in what has been described as the biggest and deadliest raid of the war up to that point. A man was killed instantly when a large explosion occurred at the junction of Bouverie Road and Cherton Road. Other bombs fell in various locations but it was Tontine Street that was the scene of the greatest devastation. In all, seventy persons were killed and over one hundred injured during the raid. The town did not suffer any further bombing of any significance.

Many Folkestone men served in the armed forces at this time. A former pupil of the local Catholic School particularly distinguished himself. Acting corporal Richard Cotter was in the 6th Battalion, East Kent Regiment (The Buffs.) He had already been blinded in one eye when, early in 1916, he was involved in heavy crater fighting around the Hohenzellern Redoubt. His right leg was blown off below the knee and he was wounded in both arms. Yet, he succeeded in making his way unaided some 20 yards to a crater where he took command of several men of his own company. He rallied their spirits and organized them to resist further attacks successfully. His cheery, gallant leadership was an inspiration, even though his wounds, which were to prove fatal, were not dressed for two hours and he was not moved for fourteen. However, his Victoria Cross was arrived so swiftly that his Corps Commander, Sir Herbert Gough, was able to pin the purple medal ribbon on Cotter before he died as he lay on his hospital bed. After the Armistice the country started to get back to normal.

They kissed goodbye and went their separate ways. Michael headed for work and to share the events of his trip to Mallorca. CC for the train station and a trip into Charing Station and a visit with her friend, Annie Ackley,

CC always enjoyed the train ride into London. Sitting by the window and watch the rural English countryside go by. Gentle rolling hills, dairy farms and cows grazing, and one hour later a complete change of landscape. First, small seaside village along the coastline, then suburban blue-collar working communities, and then the skyline of the city. High rise buildings reaching to the sky. The Thames River. Westminster Abbey. As many times as she has seen the view it always impressed her.

The train arrived right on time. She gathered her personal belongings, left the station, and down the steps to the Charing Cross tube station. Minutes later she arrived at the Piccadilly Circus station. She had agreed to meet Annie Ackley at the breakfast restaurant on Shaftesbury Street, a short block from the tube station, home to the theatre district in the West End.

While sitting there waiting for her friend the thought of Piccadilly Circus came to mind. She remembered hearing of "Piccadilly Circus" when she was a young woman growing up in Folkestone. Her thoughts were, it must be some type of circus in London. Wrong! So, she decided to check the history books and find the origin of the term.

To her surprise she discovered Piccadilly Circus is a road junction and public space in London's West End. The road was built in 1819 to connect Regent Street with Piccadilly Street. In this situation "circus" comes from the Latin word "circle" meaning a round open space at a street junction.

The name Piccadilly was another story that she found fascinating. The street Piccadilly first appeared in 1626 named after a house belonging to Robert Baker. He was a tailor famous for selling piccadills, a term used for various kinds of collars.

Thus, the term "Piccadilly Circus." She smiled as the thought of her original research came to mind. Today, Piccadilly Circus is the heartbeat of central London. Home to the theatre district of the West End Shopping of every form imaginable. Art Galleries of every form. Painting. Sculpture. Jewelry. High end artists and struggling newcomers. People and tourists everywhere. The "Circus," as it is referred to by the locals is quite similar to Times Square in New York City.

Simply sitting and waiting CC could feel the electricity. She visited the area often since becoming an adult and always enjoyed her time there. A few minutes later she heard her name being called. She came out of her thoughts and recognized her friend, Annie. They hugged and Annie asked if she had been waiting long.

"Not at all. I always enjoy being in Piccadilly Circus. It is exciting just sitting and watching the people and all of the activity," she replied with a smile.

The two of them headed to Annie's Art Gallery in the Haymarket area on the corner of Coventry and Glasshouse Street.

This was CC's first visit to the gallery. A three-story building with several rooms. Each of the rooms were filled with specific art forms. Sculpture. Water paintings in one room. Acrylic in another. Ceramics. Annie was obviously a very talented artist and widely respected. Being a bit on the curious side she peeked at the prices. Wow! She was not only widely respected, she was indeed highly expensive.

After a tour of the gallery they retired to the third floor. The entire third floor flat was Annie's living quarters. Beautiful. Tastefully, and artfully decorated with pieces from around the world in addition to her own creations. Annie told CC to sit on one of the chairs that came from Hong Kong and relax. Annie went to the kitchen to prepare tea and biscuits. CC was thoroughly impressed and could not help but wonder why a woman with such immense success would want to come to their little art school in small town Folkestone.

Shortly after Annie returned with freshly brewed tea (no tea bags for her, she has an expensive tea box from China, and of course filled with imported tea) and freshly baked biscuits from a bakery a few doors down. Along with the biscuits she brought cheese and fresh sandwich sliced ham, and a variety of fruit pieces. How nice. CC thoroughly enjoyed the company of Annie. And she thought to herself I think she just might enjoy being in my company. That thought brought a small smile.

Annie spoke up, "This morning has been crazy busy and I want to just relax and enjoy our visit."

CC replied, "Sounds great to me. I have so many questions to ask you. I hope it will be okay and trust that you will not think I am being nosy. I am so impressed with your talent and success. You are a world traveller and certainly know your way around in what most consider a man's world. I admire you and you serve, whether you realize it or want to, as a real role model for me. I aspire to emulate you and what you have accomplished as a woman. If you are willing, I sure would like you to share about your early life and how you arrived where you are now."

Annie and CC were about the same age-early forties. Annie was an attractive woman, always well dressed. Even in casual clothes when she was in Folkestone. A world traveler. Had contacts in such exotic places as Hong Kong and Singapore. She had a great presence and could hold a conversation with anyone.

On the other hand, CC felt inadequate in a social situation with people of wealth and power. She rarely left Folkestone, and then only for a trip to London. A very humble background. Surely, Annie must have been raised in an upper-class family background and social status. She had no idea what she was about to hear.

Annie smiled and said, "Okay, sit back and relax."

With that said Annie began talking. She explained that she was raised in a small village on the southern coast of Wales. One of seven children. A modest home at the foot of the Cambrian Mountains in the peaceful Elan Valley. The small village of Tenby. A mining area.

Wales for centuries has depended on the mines for a way of life. For generations her family worked the mines. Her six siblings still live there. Four of her brothers are miners and her two sisters are married to miners. They are all content. Have nice families and comfortable homes. A good life.

Annie on the other hand could not wait to get out of school and go see the world. She had no real interest in finding a husband. Over the years she has had some meaningful relationships. But none that she was willing to marry. Her art and travel was what motivated her. Maybe one day she will settle down and marry. But for now, she found no need for a man to complete her life.

When she was just a little school-kid she became aware that she just might have some artistic talent. Their neighbors were an older couple and they had no children-Mr. and Mrs. Thomas Woolam. He was a retired miner and Mrs. Woolam was an art teacher in the village school. Before long she could see that Annie had talent. She began to take a genuine interest in Annie. As a matter of fact the two of them became like surrogate grandparents. All through her school years Mrs. Woolam became much more than a teacher. Always pushing, doing research on how and where she could pursue and continue to develop her talent. She also encouraged her to leave the village. Certainly, with the talent you have there is no future here.

Annie always listened and she was a dreamer. When she finished her local schooling (with the help of Mrs. Woolam) she was able to move to London, find a job in an art studio, and attend art school at night. She was forever grateful for Mrs. Woolam. She also made a commitment, and a promise to God, that if she ever had any success, she would help other young people that came from similar backgrounds as hers. Thus-her devotion to the young people of Folkestone and the Art School.

"Wow," exclaimed CC.

She went on to say she was surprised to hear her story. Their stories about family and growing up were similar. They both came from modest backgrounds, but Annie has developed an incredible life. World traveler. Successful art career. Full of confidence. The list went on and on. CC on the other hand was a shy young person from a small town. Married her high school sweetheart and mother of two young children-a son and daughter-about to graduate from high school.

She went on to tell Annie that she would never be able to hold her own in sophisticated conversation with power people, politicians, business leaders, and world travelers.

Annie went on to tell her, "Don't sell yourself short. Believe in yourself. Work hard and you will succeed. That was the advice Mrs. Woolam gave me years ago. Guess what she was right."

CC asked for Annie's help in helping her make that happen. Annie said she would. CC was about to embark on a life that was beyond her wildest dreams.

The day was coming to a close. Annie walked CC to the underground station that would take her to the train station and her ride back to Folkestone and Michael. They gave each other a big hug and Annie said that she would be down to Folkestone the following week.

CC boarded the train and in a matter of minutes the train pulled out of the station bound for her hometown. Normally, whenever she left London for home, she used the time for a nap. Not so today. She was so excited to get home and tell Michael about her day. Maybe with Annie's help and guidance I can become a successful artist. Hold her own with other successful people-both men and women. Spread her wings. Have a vision for the future. Michael seemed to have that ability. He is going to expand his business to Mallorca.

The train was arriving in Folkestone. The ride simply flew by. She looked out the window and saw her best friend and lover waiting on the platform.

He asked how her day went.

"Oh, Michael I can't wait to get home and tell you. I had an amazing day. Annie is a wonderful person and indeed a special friend," She responded.

Indeed, she could not wait to get home. Michael no sooner started the car and CC began talking. Non-stop. All the way home. Up the steps to the porch. She steered Michael to their favorite rocking chairs on the porch, took him by the hand, and instructed him to sit. All the while talking, and talking, and talking. This was a bit out of character for her. CC was always the one listening. Listening to Michael. Listening to their son Jimmy and his dreams. Listening to Molly and her vision of going to University in America. Always listening. Not so this day. Michael began to laugh and told her to slow down he couldn't follow everything she was saying. Jumping from topic to the next. What a great friend Annie Ackley is. How talented she is. Her home and gallery are beautiful. Annie thinks I have talent. She offered to let me put a few of my pieces in her gallery. Annie believes they will sell. Can you believe that. She believes someone would actually buy a piece of my sculpture!

Finally, she sat back and tears came to the corner of her eyes. Michael got up from his rocker and gave her a big hug and a kiss. He went on to tell her how happy he was for her and explaining that he always believed in her talent. Whenever he expressed that belief CC dismissed it as flattery from a husband. But now a highly successful artist was telling her. She put her head on his shoulder and both were silent for the next several minutes. They got up from the chairs and went off to bed. A couple powerful hours and the beginning of a new chapter in her life.

cyh

The next few years flew by...

Michael and his Mallorca venture were exceeding his wildest dreams. In large part through the efforts of his good friend, Eddie Boyle. He told Eddie that he wanted to share the profits with him. True to his low-key character he dismissed that idea as nonsense. He claimed that all he did was to introduce a few key people to Michael and his workmanship did the rest. Michael insisted and Eddie finally agreed to accept some of the profits. Far less than Michael was offering.

CC was working hard on the after-school art project with the children of Folkestone and her own art and sculpture project with incredible guidance and direction from Annie. Her pieces were selling routinely to some of the true connoisseurs of art in London. As a matter of fact, Annie gave her a private room in the gallery for her exclusive use. CC offered to pay rent. Annie refused, simply saying that all she was doing was a form of gratitude to the family in the south of Wales who helped her many years ago.

Jimmy Magee completed his studies at the London School of Economics. He expressed gratitude to his father for somewhat forcing him to attend this highly regarded university of higher learning. He was convinced that it was time well spent and time thoroughly enjoyed. The education would serve him well in the business aspect of their company.

Molly Magee completed her studies at the Catholic University in Washington, DC. and would continue her education at Villanova University in Philadelphia earning both a Masters and PHD in theology and spirituality. She definitely found her calling-travelling the world and guiding individuals on their path towards a spiritual life. While attending Catholic University she made a strong, and lasting connection with the Maryknoll Sisters of St. Dominic. The Sisters devote their lives in service around the world. Through their efforts Molly found herself in the island nation of Visby located in the middle of the Baltic Sea some 100 kilometers off the coast of Sweden Cap'n Fitz continued to work with the young people-both boys and girls-of the after school project at the Folkestone School of art. Teaching young people how to work on sailboats and how they are built. He loved it. He often thought of one day retiring from his shipyard. Leaving all the pressure and stress of the business. The business part especially. He did not like the business end at all. Working on boats and building them was another story. He never envisioned he would be doing what he was doing. He loved young people and he loved working on boats. He could not be happier.

Father O'Rourke was actively involved with the War Memorial project and his many other projects of the parish. Michael felt deeply indebted to his old school chum.

All seemed well in their world and the world in general. World War II was over. The world was at peace. Their individual careers and lives were going well. Everyone was healthy. Life could not be better... Or so they thought...

It was a typical Monday morning. The beginning of a new work week. Michael and CC had their typical breakfast of porridge, tea, juice, fruit, and toast. He gave CC a kiss on the cheek, a goodbye with a smile, and began the ten-minute walk to work. He thought to himself as he waved to some of the neighbors that it was an unusually sunny morning. Most mornings at this time of the year tended to be a bit on the cloudy side. He thought, oh well, I guess it is a good sign.

As he entered the shipyard he waved and offered a good morning to several of employees already hard at work. He was very proud of his employees. They often came in early without any prodding from him. They took pride in their work and if that meant coming in early to meet a deadline on some project that they did. From time to time he would ask Cap'n Fitz if he was paying them adequately. The good Cap'n always responded with the same words, "Why do you think they arrive early so freely. Yes, you compensate them more than adequately."

That was a lesson Michael learned a long time ago. Cap'n Fitz always paid him more than adequately. The good Cap'ns philosophy was always treat your employees fairly and they will more than compensate you. A philosophy Michael lived by.

As he entered his office, he saw Paddy O'Connor, his CPA accountant, sitting near his desk. Michael thought that a bit strange. Paddy rarely came to the office without telephoning first to make certain that Michael was there and able to spend time with him.

"Paddy, what brings you here at such an ungodly time of the morning," he asked. Paddy was always smiling. A cheerful, upbeat big Irishman if there ever was one. Not so this morning. He had a very somber look on his face. Definitely out of character for his old friend and schoolboy chum.

"Michael, I have some extremely difficult news to deliver. I don't know where to start." was the response of Paddy.

Michael became filled with anxiety and blurted out, "Damn it Paddy. Just tell me the news."

"You are broke and in debt," Paddy replied in a quivering voice.

He then went on to explain that their good friend, the young man they grew up and went to school with, and most importantly your banker, has been embezzling funds from your bank account for the past two years.

"Tommy Doyle!" shouted Michael.

"The one and only," Paddy sighed.

Michael went on to ask how it could be. He would trust Tommy with his life. He worked so hard to arrange the financing for Michael. Tommy knew both Michael and CC since they were little kids. Tommy knew this business was my life. He went on to say I just can't believe it. No not Tommy. How did this happen.

Paddy began to explain, "He created a Ponzi scheme. And as always in ventures of this type he got in over his head. Seems he had a gambling problem for quite some time."

"What in the hell is a Ponzi scheme," Michael screamed out.

Paddy went on to explain what a Ponzi scheme was and how it got its name. The scheme was named after Charles Ponzi a Boston businessman who operated in the 1920's. It is a fraudulent investment operation where the operator generates returns for older investors through revenue paid by new investors. The trick to making the plan work is finding sources of new revenue to replace the funds withdrawn from other accounts. Sooner or later the system collapses as the operator gets in over his head. He can only manipulate funds for so long. Taking money from one client's account and moving into another. Basically, it is like building a house of cards. That is exactly what happened here. It took a couple of years but eventually Tommy ran out of sources to replace the revenue.

The only thing different was that Tommy did not seek new investors. He simply manipulated funds of current bank customers. And most importantly these were people, much like yourself, who had complete trust in him. That is what makes it so difficult to understand. Lontime friends and neighbors.

"So what happens next. What does Tommy to say about all of this," Michael asked.

Paddy continued talking about the recent events explaining it all came to a crashing end last night. Tommy told his wife he was going out to the garage and check for something that he left in the car. Some fifteen minutes passed and he had not returned. She began to become concerned and went out to the garage. When she opened the door, she was overcome with the odor of carbon monoxide. Tommy was draped over the steering wheel and the motor was running.

She screamed. Turned off the motor. Dragged Tommy out and onto the ground. He was still breathing. She called the emergency people. They were there in minutes and took him to the hospital.

The police arrived on the scene and began searching the car. They found a suicide note explaining what he had done and how he had betrayed his wife, family, best friends and neighbors. He went into detail why he did what he did. In a word-gambling.

The note stated while he was the President of the bank he did not earn a great deal of money. So many of his friends had become successful businessmen (like Michael) and he felt he was a failure. He "borrowed" some money, gambled and won. Repaid what he had "borrowed" and things were going well. Then the reversals. Huge reversals that he could not repay.

He then went on to say that he could not go on any longer and had no choice but to end his life.

When they showed the note to his wife she collapsed and fainted. Another ambulance arrived and took her to the hospital. The entire scene took place in a matter of minutes.

Michael was in shock. His emotions were all over the place. Anger. Rage. Disbelief. Shock. Pity. Then the obvious question. So, what will happen to Tommy now.

Paddy said that he talked to the police and they informed him that he will be placed under arrest and charged with several crimes. Then he will be held for trial and results will follow. He has admitted to the crimes and most certainly will go to prison.

Michael's head was spinning. He simply could not process what he was hearing. Paddy suggested that he drive Michael home and the two of them present the information to CC. Michael agreed that it was a good idea. He did not think he could handle the matter by himself. Paddy was much more than his accountant. A lifelong dear and close friend. Much like Tommy.

Paddy suggested that they walk the few blocks to the house. He thought the walk would give Michael a chance to compose himself and relieve a bit of anxiety. Michael agreed. There was little conversation. At times the silence was deafening. As they approached the house Paddy asked Michael how he was doing. He suggested to Michael it would be important to maintain composure. If he lost his composure the situation would only worsen. He assured Paddy that he would keep himself together. The last thing he wanted was to see CC fall apart. He would try to convince her that they would work through the problem.

As they walked up the front porch steps the top one creaked.

"Damn it! I keep meaning to have that fixed, Michael thought to himself. When he looked up, he saw CC standing at the front screen door.

"What is going on. Why are you here," she said with a nervous look on her face "What is wrong?"

Michael took her by the hand and guided her to the two-seat swing they enjoyed so much. He put one arm around her shoulder and held her hand with the other. This did not comfort her. She pulled away and asked again, "Tell me. What is going on."

Michael cleared his throat and told her that Paddy has something to tell us. He explained that it was not good news. Then added that we will get through whatever the final outcome of this situation may be.

He looked over to Paddy who was sitting in one of the maple rockers. Paddy looked back seeking approval to begin talking. Michael nodded his head, once again putting his arm around her shoulder and holding her hand.

With that Paddy began to tell the story from the beginning. Every detail. CC was stunned. She would look at Michael and then Paddy. Her expressions were saying-I can't believe or comprehend what you are telling me.

Paddy continued. CC became extremely angry. Agitated. Hysterical. Tears. Anger. Shock. Disbelief. Michael tried to calm her down. She fell into his arms and asked, "What are we going to do."

He assured her that they would get through it. He went on to say that he was not exactly certain just how it would happen at this moment. They needed hope and a lot of faith. He reminded her that England survived World War II the country recovered, and there was peace in the world. If they could survive something of that magnitude, they could surely survive a financial setback.

CC replied in a bit of subdued sarcasm, "Oh yes, you and your eternal hope and optimism. So, what is next."

He went on to suggest that their next move would be to talk to their friend and spiritual director Father O'Rourke. Michael definitely felt that they needed to get rid of some of the anger and hostility raging inside both of them. Carrying that around would not help the situation for anyone. Next, he would telephone Eddie Boyle and advise him that he would be coming over for a visit in the following days to discuss some issues regarding the business. It is too involved to deal with on a phone call. Not to worry. I have not been over in a few months anyway.

Lastly, he wanted to meet with Tommy and have a discussion about the entire mess. He knew that this conversation would be extremely difficult to put it mildly. Nonetheless, it had to be done.

Michael all of sudden realized a strange feeling was coming over him. He was beginning to believe what he told CC – somehow, we will get through the situation. He was a very spiritual individual-had been all of his life. In his heart he knew that rage and revenge was not the answer. That would solve nothing.

Paddy offered to go with them when they visited with Father O'Rourke. Michael thanked him but said that would not be necessary. CC and he would be fine. He got up from the swing and gave Paddy a big hug, a kiss on the cheek, and thanked him for all of his help. He then added that for sure more help would be needed. And thanked him for being such a good friend in this most difficult of times. Paddy responded with a hug and assured Michael that he will be by his side and help in any way that he could. As he walked down the steps and up the street Michael thought how fortunate he was to have a true friend like Paddy.

He guided CC into the house holding her hand and smiled, "I will call Franny and see when we can meet with him."

"Okay, I am still frightened and angry, but feel a smidge better."

Michael dialed the phone and by a stroke of good fortune Father O'Rourke himself answered the phone. That rarely happened. Maybe a good sign. Without going into detail, he asked if they could meet.

Franny responded, "Of course. Anytime you want. I will be tied up with the Parish Council for the next couple hours. After that I am available."

Michael knew well how those "meetings" went on for hours. Both he and CC were exhausted. It was getting to be late in the day. He suggested breakfast in the Rectory at nine o'clock. That was fine with the three off them. The meeting was set for the morning.

After a restless night's sleep, they were up and ready to go well before 9:00 am. They decided to walk along the Leas and sit for a few minutes on one of the benches that overlooked the Channel. The sun was coming up, the water was shimmering, calm and peaceful. That old adage, "Things will look better in the morning" certainly applied here. Somehow that seem to apply at this moment. Both were still uncertain of what to do next. But with their faith and hope to guide them they did believe answers would come. At least the anger and rage had dissipated. Fear was still alive and well. They shared some thoughts for the next several minutes....they had good health... their children were doing great-and healthy... were on track with developing careers... CC was doing great with her artistic endeavors... her friend and mentor, Annie Ackley, was there for her... the after school project was developing... with the help of Cap'n Fitz the young people of Little Dublin were developing skills and enjoying boating on the sea.

A brief kiss and off to Our Lady and their friend Father Francis O'Rourke. Whatever the dire situation was after an hour or so visit with Franny things always appeared to be at least a bit better. That is just who he was. An eternal optimist who projected both faith and hope. Maybe he will be able to transmit some of his "magic" on this visit. He greeted them at the door with huge hugs for both of them and a big smile. He would have been a fantastic salesman thought Michael. Followed by the thought, "I guess in a sense that is what he is." One thing was for sure-he thoroughly believed in what he is selling.

He led them into the kitchen. No formal dining room for these life-long friends. After a few minutes of casual exchanges Father O'Rourke asked the obvious question, "So what is going on. Michael, you sounded pretty serious last night."

"Well Franny it is serious. I mean really serious." He then related the events of the last 24 hours. In detail. Painfully and slowly. A couple of times he lost his composure and his voice cracked. He paused and then continued. Finally, he stopped and asked the obvious question, "What do we do now."

Father O'Rourke sat back in his chair, sighed and began to speak-This is difficult to believe to put it mildly. Tommy has been a part of our family of friends since we were kids. I will tell you this he is not the first one in Little Dublin to get into gambling problems. I have done some research and discovered that there is an organization that deals with the problem. A fledgling group known as Gamblers Anonymous. They have had some success. Not complete success. But some success. There is a group that meets in Dover on a regular basis.

Michael interrupted, "That's fine, but how in the hell is that going to help me and CC. Frankly, at this time I am not too interested in helping Tommy."

"I understand. I get it. But we both know Tommy and one thing we know for sure he is not a thief. I also agree that he must pay the penalty for his actions," replied Father O'Rourke.

He went on to say that he would meet with Tommy and see how he is doing. Certainly, committing suicide is not the answer. Both Michael and CC wholeheartedly agreed with that. Tommy had a nice wife and two great children. No doubt this is taking a huge toll on the entire family. CC and Tommy's wife were good friend. They were both committed to and heavily involved in the afterschool program. The whole thing was one big mess.

Father O'Rourke went on in his usual upbeat manner and said together they will bring about a positive solution. He agreed that Michael should go to Mallorca and visit with his friend, Eddie Boyle, and tell him the entire situation. Eddie is well respected and connected with some powerful people there.

They were talking for more than two hours and it was time to move on with their day-all of them. Father O'Rourke spoke a few prayers and spiritual thoughts. He prayed for guidance, forgiveness, faith and hope. Michael agreed with all of the prayers-except one of forgiveness. He told his friend Franny he was not there yet. He said that he is willing to pray that he will reach the time when he will forgive-but he is not there at this point. Father O'Rourke replied that is fine.

The three hugged each other and were ready to move on. Father O'Rourke would make arrangements to meet with Tommy Doyle. Michael would telephone Eddie and arrange for travel plans to Mallorca. He would explain what they were going to discuss had to be done in person-not on a telephone, telegram, or letter. And CC would meet with her friend Annie Ackley and inform her of the recent events. A busy schedule for all of them.

Michael went directly to the office and met with Cap'n Fitz and again went through the entire story one more time. To say that it was stressful and exhausting would be putting it mildly. Each time he told the story it was difficult. It simply did not get any easier.

Cap'n Fitz being an older man had been through some difficult time of his own over his long life. His efforts were along the lines of trying to get Michael to believe that they would get through it all. Of course, he knew Tommy. He knew him well. Tommy had helped the Cap'n on more than one occasion when things got tough financially. He also stated that Tommy was not a thief. A family friend that got in over his head gambling. Same old story-starts out with a few pounds and snowballs into a mountain. He closed his comments with a hug and the assurance that there will be a way out of the mess. He also stated that Tommy must suffer the consequences of his action. No question of that. Michael thanked his friend and lifetime mentor.

Michael then went into his private office and placed the long-distance call with the operator. Hung up and waited for the connection to be made. In a matter of minutes, the phone rang and the operator was on the phone. She told Michael to go ahead Mr. Boyle is on the phone.

"Eddie, is that you."

"Yes, it is. What is the occasion for you to make an unannounced long-distance telephone call? What did you do, hit the lottery," he joked!

"I need to come over and visit with you and talk about some business issues. It is way too complicated to try and write a letter or telegram," Michael said in a very business-like voice.

"Sounds important."

"Well, yes. But not to worry. Besides it has been a few months since I saw you. I will send you a telegram when I get my flight and travel plans confirmed. Hopefully, in the next of couple days."

"Okay, look forward to seeing you my friend," Eddie concluded the telephone call.

Michael asked CC how she felt about his making a trip to Mallorca. She was in complete agreement. Both of them appeared to have settled down a bit over the next few days. Of course, they were still dealing with the fear and uncertainty of the future. Their time with Father O'Rourke was a huge help. He simply has a gift to help people believe that-"It will work out. Keep faith and hope." An extraordinary friend and spiritual individual.

The day was a busy one at work. He began contacting suppliers and creditors and outlining what happened. He asked for their patience and trust. He assured them that they would be paid every shilling that they were due. He also advised them that he worked hard over the years and had paid off the mortgage on their home. He was more than willing to add them as mortgage holders. Not one of the creditors took him up on that suggestion. To the contrary they said that his word was good enough. That he was a man of character, they had complete trust, and confidence that they would be paid. The reaction brought a lump in his throat and more than a few tears to his eyes. Their reaction ever strengthened his determination to work through and solve this issue.

Next on his agenda was to make flight reservations for his trip. He finalized the details and rushed off a telegram to Eddie Boyle. The routine was as usual. Eddie would go to the mainland, rent an automobile, and meet him at the Barcelona Airport. A trip and arrangement they had done countless times and became routine. In two days, he would board the train for London and the Heathrow Airport.

In the mean-time he would continue to go to work and keep busy with the endless details of the business that he truly loved. Cap'n Fitz was always there and at his side. Working was great therapy. It certainly kept his mind off the problem.

The night before leaving he took CC out to dinner at their favorite restaurant located in The White Cliffs of Dover Hotel. The hotel was built in 1841 and has been in continuous operation since. The five-star restaurant serves French cuisine and the finest of French wine. CC always felt a bit intimidated on the rare occasions they dined there. Very-very expensive. The finest of everything-silverware, china, draperies, background music. She truly loved going there. But felt that a kid from Little Dublin was out of her league. The hotel was home to Prime Ministers-Winston Churchill often stayed there-members of Parliament, aristocrats, and wealthy business barons.

When the evening was coming to a close CC went on to share her thoughts about the hotel. She reflected on the history. Somehow the structure survived two world wars and countless weather disasters over the past century. A magnificent building like an elegant grand lady sitting atop the world-famous white cliffs providing a safe port for the people of England.

Michael gave the auto keys to the valet and said he knew how much she liked the hotel. He went on to say that she deserved a special night. He added that she was the equal to anyone that visits here-you are first class in every sense of the word. Our ancestors are people that we can be proud of and we can hold our head high. Do not ever forget that. She smiled, kissed him on the cheek, squeezed his hand and gave him a big thank you.

A special night was had by all.

Early the next morning he took the train into London and not long after he was on the plane and heading for Barcelona. While he did not fly that often he was usually able to sleep through the flight. Not so today. He simply could not shut down thinking-rehashing in his mind the events of the last few days. Also, he was too excited about telling Eddie the story. He definitely was still dealing with some true anxiety.

Two hours later he saw the skyline of Barcelona and the beautiful Mediterranean Sea. He perked himself up and prepared for the landing. Minutes later he was in the terminal and met with his friend. Eddie immediately asked what the hell is going on. Why are you here with all of this mystery? Michael told him to relax we will talk about it when we get out to Mallorca. Let's catch up on what is going on in your life.

How about AA. Have you taken anyone on any big fishing trips? Any new business prospects. Eddie got the message-Michael is not going to talk about anything until he is ready. So, they settled back and made small talk and before long they were on Mallorca and Eddie's boat.

Following a short lunch Michael took a shower and came to the deck where Eddie was anxiously awaiting his friend and whatever the message that he knew was coming. Eddie had no idea what the message was to be, but he felt certain it was not going to be good news.

They both settled back into the deck chairs and Michael began. Explaining in painstakingly detail the events of the past few days. He told Eddie they would probably have to cease operations in Mallorca. Michael said that he felt terrible for Eddie after all the hard work he had put into the operation.

Eddie let out a deep breath and began to smile. Michael jumped up and began to holler, "What is so funny! I tell you we will be bankrupt and you laugh."

Eddie replied, "I thought you were going to tell me someone was fatally ill or something happened to CC or the kids. You tell me you have financial problems. That is it."

"Do you have any idea as to how we will solve this problem."

"Of course I do. In two words. Ralph Wilkinson."

He went on to tell Michael how impressed Mr. Wilkinson was with Michael's talents and the quality of boats that he built. How he, Mr. Wilkinson, had told Eddie that if Michael ever wanted to expand their operations, he would jump at the opportunity to invest.

Michael lost his composure and broke down. He simply could not believe what he was hearing. Eddie explained that Mr. Wilkinson was enroute from Sydney, Australia where he had vast holdings in various business ventures. He would be arriving in Barcelona in the next couple of days and Eddie believed without a doubt that Mr. Wilkinson would be interested in talking on two levels. First the business opportunity and secondly, the chance to get into the boat building business.

"Are you sure. Can this possibly happen." Michael was still in a state of disbelief.

"I know this man really well and I will be shocked if he turns you down."

Eddie went on to tell Michael that Mr. Wilkinson had his share of business difficulties getting his business career started in his early days. He never forgot those problems and he made a promise to God that he would share his experience and resources wherever and whenever he could.

Michael went on to tell Eddie that he needed to call CC as soon as possible and share this information. Not a problem. We will go into the Harbor and place the call. The two hugged and began the short walk to the Harbor.

Michael placed the call, and in a few minutes, CC was on the phone. He went on to tell her the conversation with Eddie and yes, he was excited. But remember nothing has really changed and won't until they have the conversation with Mr. Wilkinson. However, there does seem to be some hope. They were both choking back tears. Could this really happen. He told her that he loved her and would call her as soon as he has the conversation.

Sure enough, two days later Mr. Wilkinson did arrive and was greeted by Eddie and Michael. They had met before and knew each other casually. Mr. Wilkinson had a great deal of respect for Michael. Eddie had told him the details of how Michael became owner and worked hard all his life building boats. Mr. Wilkinson was always impressed with success stories of this type.

Eddie went on to tell Mr. Wilkinson there was a business proposition that Michael wanted to present. With that Michael began nervously to outline in detail the events of the past few weeks. The longer he talked the more relaxed and confident he became. Mr. Wilkinson interrupted a few times with questions and seemed more than simply casually interested. After almost two hours of dialogue he sat back in his chair and sighed a deep breath of relief.

Now it was Mr. Wilkinson's turn. His opening remarks were more than comforting. Nice words about Michael's work ethic. Dedication to the business. The manner in which he treated his employees. Integrity. The list went on.

He then talked about financial matters. Yes, he would be willing to make an investment in the company. He explained that he was an extremely wealthy individual but he did not believe in simply accumulating money. That does not help anyone. Putting money to work helps on many levels. The economy. Employees. Investors. Creativity.

He offered to pay all the creditors and advance cash for expansion. In return he would like ten percent ownership in the company. With a smile he explained that he would now be able tell his wealthy friends that he was a proud part owner of boat building business. He has always loved boats and owning a part of a company would be like a dream come true. They would keep the funds from his ten percent ownership in a separate account. He did not need the money and one day they would determine how those funds could be best put to work.

Next on the agenda the subject of expansion. Australia is a huge boating market. Mr. Wilkinson explained that he had many contacts in Sydney. Both professionally and personally. He had various business in Australia and travelled there several time during the year. He owned a hotel in Cremorne Point on the north shore overlooking the Sydney harbor. A short ten-minute ferry ride to the heart of the financial district and The Rocks, an area that the United Kingdom sent hardened criminals to in the 1800's. Now the area is a highly desirable commercial port and several marinas for boats of all size. In the event that Michael has an interest in expanding to that part of the world that could be arranged.

AMP Limited is a financial service banking facility that date back to 1849. Mr. Wilkinson has strong connections with the senior officers (several are boating enthusiasts.) He would make proper introductions and assist in any way that he could.

Closing with that comment he said, "So what do you think of my offer."

Michael was dizzy with thoughts. He said, "It is almost like the whole conversation was some magical dream."

"To be sure it is not." Mr. Wilkinson replied.

He then suggested that Michael go back to Folkestone discuss the offer with his wife and the event that she agrees they would proceed with the proper details and necessary paperwork. Michael got up gave Mr. Wilkinson a big hug and handshake.

The next morning Michael told Eddie that he needed to get home as soon as possible. Eddie agreed and the arrangements were made to Barcelona and flight home.

Before he realized it they were back on the mainland heading to the airport. Michael could not stop telling Eddie how indebted he was and could never thank him enough. Eddie replied with usual low-key personality, "No problem. I did not do much. I know you and I surely know Mr. Wilkinson and felt 100 percent confident that things would work out."

Work out they did. Indeed, they did.

Back in Folkestone he told CC that he wanted the two of them to have a conversation about the details of the plan and then meet with Father O' Rourke. Next, he wanted them to meet with Cap'n Fitz and Paddy O'Connor, their CPA. Finally, he wanted the two of them to meet with Tommy. CC knew Tommy as well as Michael did. CC asked Michael what he planned to say to Tommy. He responded that he was not sure. God would give him the words when the time came. All he knew was that he had to talk to him and ask him why. Why?

It had been an incredible 48 hours and he was exhausted. He needed some sleep. First, he would call his friend, Franny, and try to set up and appointment for the morning. He called Father O'Rourke and arrangements were meet in the rectory following 7:30 mass. He told his friend he had some incredibly positive information to share. Off to bed he collapsed and fell into a deep sleep.

Indeed, yes it was an amazing 48 hours.

They were both up early the next morning. A quick breakfast and off in plenty of time for the 7:30 mass. Father O'Rourke gave them both big hugs (He was famous for big hugs) and over to the rectory for tea and biscuits. He smiled at Michael, sat back in his favorite chair, and with outstretched arms said, "Okay, let us hear this good news."

For the next thirty minutes Michael told him the events of the past few days. How blessed he is to have such great friends and supporters in Folkestone.

Eddie in Mallorca. The generosity of Mr. Wilkinson. How he will be able to pay all of his creditors. People like Cap'n Fitz. Paddy O'Connor. Father O'Rourke. The faith that Father O'Rourke helped him to develop.

Father O'Rourke said that he just knew that God would answer their prayers. But he had to admit he did not think that the answer would come so fast and so generously. He then went on to ask the question, "How are you going to deal with Tommy Doyle."

Michael went on to say that he prayed on the matter and decided to have a conversation with him. It would not be an easy conversation, but he knew it was one that he absolutely needed to have. He said that CC would go with him.

CC then spoke up, "Michael I know that you said you want me with you. I thought about that during the night and do not think I should go with you. It will be difficult enough for you and I believe that I will just increase your stress. Maybe at a later date, but not now. I am still very angry and you are definitely more accepting. I might lose my temper. I know how hard you have worked. How you trusted Tommy and what difficulties he created for you. No, I think it best you go alone. Father O'Rourke smiled and then said, "I agree." Breakfast was over. They hugged and moved on.

Michael walked the few blocks to his office and CC went home. He arrived and Cap'n Fitz was already there. Michael called Paddy and asked if he could come over and the three of them meet for an update on the recent events. Paddy replied that he would be over in thirty minutes.

Once he arrived Michael prepared to repeat the story that he shared with Father O'Rourke. Both the good Cap'n and Paddy were anxious with anticipation. Michael began with, "It is all good news. Almost too good to be true." Once he finished both of them were astounded and said – Yes, it is too good to be true. Of course, fantastic news.

One final meeting and that would be with Tommy Doyle. But not today. Michael was emotionally spent and certainly not ready to meet with the individual that created all the chaos. Tommy was still out on bail. His legal issue and problems were yet to come. Michael would call him in the morning.

Michael told them for now he was heading home and some time with CC. Telling and retelling the story, even though it is great news, is exhausting. He thanked his two friends for standing by him through this ordeal and told them how much their friendship meant to both him and CC. They reminded Michael that they all have been friends for a long time and believed that he would be there for them if there ever was a need.

They hugged and Michael started the few blocks walk home. He began to think how fortunate he was to have people like them in his life. God certainly blessed him. Father O'Rourke provided the stability and balance that he needed when his faith wavered. And there were times that it happened. But he always recited Father O'Rourke's rock-solid statement-"With God all things are possible." Then he thought of his other life-long friend-Tommy Doyle. The president of the bank that provided the loan to launch his business. He was extremely grateful for his efforts in making all of it become a reality. What happened. He did believe what Father O'Rourke said, "Tommy Doyle is not a thief."

He crossed the block and was home. He went into the house gave CC a kiss on the cheek. She suggested that they sit on the porch and rock for a bit. She told him to go out and she would bring tea. He settled back in his favorite chair, closed his eyes, and gave a big thank you to God.

CC brought the tea and some of her homemade biscuits. Oh, how he loved her biscuits. He told her how fortunate and blessed he was. A wonderful wife. Good friends. Healthy children. A lovely home that she created. The list goes on. After about an hour rest and recuperation he told her it was time to make the last phone call and appointment – Tommy Doyle. CC smiled, "You will be fine. Reflect on what has happened so far. Keep your faith, say a prayer, and give him a call."

Michael went into the house, picked up the phone, and dialed the number. A few rings and the voice of Tommy's wife answered. The next minute or two was a bit uncomfortable for both, but she told him to hold. She summoned Tommy to the phone.

In an obvious nervous voice Tommy said, "Hello Michael. How are you."

Michael thought to himself-How the hell am I. Let me tell you. He knew that was not what he wanted to say. Cooler heads must prevail. He responded by saying, "Tommy, we need to sit down and have a conversation."

"Of course," replied Tommy still with a shaky voice. "When do you want to get together."

"How about first thing in the morning-the breakfast shop across from my office at 9:00 am" Michael replied.

"Absolutely," Tommy.

"Okay, see you in the morning," Michael said in a very controlled voice. He did not want to lose his temper and it was obvious that Tommy was very nervous.

They hung up the phone. The meeting was scheduled. Michael would pray again before they met. He decided to walk over to the rectory and try to have a few minutes with Father O'Rourke. As he approached the rectory and as luck would have it Father O'Rourke was pulling up in his car.

They shook hands and Michael told him that the meeting with Tommy was set for tomorrow morning. "Franny, you need to give me some of your wisdom. I do not want this meeting to come off badly."

"You will be fine. Just remember losing your temper will not solve anything or make the situation better. I realize the depths of your betrayal. Say a prayer and ask for the guidance that you seek," was the good Father's wisdom.

"See, that's is why you are so great to all of us," Michael said with a smile. A few minutes later following some small talk Michael was on his way back home.

Not surprisingly he did not have a good night's sleep. Tossing and turning he played out the script of what he would say... how Tommy would respond...he knew he was disturbing CC... got out of bed and downstairs and on to the porch and his favorite rocking chair... calmed down a bit...back to bed. Finally, he drifted off ...

Up early and dressed ready to go. CC asked if he wanted something to eat. He told that he was too anxious to get this conversation behind him. He gave her a kiss and hug and asked her to say a prayer for the three of them. In a matter of minutes, he was approaching the breakfast shop. Took a deep breath, asked for God's guidance, approached Tommy with, "Good Morning." No handshake or big smile. Tommy replied similarly.

The waitress took their order. Silence. Then, "Tommy, why. Why, why. What were you thinking?" He went on to say that they were friends all of their lives. School. Church. Beach. Everything. We shared everything. If you were in trouble why did you not come to me. We could have worked something out. For God's sake you did all the work and figured a way for me to buy the business from Cap'n Fitz. As he fought back tears, his voice trailed off he said in a shaky voice, "Oh, why Tommy."

Tommy responded explaining yes he was president but it was more title and not much in compensation. The other members of their little circle were successful. Michael had a thriving business. Paddy had built his own accounting firm and was well respected in the community. Franny was a pillar in the church and community. People always went to him for guidance.

He felt if he could accumulate some financial success, he would gain respect in the community. A bigger house. Car. It started small and he did have some financial success. He put the money back. He thought he had the situation under control. With the passing of time it grew and he knew he was in trouble. He did not want to come to Michael. He was embarrassed. He saw no way out.

Michael then went on to say thank God you did not succeed in ending your life. We will work together to help you. Father O'Rourke said we all know one thing – Tommy Doyle is not a thief. Of course there will be consequences for your action. Yes, you became addicted to gambling. But that is no excuse. You will be going to prison for sure; however, you have a number of character witnesses who will speak on your behalf. Tommy, somehow you will have to figure a way to turn this into something positive.

With that said Michael got up and gave Tommy a hug. Michael told him that he would try to get past what was done. He also said that it would not be easy. CC is truly struggling with what you did-but she is trying and praying. As our good friend Franny O'Rourke always says-forgiveness is always the answer. Seems as though he is always right. So let us move on.

Tommy continued out on bail and his trial would be coming up shortly. In the mean-time Michael would be tied up and very busy with arranging for the financial transaction with Mr. Wilkinson. Among other things it would involve a trip to Australia.

⌁

JIMMY MAGEE AND DELANIE

Back home he told CC that the meeting went well. At least as well as can be expected. He would have to get in touch with Mr. Wilkinson and make arrangement for the long trip to Australia. He would most likely be gone at least one month, probably a bit longer. All of the creditors had been contacted and he explained that arrangements were being worked out to pay everyone 100 percent of the debt. While he was out of the country his son, Jimmy Magee, would be running the business and that he would keep everyone on the progress.

Jimmy had completed his studies at the London School of Economics a couple years ago and was involved in all aspects of the business. Like his father he liked the hands on of actually building boats and not so much the business and financial day to day operations. But he committed himself and developed into an excellent manager of business affairs.

Michael usually sent him to different conferences, networking events and conventions in London. He explained to Jimmy this was an important part of business. You just never know who you will connect with that could develop into someone that would be of benefit in the pursuit of new possibilities and avenue to new business.

Jimmy agreed to attend these events but usually found them boring. He did manage to connect with a few people over the past couple years that indeed proved to be a source of business. He was scheduled to attend one in the next few days as the result of a change of plans for his father.

He left for London and planned to be there for three days. The convention was held in the Westminster section of the city. He arrived early and did his usual routine. With a name tag on his suit he introduced himself to various people and made small talk. Oh, how he hated this activity. Finally, he wandered over to the bar and ordered a glass of wine. He was not much of a drinker, but thought with drink in hand he might get rid of some of his uncomfortableness. While waiting a beautiful young woman came to the bar and ordered a glass of the same wine.

Wow, he thought that might be a good ice breaker. And that is exactly what he did. "Hello, my name is Jimmy Magee, and we both just ordered the exact same glass of wine.

She did not seem to be too impressed thinking just another guy hitting on me. He persisted and continued to talk. He asked her name. What are you doing here? What type business are you in. Do you attend many of these affairs?

She started laughing and said, "Whoa. Slow down. Take a breath."

"I am sorry. I just find these things so boring. I found you attractive and just wanted to have a bit of conversation," He replied with a smile. And he asked her name.

"My name is Delanie-Delanie McGettigan. I am a fashion designer of women's clothes."

"Good God what are you doing at this thing."

"Well you never know. There are more than 200 people here from business all over the UK and even Paris and Rome. You just never know."

Jimmy suggested that they go over to a corner and get to know each other and enjoy their wine. Delanie agreed. Removed from the crowd they relaxed and enjoyed getting to know each other. Jimmy explained that his ancestors came to England during the Irish famine in the 1800's. They helped build the railroad across England to the English Channel in Folkestone. His father was in the boat building business Jimmy is also involved and has been since he was a young boy. In the middle of a sentence he smiled and said, "Delanie it is your turn."

They both laughed and Delanie went on to say that she was enjoying hearing his history. Then she began by saying that her history was a bit more convoluted. Yes, her father was from Ireland and he did make it to Paris. He was an alcoholic and left his family. Her mother was still living in Galway and heavily involved in the Catholic Church. And unlike Jimmy she did not know much about her ancestors-other than that we were Irish.

Before they realized it the event was closing for the evening and it was time to leave. Jimmy suggested that they continue in the neighborhood cafe and have tea and a biscuit before he escorted her home.

Delanie thought to herself this guy is a real gentleman. Not one of the usual cast of characters that are always hitting on her. She liked him. They finished their tea and ready to leave. Jimmy summoned a taxi and they took the short ride to her apartment in the Belgrade neighborhood. An upscale area where many of the large homes from another era were converted into apartments.

He walked her to the front door, shook her hand, and said that he hopes they get together again. She agreed and they exchanged phone numbers. Jimmy said that he usually gets to London at least once a month. He promised that he would call before he got to London.

They said goodnight and he left with the taxi. Delanie went into her apartment and settled into her favorite chair and began reflecting on the events of the evening. She thought-Wow! This is one nice guy and a gentleman. That was a pleasant evening. No heavy drinking. Not trying to get into my pants. It has been a long time since I had a night like that. I sure hope he calls again.

Not to worry. This was the first of many such nights. Indeed, the beginning of a beautiful relationship.

Jimmy took the taxi back to the hotel and reflected on the events of the evening. Maybe things do work out the way they are supposed to. My father is always telling me that when I become impatient and frustrated. I did not want to come to this event and reluctantly agreed. So what happens I meet a beautiful young woman and we seem to hit it off immediately. My mother always told me when you meet the right woman it is like magic and you will know. Tonight sure felt like magic. And I think Delanie wants to see me again.

Up early he went to the Charing Cross train station and back to Folkestone. He settled into a window sheet and watched the landscape and got lost in his thoughts while the click-clack of the tracks sort of hypnotized him. His thoughts concentrated on Delanie. She was not only a beautiful woman, a strong and pleasant personality. A successful career and not easily influenced. She had strong and definite plans on where she wanted to go and obviously would not be distracted. In a word he liked her. He liked her a great deal.

As the train pulled into the Folkestone station he gathered his few things and was ready for the short walk home. His mother was home and Jimmy could hardly wait to share what happened last night. They sat out on the porch and he began to share. It was quite obvious to CC that Delanie had made quite an impression.

Following about an hour of give and take about Delanie they moved on to a few other personal and business topics it was time for dinner. CC expressed her impressions that were formed while listening about Jimmy Magee's special new lady friend. She like what she heard and hoped that he would invite her down to spend a weekend with them at the seaside. He assured his mother he would make that happen.

On several occasions over the following months Delanie became a regular visitor. She loved the seaside and thoroughly enjoyed sailing on Jimmy's sailboat. In addition, she was quite impressed with his sailing skills. Jimmy explained that he grew up hanging around his father's boatyard and had been sailing boats since he was a little boy. He loved everything about the sea. Just about everyone in Little Dublin felt the same way.

Christmas was coming and Jimmy thought that would be the perfect time to pop the question. Pop it he did and Delanie said yes. CC, Michael, and Molly loved her. They all agreed that she would be more than welcome as a new member. Their family friend would perform the ceremony.

Delanie was delighted beyond words. She was an only child. Her mother lived in Ireland. They saw very little of each other. There was not any problem. They not only lived in different countries but really different worlds. Their views were different in many ways. Sadly, she and her father tried to connect but just could not make a go of things.

He left when she was a little girl and developed alcoholism. After travelling around the world he got sober and settled in Paris and became a successful author.

He lived with the love of his life-a beautiful woman, Quinn, until his death while sailing his beloved sailboat, ODAT, off the coast of the French Riviera. Quinn was extremely instrumental in seeing to it that Delanie attended the Sorbonne and became a fashion designer. The same profession that Quinn was extremely successful in.

Quinn and Delanie had a marvelous relationship, but Delanie and her father just could not make it. They both loved each other and gave it a good try. But try as they might it did not work out.

Coming from such a confusing background the chance to have a real family was simply more than she could imagine. The wedding date was set-February 20-her birthday. Delanie, CC, and Molly worked together planning the wedding. The more time they spent together the stronger their bond developed. Over the next few months they became good friends and truly enjoyed each other's company.

Delanie had drifted away from her catholic upbringing and was finding her way back. She became a regular at Our Lady, and liked Father O'Rourke. Of course it was pretty difficult to not like the big gregarious Irishman. He was instrumental in helping with wedding plans. The church would be decorated and the reception in the adjoining parish hall.

Jimmy Magee stayed in the background while all of this was taking place. He did this by design. He wanted Delanie to feel comfortable with the entire process. Getting to know his parents and Molly. Father O'Rourke. The church. The community. Their friends. The plans were to live in Folkestone following the marriage and their honeymoon on the French Riviera. Delanie could do her job as a fashion designer wherever she lived. Traveling to fashion shows across the UK, Europe, and New York was where the business was conducted. Living in London she conducted business from her apartment. Living by the sea would be ideal.

The big day arrived. A glorious morning. Even some bright sunshine (a rare event February in Folkestone.) Standing in the front of the church Jimmy saw her being escorted from the rear by his father,

Michael. That was Delanie's decision. The family was surprised to say the least when he was asked to perform this honor and Michael asked, "Are you sure that is what you want."

"Absolutely," was her one word response.

As they walked up the aisle and with the organ playing beautifully Here Comes the Bride Delanie began to tear up. Her thoughts went immediately to her father. Jimmy Magee focused like a laser on her. She was absolutely gorgeous.

Father O'Rourke was his usual masterful self. Delivering remarks that brought the entire church to sniffling and tears. He was simply the best. Following the ceremony, they went directly to the parish hall and a genuine Irish party. A party that only the Irish could put on. Music. Dancing. Irish Guinness Beer. Little kids running around. The Irish jig. A great time was held by all.

Following a night of celebration, the young couple were ready to leave on their honeymoon. Jimmy suggested the French Riviera. Delanie was ecstatic. She went on to tell Jimmy that she spent her earlier years in both places. Yes, she would love to take that trip.

Paris is where she reunited with her father and met Quinn. She went to school at the Sorbonne and sort of grew up on the French Riviera in a small village just outside of Cannes.

Jimmy had been thinking about a sea adventure for several years. This seemed to be the ideal time and the right event to undertake such an adventure. He had total confidence in his sailing skills and not in the least intimidated. Delanie was certainly an adventurous woman and signed on immediately when he proposed the trip.

Following a big breakfast with several of the people who attended the wedding they were escorted down to the shoreline and his sailboat. The boat was a 65 foot, three sail Ketch. A beautiful boat that he helped build with his father and a couple of the employees. It took a couple of years to build. Some of the highlights include a full galley. Two separate and private sleeping quarters. Topside plenty of room and all the comforts of home. The bulkheads below were covered with photographs of the family ancestors. Letters between family members that gave the history of their migration.

Delanie quickly saw that this was a family proud of its history. She could not help but think how different it was from her own history. The boat's name was emblazoned aft, below the stern-"*PADDY" March 17, 1860-*

The name of the boat was to recognize their ancestors. With not much more than hope and faith the small group left Ireland on that date. Paddy being a symbolic Irish name. Jimmy was extremely proud of his heritage. When Delanie heard the story, somehow, she felt a connection and for the first time had pride in her Irish heritage.

On board the two settled in and received a hearty Bon Voyage from their friends on the beach. A perfect day for sailing. As they sailed along the shoreline of the English Channel Jimmy began to review the details of the sailing plan he had researched:

"Sail through the English Channel...on to the Bay of Biscay off the coast of Spain... Down the coast of Portugal...Through the Strait of Gibraltar... into the Mediterranean Sea... and finally to port of Cannes, France."

Statistics-Total distance of 1,981 nautical miles

Average 10 knots

18.2 days

Jimmy was in no hurry. Delanie agreed. The decision was made to take one month for the entire trip. They made certain that they had more than the necessary supplies-medical, food, tea, and drinking water. Jimmy made plans to stay relatively close to the shoreline for the trip. They would make several stops along the way. Cadiz, Mallorca, Barcelona, and Nice. If they like a particular port they would stay a little longer.

The trip was indeed a romantic adventure. The days passed, the weather was beautiful, and winds gentle. Perfect for sailing. Delanie begged Jimmy to let her sail the ship and take control of the steering. Reluctantly at first he did, and days later he gave her a bit more freedom. She loved it. She smiled and in a loud voice and shouted, "I am a sailor, and I love it." She could not help but to reflect on her many failed relationships. Life is truly worth living. God placed the right man and right family in my life-finally.

The final two days Jimmy told her that he would have to do the sailing as they approached the Bay of Cannes. They arrived at the harbor, secured the boat, and found the Dockmaster. Arrangements were made to dock **Paddy** for the next several days. They strolled the waterfront and had lunch in a quaint French harborside cafe'. The Cote d' Azur (French for the French Riviera) was a spectacular sight. Beautiful harbor. Frenchmen singing. Flowers everywhere. Smell of French Bakeries.

Delanie explained that she was quite familiar with the village and the harbor. Her father kept his boat, ODAT, (One Day At A Time) in this very marina. Maybe if they asked around who knows the boat and the man who built it, Jean-Claude, may still be here.

Jimmy said the one person who could answer that question would be the Dockmaster. In a few minutes they were able to locate him and ask the question. Bingo! Yes, the boat is here and it is a beauty. Yes Jean-Claude is definitely still here and most likely will be forever. He is not here at the moment but he will be in from the water as the sun sets.

Delanie was thrilled beyond words. Her thoughts were about Jean-Claude. Is he still there?. Then "Serenity Patch" and Michel is he going to be there. Her next thought? The beautiful home on the outskirts of the little village of Auribeau is nearby. This was all just too exciting. As she began to relate the story of her past, she felt overwhelmed. She began to cry and fell into Jimmy's arms. Jimmy hugged her and told her to take a deep breath. All will be fine. He promised to help in the search. The developments were simply more than could handle. God truly does work his miracles in amazing ways.

The Dockmaster led them to Jean-Claude's boat slip and again confirmed that he will be returning most likely in the next hour. He explained that Jean-Claude conducted tours for the visitors who came to the French Riviera. He sailed the Bay of Cannes and a few of the nearby islands and coves.

Delanie and Jimmy got an espresso from one of the cafes' and sat on a bench near the slip. The sun was indeed setting, a cool breeze, and ideal weather. Before long they saw a beautiful sailboat on the horizon heading in their direction. The boat was carefully guided into the boat slip and the Captain secured it and assisted his tourists off the boat. He thanked them for their business and sent them on their way. He was a busy sailor for about half an hour. Being a sailor himself Jimmy took in all of the activity with great interest.

Jean-Claude began walking on the dock and Delanie simply could not contain herself. She ran toward him yelling his name and gave him a big hug. Of course, Jean-Claude was startled and confused. Who is this woman? What is she doing? Delanie, in a very excited voice, said, "Jean-Claude it is me. Delanie. Jimmy McGettigan's daughter." He collected his thoughts and instantly realized who she was. Then he began in French, "Oh. my God. It is you. I cannot believe my eyes. How often you are in my thoughts. Your father. Quinn. Here, let me give you another hug as he kissed her on her forehead." Delanie replied, "In English... In English" The entire scene was extremely emotional. Jimmy stood on the side and took it all in.

With that Delanie introduced Jimmy as her new husband. That they are on their honeymoon. They sailed from Folkestone several weeks ago. The trip was amazing. Jimmy is a sailor just like you. An amazing reunion.

She then asked about Michel and Serenity Patch. Jean-Claude replied that the two of them get together regularly. He said that they could all go out there in the morning. Michel will be ecstatic to see both of you. Yes, he takes care of the place as he always has. As a source of revenue, he has converted Serenity Patch into a bed and breakfast. Not really what he wanted to do, but needed the revenue to maintain the property in first class condition. And you know Michel and how feels about the property. How he feels about your father and Quinn. Trust me you will be impressed.

Following dinner, they strolled along the waterfront and continued to talk and visit. Getting to know Jimmy better and bring him up to speed on the past. The hour was getting late and time for rest. Arrangements were made for an early meeting and they returned to their boats for sleep.

A highly emotional evening and a wonderful reunion. Once again, God unfolding more of his mysteries and miracles. Delanie reflected on the events of the day with thoughts of her father, Jimmy McGettigan, the famous Irish author. He was not only famous in his homeland,

Ireland, but in this part of the world as well. Not only for his literary talents. He was responsible for introducing the fledgling organization, Alcoholics Anonymous to the Riviera. She would ask Jean-Claude in the morning if the organization was still assisting people with alcoholism in the area. Drained of adrenaline she drifted off into a deep sleep.

The three regrouped as planned at the small breakfast cafe' just a few steps from the dock. Coffee, baguettes, and cheese for all. The sun was rising over the bay and reflecting on the beautiful blue water.

Delanie asked Jean-Claude about her Dad and the Alcoholics Anonymous organization in the area. He assured her that it is not only active but has grown exponentially over the recent years. The group is still meeting at the Notre Dame Church. The group decided to recognize Jimmy's efforts by naming the group-One Day At a Time-ODAT, the name of his sailboat. The boat that was built by Jean-Claude and given to him by Quinn when Jimmy died while sailing it. Following breakfast, they visited the church (Notre Dame d' Esperance) and then headed out to visit Serenity Patch and Michel.

Delanie was concerned that he might not be there and she would not be able to visit with him and introduce her husband to this wonderful man. Not to worry was Jean-Claude's words. They began the few kilometer drive and passed through the charming village of Auribeau. How charming. Delanie remembered it well and served as tour guide to her husband, Jimmy. Oh, such memories flashed through her mind. The locals hustling about during their days' activities. Fresh flowers on display outside of the various little shops. The women of the house sweeping their front steps and walks. A tradition was the older men riding their bicycles and singing in French. Truly a sight to see. Jimmy Magee took it all in and was quite impressed to say the least. He told Delanie that he had no idea their honeymoon would be such a memorable and beautiful event.

After a few kilometers of twists and turns they were approaching the small farm and the slice of heaven known as Serenity Patch. Quinn and Jimmy certainly gave the place the perfect name. Jean-Claude parked the car and led the way to the main house calling out Michel's name. Almost instantly came a response. Michel came out the side door from the kitchen where he was preparing breakfast for his overnight guests.

He recognized Jean-Claude of course but he did not recognize the couple with him. He assumed Jean-Claude had taken them on his boat and bringing them out to be guests of the Bed and Breakfast. Wrong. Very wrong.

Delanie quickly ran to Michel and began calling his name, "Michel, it is me Delanie. Quinn. Jimmy's daughter. Remember. Can you believe I am back. We are together again."

In that instant he realized that indeed it was Delanie. The memories came rushing back to him. How he tried so hard to make things right between Delanie and her father. How sad he was when Jimmy died and the family, including him, were torn apart as the result of his death. Could this all be true. Is she back? It all seemed surreal.

They embraced and he instantly knew – yes, it is true! How did she ever find her way back to this special part of the world? Delanie then introduced Jimmy Magee to him and that they were recently married. How they were on their honeymoon and sailed from Folkestone several weeks ago. Jean-Claude remained a few steps in the background and took it all in. An incredible scene and a wonderful reunion. He could not help but wonder what would happen next. How will this all unfold. Surely Delanie and Jimmy Magee would not simply stay for a few days and sail off out of the lives of Jean-Claude and Michel.

Michel suggested that they all go into the kitchen and have espresso baguettes, and some egg souffle. Delanie told Jimmy that Michel was an excellent French chef as well as a great farmer.

They sat and talked for a couple of hours catching up on everyone's life over the past few years. Jimmy Magee sat quietly and took it all in. An amazing turn of events. It was quite obvious that the three of them were delighted to say the least with what was happening. He agreed wholeheartedly with the statement that they could not simply sail away in a few days and end the reunion. He turned his thoughts to how they could reunite and develop a permanent relationship. A few ideas entered his mind. But this is not the time to bring them up. When he and Delanie were back on the boat later that day, they would discuss some of his thoughts.

Delanie asked Michel if she could take Jimmy Magee on a little tour of the farm. Michel said of course. He suggested that just the two of them go off alone. Holding hands, the two began to walk around on the five acres. She began to explain. First stop was the barn and stables. One part of the barn was bright and airy. This is where Quinn did her art. There was still evidence of her efforts. Canvasses. Some with paintings partly finished. Brushes. Paints. Tripods. It looked as though she was painting there every day. Then they entered the small stable area where her father did his creating and typing. One small opening window area that overlooked the garden of flowers. One straight back chair and his old typewriter. She showed him the flowers and vegetable garden. Everything looked the same as she remembered.

After almost two hours they found their way back into the main house. The first question she asked Michel was why have you not changed anything on the farm. Quinn's studio. Her father's work area. The same flowers that Quinn loved so much. The place looked exactly as she remembered.

Michel smiled and replied, "I never thought about changing one single thing. The farm belonged to Quinn and Jimmy. It always will. Quinn may have changed the deed to me. But I am the caretaker only. I will never change anything in the barn and stables. And that definitely includes Quinn's studio and your father's work area. He created some great literature in that little stable. Quinn loved the different flowers that we grew together. There is another reason I did not change anything. Whenever I entered the barn, I thought of them."

They all relaxed in the kitchen and continued to reminisce. Conversation flowed easily and Jimmy Magee took it in. He was quickly falling in love with the entire area. The waterfront. Auribeau. This beautiful farm area. The entire countryside. The more they talked the more excited he became about the plan he was going to suggest. The sun was beginning to set so it was time to head back to their boat. Hugs and kisses were exchanged by all. It was agreed that they would get to together again over the next few days.

Back in the harbor it was nearing time for bed. Indeed, an emotional and full day to say the least. Jean-Claude went to his boat and Delanie and Jimmy Magee strolled on the pier for a while and settled topside on their boat.

He began the conversation with the thought of a plan that occurred while they were all together at *Serenity Patch.* The first thing he wanted Delanie to hear was that he loves the area. He went on to tell her that she obviously has a great deal of history both with the area and these two wonderful men.

He went on to say that we need to put together a plan to make this area an important part of our lives. First and foremost, this has to be something that you would want to do. The idea of sailing on the Mediterranean and Adriatic Sea has always been a dream of his. Both bodies of water are famous for their azure waters, fantastic fishing, and beautiful cities and picturesque villages throughout the entire region. His thought and hope was that they would be able to moor their boat in the area. Hopefully, Jean-Claude can help us with the possibility of making that happen.

Delanie was ecstatic. She gave him a big hug and choked up. Something that she would want to do. Are you kidding me? Coming back to this part of the world would be beyond her wildest dreams was her reply.

She then asked if he thought it would be possible to take a train to Paris and visit the Marais section of Paris where she lived with Quinn and her father. Maybe Simon, the baker, would still be there. They could tour the Sorbonne where Quinn arranged for her education. She would take him to the Cathedral of Notre Dame where they attended mass. There was so much to do. When can we go? I rode the train to Paris often. We can do it again. She was so excited she could hardly keep her composure.

Jimmy began laughing and replied-Of course we can do all that and more. He suggested that they spend a few more days locally. Maybe they could sail to Monaco and see the sights. Delanie told him that she worked there in a high fashion women's clothing store. By train less than one hour. How thrilled she would be to recreate this special part of her world.

Jimmy then began to talk about the rest of his plan. First, they would work out the details with Jean-Claude and Michel. When they return from Monaco, they would take the train to Paris and stay for maybe one week. From there they could take the train to Calais. That would give them the opportunity to visit the world-famous Mont St Michel Abbey on the French coast. When it was time to return to England, they would take the ferry from French coast to Dover England.

Jimmy Magee was a dreamer, no question about that. Delanie was thrilled with his dreams. Her only question was when they wanted to visit at another date how would that happen. He saw a very simple solution to that issue. Fly from London to Paris and then a two-hour train ride through the Provence wine country to Auribeau.

Delanie saw one other issue. How would he handle leaving his boat on the French Coast? How would he go sailing when they are in Folkestone. That was the least of any logistical issues that they would have. He went on to say the family has several sailboats that they have acquired over the years. He then told her he planned to teach her to sail.

She was flabbergasted by these ambitious plans. The whole plan was more than she could comprehend. Nonetheless, she loved every little detail. Their married life was off to an amazing beginning. And she loved it.

They were both awake early and went looking for Jean-Claude to discuss their plan with him. He was busy on the ODAT preparing for the tourists that scheduled for an outing later in the morning. Jimmy opened the conversation with the proposal. No sense beating around the bush. He asked Jean-Claude to be direct and honest. Does the idea have any merit? "Absolutely," was the one word reply from Jean-Claude. There are any number of boats that are moored here by individuals from other parts of the world. He reminded Jimmy that this is one of the wealthiest ports of call in the world. He also said that there would not be any expense. He would take care of PADDY and make sure it is safe. After all, it was the least he could do after Quinn gave him this beautiful sailboat, the ODAT.

Great news. One part of the plan was now in place. They told Jean-Claude they planned on leaving by noon on a three day adventure along the coast of the Mediterranean. Hopefully, spending one day ashore in

Monte Carlo. Once back they would visit with Michel and see what he thought of the idea. The idea being that they would pay the expense to maintain Serenity Patch and an income for him. He would no longer have to operate a Bed and Breakfast. Jean-Claude said Michel will be ecstatic. He hated operating the Bed and Breakfast. The place meant far too much to him. But he could not afford to operate the farm any other way. It all sounded too good to be true.

They all hugged and went about their business. Jean-Claude and his tourists. Jimmy Magee and Delanie readied PADDY for their little adventure. A perfect day for sailing. Gentle breezes. Blue skies. Sunshine. Mild temperatures. Does not get any better.

Supplies and provisions were aboard and they set sail shortly after noon. The next few days they visited St. Tropez, Monte Carlo, and a couple small private islands. While in Monte Carlo they visited the Internationally famous casino. Jimmy lost a few French francs at the crap table. Strolled the main shopping district and Delanie stopped at the fashion shop where she worked. Ownership had changed and she did not know anyone. But a fun stop.

The time had come for the return trip. They both agreed it exceeded any of their expectations. It would take the better part of two days to make it the entire way. Up early they began to sail. After a full day at sea they decided to simply anchor offshore watch the sunset and sleep aboard. Following an amorous evening together they drifted off to sleep.

Jean-Claude had provided Jimmy with some nautical maps of the region and handmade notes and maps. They proved to be invaluable.

Early in the morning they set sail. Jimmy was thoroughly enjoying the sailing experience on the beautiful Mediterranean. As a sailor it was a super experience. They sailed all day and as the day was coming to a close they glided into their port and came to rest in their slip.

They were walking along the harborside and ran into Jean-Claude. Big hugs were exchanged. They thanked him for his help in the planning of the trip and the maps and documents that he gave them. It was obvious to the three of them that a relationship was developing. Developing quickly and strongly.

Delanie asked Jean-Claude if he would take them out to the farm in the morning. It was time for them begin the journey back to Folkestone. No problem was his answer. He said he was sure that Michel would be home but he would telephone him just to make sure. He smiled and told her not to worry he would not talk about the plan they have in mind about making *Serenity Patch* a part of their life. He did say that he wished he could be there when they asked Michel how he felt about the proposal. Both Jimmy and Delanie thought that was an excellent idea. They would love to have him there when they asked him."

"Great!" was his reply, He would be delighted and honored to be there. Seeing Michel's expression would be priceless. It was agreed he would be there.

Following breakfast in the morning they gathered their personal effects and packed their travel bags and met Jean-Claude at their regular cafe' for the three kilometer drive out to the farm.

Michel greeted them with a huge "Bon jour" Bon jour" hugs were exchanged and they gathered in the breakfast area. Jimmy told Delanie that she should be the one to bring up the subject and detail how it all would work out. She was grateful. Trying to reconcile with Michel and the farm was beyond her wildest dreams.

She took a deep breath and began talking. The nervousness in her voice quickly disappeared in a minute or two. She explained. We will leave our boat to Jean-Claude and his care. We would fly from London to Paris whenever we were able to come over. We would come over whenever our schedule would permit. Jimmy will look into the possibility and prospects of beginning an operation on the Riviera. Boating is a major industry along the coast. Jean-Claude has all the right connections.

Once they arrive in Paris, they would take the train from the Lars Station in the Montemarte section down to Auribeau. Michel was overwhelmed. In tears, he asked "How will you get back to England." Delanie replied not a problem. When they had to return to Folkestone they would reverse the routine.

She went on to tell Michel that he has lived out here long enough without transportation. They will purchase a service vehicle for farm work and personal use. Michel jumped out of his seat and gave her a hug and kiss and ramble on in French. Then he rushed over to Jimmy and again went on and on in French. Everyone broke out in laughter.

Delanie was finishing her remarks and asked Michel if he was okay with the plan. No more Bed and Breakfast. No more tourists. Jimmy Magee and Delanie will provide the finances necessary, including compensation to Michel.

Once again, he broke into French. Jean-Claude began laughing, "Michel, Michel English. English my friend. Everyone was hugging and ecstatic. There was definitely a plan in place that everyone was delighted with.

Jean-Claude said that he needed to get back to the harbor. Tourists were booked for early afternoon.

Jimmy and Delanie decided to spend a couple days on the farm before starting the journey back to Folkestone. Delanie asked if it would be possible to take a train to the Normandy coast from Paris and then the ferry across the English Channel to Dover. Doing that would give them the opportunity to see the French countryside and what World War II did to it. Jimmy saw no reason why not. No problem. So that became part of their plan.

Michel escorted Delanie to her bedroom. The bedroom she occupied in years passed. To her surprise he had saved some of her personal effects and pictures and arranged them just as the room was when she left. Yet another emotional experience. She hugged Michel and thanked him. He truly was a good friend and supported her in time past.

The next few days they relaxed and took in the local flavor. They walk the couple kilometers into the village of Auribeau. Enjoyed Michel's outstanding French cuisine. Jimmy enjoyed walking the grounds of the farm. Trying to capture what it must have been like for Delanie. Living here with Quinn and her father. He found it hard to process how there could have been difficulty between her and her father. Of course, he was fortunate and blessed to grow up in a united family filled with love and caring. Delanie came from a fractured family that included an alcoholic father who and abandoned her. Her mother was not very good about talking. Silence and denial seemed to be the order of the day.

During the last day of their stay Delanie and Jimmy took a cup of tea and went outside and found a cool spot under a huge oak tree and were quiet. Just sat and meditated on their own thoughts. Finally, Jimmy spoke up.

"So, what do you think. Would you like to reconnect with Quinn," Smiling as he asked the question.

Delanie replied, "Yes. I think so. I am not sure she would be willing to meet with me. I was kind of a jerk at the end. She handled it well. But I really did not treat her right. Especially in her time of grief. Actually, we were both grieving."

"Do you know where she is living," he responded.

Delanie believed she was living on an island off the coast of the Connemara Region in Ireland. Hopefully, we would be able to track her down.

Jimmy thought, that should not be too difficult of a challenge. We have a great deal going on in our life, but it will become a priority when we get back home.

Early in the morning they said their goodbyes to Michel at the train station for the short trip to Paris. The train arrived right on time. Delanie smiled and told Jimmy she was not surprised. He smiled and thought the trains are always on time.

They promised Michel that they would stay in touch and before long would be back in that little special place in the world.

The train pulled away and they sat back and relaxed for the short trip into the city. The scenery through the beautiful wine country of Provence made the journey a pleasant trip. They both drifted off not long after the train left the station. The honeymoon turned into something that they could never have imagined. It would certainly be remembered the rest of their lives. Jimmy is a strong spiritual individual and thought of the words-God truly does work his wonders in mysterious ways.

He thought the two of them were going on a nice honeymoon to another part of the world. Little did he know that he would be reconnecting with a huge part of Delanie's life. Plus, the real possibility and probably of beginning a boat business on the French Riviera.

He began to truly believe that God indeed has a Master Plan. If he did not fill in for his father at the business conference, he would not have met Delanie and all that followed. He smiled and thanked God.

Once in Paris Delanie directed them to a hotel on the South Bank of the Seine. In the middle of all the action. Notre Dame Cathedral nearby. The Sorbonne. Quinn arranged for her to attend. Internationally known Louvre Art Museum (home to the famous Mona Lisa.) Champs-Elysees. Arc de Triomphe. The South Bank was an exciting part of the city.

Clearly, Paris is one of the most famous and beautiful cities in the world. The French language is beautiful. Shopping on the Champs-Elysees was an incredible experience. Of course they strolled that famous avenue. Delanie loved the city and enjoyed showing Jimmy all the sights.

They spent a few days seeing all the sights and began thinking of moving on and taking the train to the northern Plains of France and the seaside village of Calais. Delanie had one more request. Jimmy took a deep breath, smiled, and jokingly said why not.

Delanie said that she wanted to visit the Marais section of the city. She explained that it is close by. She remembered the Avenue name-Rue de Rosier. A quaint area with homes. Simon, the baker, lived across the street and was the man who helped her father get his start in Paris. She would love to see him again. With that said they took a taxi to the neighborhood. Nothing had changed. Kids playing in the streets. Young mothers pushing baby carriages. Old men playing chess. Music-music everywhere. The smell of fresh bread baking in the shops.

Bingo! There it was. Simon's Bakery. Delanie walked in and gave a big "Bonjour". Simon looked a bit confused but responded with "Bonjour" and thought to himself-do I know this woman.

Delanie smiled, "Simon, it is me. Delanie. Jimmy McGettigan's daughter. Quinn. Of course you remember Quinn.

Certainly he did. But it has been so long. Questions just kept popping out from him. Another reunion. They talked for a few hours. Delanie explained what the two of them were planning. They would be coming to Paris on a somewhat regular basis.

Simon asked that they stay for a few days. Delanie said that would not be possible on this visit. After she went into the details of their time on the Riviera he understood. Not to worry. We will be back.

The next morning the final leg of the trip homeward began.

A short taxi ride to the train station and they were on the way for a 180 kilometer train ride to Calais. A charming small city on the banks of the English Channel and close to the Belgium border. A beautiful ride. Delanie was excited to see the Ardennes Mountains. She had heard much about them while living in Paris. Unfortunately, she never got that far north. An area that approached one of the most famous battles of World War II-The Battle of the Bulge.

Once they arrived in Calais, they realized how close they were to home. They both agreed to spend just one night and get an early ferry for the 26 mile crossing of the Channel. Excited to get home and share the events of the honeymoon. They definitely agreed that the trip was a great deal more than a honeymoon. And an event that they would not soon forget.

Once they were settled in their hotel room, they made a transatlantic phone call to CC. Jimmy began to explain to CC where they were. Needless to say, she was startled to say the least

"What are you doing in Calais. How did you end up there? Is everything alright," she fired one question after another.

Jimmy laughingly replied, "Not to worry everything is alright. As a matter of fact, things are more than alright. Just meet us at the Port of Dover at 10:00 am. We have an amazing story to share with you. Goodbye for now. Love you."

A pleasant dinner. Some robust French wine. And off to bed. A good night's sleep.

Up early and a taxi to the port. A beautiful morning made for the Channel crossing an easy trip. The ferry docked in Dover right on schedule. The checking of passports and other proper documents went smoothly. The two of them walked out of the terminal and sure enough there was CC. Waving excitedly, she ran to the two of them. Tears of joy were shed by CC and Delanie. Jimmy showed little emotion. Inside he was about to burst with joy. He was delighted that his mother and Delanie got along so well.

CC spoke up, "Okay tell me what the hell is going on." Jimmy said let us wait til we get home. There is a great deal to share. CC did the driving and they were on their way for the twenty-five kilometer drive to Folkestone.

Once home they gathered on the front porch and squeaky rocking chairs. CC then asked once again, "So start talking."

Jimmy replied, "Okay, okay. But first one quick question. When is Dad coming home,"

"As a matter of fact, he is on his way. He should be arriving in London tomorrow. He has some business to attend in London and should be in Folkestone by the weekend."

"Great. I have some business possibilities to discuss with him." Jimmy told her.

CC smiled and said you have delayed me long enough. So, start talking buster.

With that Jimmy did indeed begin to talk. For more than an hour. He discussed the sailing from Folkestone to the French Riviera. The stops along the way. How super, *PADDY*, his boat, handled the open water on the Mediterranean. The French Riviera. People from all over the world that they met. Then he looked over to Delanie and told her she could take over from there.

Delanie did not anticipate this happening. This part of the story was hers to tell. Nervously she began to share going into great deal about her past. Her father and their struggles. How wonderful Quinn was to her. Jean-Claude. Michel. Serenity patch. How Quinn gave the gorgeous sailboat, ODAT, to Jean-Claude. The very boat that he, Jean-Claude, built himself. Paris and attending The Sorbonne.

They talked for hours long into the night. CC was mesmerized. What a story. She thought how amazing life is and how it unfolds. Delanie was in tears as she told parts of the story. Especially about her father. She truly did love him. He was a good man. How her family life was a story of struggle. The fact that Delanie and her mother could never really talk. Her mother was a good woman. Devoted her life to the catholic church.

Then she talked about this family that she married into. A family strong in their faith. Always caring about one another. How they have supported Molly on her life journey as a Spiritual Director and writer. Her travels around the world.

CC got up from her rocker, went over and hugged Delanie and said that you will always be a member of this family.CC did indeed loved her as a daughter. And told her so. They both were in tears at this point.

It had been a long and emotional day. Everyone was ready for a good night's sleep. Off they went. The next couple days were spent just visiting and sharing. Jimmy went to the office and did some work and caught up on recent activities.

Everyone was waiting for the next big event. The arrival of Michael. That day came soon enough. Saturday morning while CC and Delanie were busy in the kitchen Jimmy drove to the train station. He was anxious to see his father and discuss the business opportunities on the Riviera. And of course, retell the stories he and Delanie shared with CC. Certainly, a great deal of big events were unfolding in the Magee family. Not the least of which will be Michael's updating on developments in Australia.

The train pulled into the station. The two men met. Hugged and started for home.

〜

MICHAEL AND THE AUSTRALIAN DEVELOPMENTS

CC prepared a nice dinner and a coconut custard pie (A favorite of Michael's-although as he always said he never met a dessert that he did not like) The family gathered around the dinner table, shared saying Grace, (Delanie felt a bit uncomfortable. She was not accustomed to Grace) and enjoyed a great meal. CC took control of the conversation and suggested that they have tea and dessert on the front porch. She also suggested that they wait until tomorrow to talk about Australia and the long honeymoon and subsequent events.

Everyone agreed. Michael mentioned that he was exhausted from the long journey and travels from Australia. Of course, Jimmy and Delanie did not want to rush into their story. They both said that they would wait. Michael and the possibility and probability of expanding their operations internationally is of huge concern to the whole family.

Without question that should be the first topic. And, yes discussing it when everyone is adjusting to being back home should wait until the morning.

CC said, "Fine, discussion over. We will just relax, have tea and dessert, thank God for getting everyone home safely, and all get a good night's sleep." When it came to the family everyone knew and realized that CC was the decision maker. Everyone also realized that it was one hundred percent okay with all family members.

Tea and dessert was finished. It was obvious that Michael was almost falling asleep in his rocking chair. CC called the evening as over. Everyone went to their bedroom. Delanie asked Jimmy if she could share a few thoughts she had. "Certainly," was his response.

She went on to say how blessed she felt to be a part of the family. How different from the environment she grew up in. An alcoholic father. A mother who did not like to talk about anything. No sharing of information. Just totally different. Every member has an opportunity to make suggestions and have input. The one striking similarity was Faith. Her mother was committed totally to the catholic faith. Obviously, the Magee family was too. Then she abruptly said, "that's all, turn out the light." That he did. Lying in each other's arms they fell asleep.

Early the next morning they were all up and had breakfast completed before 8:00 am. They were all anxious to hear from Michael. He started out with the comment the trip exceeded his wildest dreams. Mr. Wilkinson arranged for me to stay in his hotel on the north bank of Sydney Harbor. The charming community of Cremorne Point overlooking the harbor.

We met in the lobby the very next morning after arriving. Took the ferry across the Harbor with the skyline on the horizon. A beautiful view. A few short blocks to the AMP Limited Bank, established in 1849. Mr. Wilkinson was connected both socially and professionally with the senior officers. They were escorted to the conference room and greeted by three of the senior loan officers. Michael went on to say that he was definitely more than a little nervous. A walnut paneled boardroom with plenty of marble throughout. A most imposing setting.

Mr. Wilkinson then introduced everyone and took a seat. He looked over to Michael and said with a smile, "It is your show. Tell these fine gentlemen why they should make a loan to you of more than 100,000 pounds."

Michael began talking. Unsure of himself as he began. But a few minutes later he was confident and projected that image. He realized that he was talking about the sailboat business. And if he knew nothing else, he knew the boat business. He was on solid ground when talking about building sailboats.

The bankers sensed his confidence and his knowledge. They also realized that he had the support and backing of their friend and business associate, Mr. Wilkinson.

The meeting lasted a couple of hours. Questions and answers. A short break. They resumed. More questions and answers. Finally, the senior loan officer expressed the feeling of having the information that they needed and brought the meeting to a close.

They reconvened in the officers dining room for lunch. Another impressive room. Michael felt relaxed but a bit overwhelmed. This entire experience was way out of his league. His only real banking experience involved the purchase of the boat business in Folkestone from Cap'n Fitz. That involved the loan, relatively small, compared to what they were talking about here. The bank that his friend Tommy was the president of and what led to all of this. Wow! He thought to himself how life unfolds. From a small neighborhood bank in Folkestone, his friend embezzling his funds, and now meeting with the officers of a major international bank more than 5,000 miles from home. His final thought-it is true we really never know what tomorrow will bring. Also, he gave a huge thank you to God. He truly believed that He was a part of this whole story.

Lunch finished it was time to leave. Handshakes all around and the senior officer told Michael would hear from in a few days. There would probably be a few more questions. This was going to be a sizable loan from the bank.

While on the ferry for the short ride across the Harbor Mr. Wilkinson assured Michael everything would work out fine. They are simply going through normal business procedures. He also told Michael that he planned to remain in Sydney for a few more weeks and provide any help that was necessary.

They made the short trip back to the hotel. First thing on Michael's mind was a telegram to CC. He told her everything was going great. He met with the loan officers. At first a bit intimidated but became quite confident. Gave himself a lecture. You know the boat building business. Simply discuss and project your knowledge. Hopes to hear from the loan review board after the regular monthly review of potential loans next week. They reassured Michael his request will definitely be on the top of the pile.

I will keep you posted CC. I have a few boatyard sites to review over the next several days. My new friend and partner, Mr. Wilkinson, will go with me. He knows this waterfront as well, if not better, than anyone. Sure is comforting having him in our corner. He is a well respected businessman and boatsman.

Love to all. Keep me in your prayers. I will stay in touch. This has been an education in high finance and the world of business. Makes me smile when I think of dealing with our small one branch bank in Folkestone. I am not being critical. It is just that this operation is huge and has world wide connections.

The telegram was sent. Mr. Wilkinson went on about his affairs and suggested that they get together in the morning and look at some of the prospective sites. Michael agreed. He went into the hotel bar and ordered a gin and tonic and fish and chips. Settled back and said to himself-proud of you old boy, job well done.

He finished his drink and light snack and took a stroll along the waterfront. Time for bed. A full and busy day came to a close with the sun setting over the harbor.

Michael spent the next few days looking over prospective sites to locate a shipyard. Nothing seemed to hit him right. Too far from the water. Too big. Too small. Too expensive. Too rundown. The list went on. Totally frustrated when the bank suggested a location near The Rocks. A former owner had started to develop the location. Unfortunately, he had a heart attack and died. The bank knew the location, had made the loan, and were of the opinion that it would have been successful. Reluctantly, Michael agreed to look it over. His thoughts were that a bunch of bankers are not going to have any idea what a location would need to be successful.

Too his surprise he agreed. There was potential. Another business lesson learned. Keep an open mind. Do not fall prey to the expression- "contempt prior to investigation." Easy access from a deep river tributary to the bay and harbor. High ground with run off in the event of heavy rains. Storage buildings for boats to be worked on during inclement weather. Yes indeed, this would be an excellent facility for the building and repairing boats of various size.

Arrangements were made to meet with the bankers. He felt confident enough to meet with them without his friend and adviser, Mr. Wilkinson. For some reason that he was not sure of he felt a need to share this thought with Mr. Wilkinson. That he did. Mr. Wilkinson was fine with the idea. He told Michael that he understood and was delighted that he had the confidence to go on his own.

During the meeting the bankers told Michael that as part of the agreement that they made with the former potential buyer was a review of what would be the owners key management staff. The individual who would be the General Manager was a local man. They would give Michael his name and a copy of his resume'. Michael agreed to meet with him and determine his qualifications. Michael felt certain after a visit he would know if this was the right man. Michael knew that he might not have the business skills of Mr. Wilkinson. But one thing he felt unquestionable about was what it took to operate a ship building and repairing operation.

An appointment was arranged for the next morning. They met in the lobby of the hotel. Michael arrived a few minutes early for the meeting and watched for his prospect. Fifteen minutes prior to the agreed time a neatly dressed young man probably in his early 40's walked in. This impressed Michael. He is early for an appointment. Michael could not stand people being late for an appointment-business or personal. He considered that to be an insult.

The young man smiled as he approached Michael, "Good morning. My name is Eddie-Eddie Reynolds." A strong handshake and good eye contact. All important matters to Michael

"Hi Eddie. I'm Michael Magee. Thanks for meeting with me." Michael replied. He then asked Eddie to talk a bit about his background and family.

With that said Eddie began. For openers he explained that his family are fourth generation Aussies and have no intention or desire to live anyplace else. They have always lived in the Sydney area on or near the harbor.

His father worked all of his life in the boat business and was a master boat builder. Working on all type boats-motor and sail. Eddie grew up at his side. Watching, asking questions, and loving it. He admitted he was never much of a student in school. His love was boating and the water. Unlike his father, who had no interest in becoming a boss. His father was most content working on boats.

While Eddie loved working on boats he also wanted to grow and become involved in management and advancing some of his theories and ideas about boat building.

Michael was delighted. He went on to share a bit of his life and feelings about boats. He grew up on the water. Built his own sailboat as a young man.

The two hit off immediately. Similar personalities. Strong family. Strong ethics and commitment. Loyal. The conversation went on for more than a couple of hours. Both seemed pleased with the meeting.

Michael told Eddie that he would give him a call in two days. He needed to interview another candidate. He did say that he felt more than optimistic about the prospects of getting together.

Eddie offered that he knew a couple other workers that would be good candidates as employees. That was good news to Michael. They shook hands and went their separate ways. To say that Michael was excited and optimistic would be putting it mild. Eddie seemed to be the perfect candidate. Someone that he could feel comfortable with, and more importantly trust. He would put a phone call into the loan officers and ask what they know of this young man and his connection to the individual who died of the heart attack.

In the conversation with the bankers he was informed that they did not only research on the property, but the key employees that would be involved with the new operation. Without question Eddie Reynolds was the key employee. He would serve as the General Manager. They researched his work history and received nothing but glowing reports. His family has a long history in Sydney. A solid family.

Naturally Michael was delighted to hear this report. With the potential of an excellent facility and someone he can trust not only financially but with the proper skill set he was ready to execute the loan, offer Eddie Reynolds the job, and move on.

He discussed all of this with his new partner, Mr. Wilkinson, who was in complete agreement. The next couple weeks were spent dealing with all of the necessary details.

Once that was accomplished, he began working on details for the return trip. The first flight would be from Sydney to Rio de Janeiro. A day of rest. Then a flight to New York City. Finally, a transcontinental flight to the London Heathrow Airport. A long week. The 90 minute train ride from Charing Station to Folkestone. Home at last.

CC was so glad to have him home. The information was extremely exciting. She thought the entire plan was a bit risky and a bit scary. He told CC yes there is a risk. He went on to say that with big risk comes big reward. Little risk little reward. No risk no reward.

Michael then asked Jimmy about his honeymoon and the business prospects on the French Riviera. Jimmy said not now. We will discuss it later. Sounds like the Magee family has a lot going on at the moment.

Michael smiled and said, "Yes we sure do."

THE TRIAL FOR TOMMY DOYLE

It had been more than two months since the scandal had been uncovered. During that time the prosecutors were putting their case together. The trial was now ready to begin. The anticipation was that there would be a great deal of emotion on both sides.

For openers the prosecutor for the County of Kent was a cousin to Tommy. The judge was a lifelong resident of Little Dublin. A few years older than Tommy, but they knew each other quite well. Not all, but most, of the jury were local residents.

It was a bright sunny morning when the trial opened and court was in session. The lawyers from both sides made their opening remarks. Tommy's wife sat in the first row of the courtroom. She had a difficult time hearing these terrible remarks being made about her husband. Thief. Distrustful. Embezzler. Gambler. On and on. She knew in her heart that these comments did not tell the whole story of her husband. She knew him to be honest. A good father. Active member of the church community. Volunteer in several community projects to help those less fortunate.

Sadly, that is not why he was on trial. He was on trial for absconding with funds that did not belong him. Betraying the trust of Michael Matthew Magee and the bank of which he was president. The anticipation was that the trial would last five days. Michael's plan was to be at the courthouse every day of the trial.

CC had said earlier that she did not think she would be able to attend the trial and listen to all of the terrible details. Certainly, she would not be able sit in the courtroom and witness Tommy's wife go through the ordeal. The two of them were lifelong friends. Grew up together. Went to school and church together. They both had two children. A son and a daughter.

CC had discussed all of this with their mutual friend, Father O'Rourke. He told her that he certainly understood her feelings. He reminded her that he knew Tommy and his wife equally as well. CC told the priest that it was more than she could handle to just sit in the court and listen. It would be impossible. Definitely more than she was capable of.

Father O'Rourke hugged her, smiled, and said CC, "I am going to ask you to do something even more difficult. But not impossible. I am asking you to forgive him."

CC replied, "You are right. Impossible is the word. He ruined my husband's business and life's work. Destroyed his family, his wife and children. You are certainly asking a great deal."

"I realize that. I also know that you are a good Christian. Please prayer over the situation," He asked her.

She did agree to try and that she would prayer every morning during her meditation and prayer time.

As the trial went on there were several tense and emotional times. Tommy managed to maintain his composure. Occasionally his wife would bury her head and sob.

The courtroom was filled every day. Filled with residents of Little Dublin. The case garnered some attention in London. Reporters from the London newspapers were there every day. Talk was that Michael was going to become involved in politics. London reporters always chased anything that looked like a scandal.

The final day. Attorney's from both sides made their closing arguments. The judge charged the jury and they went to the jury room. Now it was just a matter of waiting. The wait was not long. In less than two hours they brought in a unanimous decision on all counts.

Malfeasance-guilty.

Misfeasance-guilty

Embezzlement-guilty

Absconding of funds-guilty

Government banking statutes-guilty

The following day sentence was made by the judge-3 to 5 years in the federal penitentiary in Canterbury, 50 kilometers from Folkestone.

Tommy dropped his head in his hands. His wife collapsed and fainted. The courtroom became somewhat out of control. The judge rapped his gavel to order. Chaos developed. A very emotional scene. Tommy had been solid as a rock in Little Dublin for many years.

Michael just sat in disbelief thinking how did this nightmare ever happen. Why didn't Tommy come to me for help. Then he changed his thoughts to how can I help him. How can I help his family? He made a decision to stand by Tommy. Yes, he will have to pay for his crime. He could never forget that Tommy went out on a limb in making the loan that permitted him to buy the business from Cap'n Fitz. Without Tommy there would not have been a business. This is something that he would discuss with their mutual friend-Father O'Rourke.

He waited a few days and went to visit his friend. Franny always seemed to find just the right words and had a comforting way about him.

They sat in the parlor of the rectory and had tea and a biscuit.

Michael said, "Franny, I feel that I am at the end of the road on this whole situation. I don't know where to turn. You need to help me. I am thoroughly confused. I feel like I have no answers."

"Faith and trust in God is always the answer. God did not bring you this far to drop you off a cliff. There is an old Irish saying about the end of the road. Goes something like this-A bend in the road is not the end of the road unless you fail to make the turn," replied his friend.

He went on to say that you may feel that your entire world has been turned upside down. You had a nice business. Beautiful family. Good friends. Then one of your best friends steals your assets. Ends up going to prison. You were forced to look for help. You found it. None of this did you either expect or want. Nevertheless, you found the help you needed. You have survived and will continue to grow.

We all agree that Tommy Doyle is not a thief. He got into trouble and made some terrible decisions. Now he has to pay for that crime. That does not mean that you should abandon him.

They continued their conversation. If Tommy is willing to find redemption you can be there for him. Tommy is a very intelligent individual. During our school days, the gang always said he was the smartest one of the bunch.

Following several hours of conversation, the two got up, hugged, and said a prayer. Michael thanked his friend and went home to discuss the matter with CC.

He asked CC if they could sit on the front porch rockers and talk about the meeting he just had with their friend, Franny O'Rourke.

The plan was to visit Tommy in prison. Father O'Rourke would go with him. They would suggest that Tommy begin an elementary education program for the prisoners. Many of the prisoners were young and were there for what you would call "poverty crimes." Stealing. Gambling. Drugs. Abandonment by their family. Broken home life.

Kids that were not really criminals. Yes, they broke the law and needed to pay for their actions. But being but in prison with hardcore career criminals they got the equivalent of a college education in crime.

Tommy could be a real role model. He would be a real example of how you could be a fine upstanding member of the community and get in to trouble gambling. Next in the progression of life is the thought that stealing is a good idea and a way of life. Next you are in prison.

Education and knowledge are power. Tommy could help them achieve this possibility. There was a fledgling organization known as GA-Gamblers Anonymous. It was founded on the same principles as AA-Alcoholics Anonymous. A support group for people struggling with alcohol.

CC could see how excited and enthused Michael was about the possibilities. She was 100 percent supportive. Michael thanked her and gave her a huge hug and kiss on the cheek. Next on the list was to arrange for a meeting in the prison. Father O'Rourke said that he would go with him whenever the meeting could be scheduled.

Michael could not have been more excited. God had blessed him beyond belief. Now he had the opportunity to not only help a dear friend but these young people in prison. Little did he know at the time, but this project would become a lifelong passion.

Over the next two years the program was a huge success. Tommy helped a long list of prisoners. He conducted courses on basic reading, math, writing and job skills. The gambling program was making some progress. Not great. But some of the inmates attended the weekly meeting on a regular basis. Tommy arranged to get brochures and books for the program from the world headquarters for Gamblers Anonymous in Los Angeles, California.

Father O'Rourke and Michael continued to visit Tommy and supported his efforts in any way that they could. The warden was also supportive and impressed with the efforts Tommy put into the program.

On one of their visits the two men met with the warden. During the meeting with the warden he told them that the guards were impressed with Tommy's commitment and overall attitude. He had definitely become an ideal prisoner. In addition to his teaching efforts he served as an altar server during the Sunday morning mass.

The warden then delivered the big news. Tommy could be considered for early release at the end of his three year minimum sentence. Six short months from today. The warden asked for their opinion on that possibility. Both of the men were 100 percent supportive.

Of course, this news made the drive home a pleasant trip. Father O'Rourke told Michael he should feel good about his efforts and contributions to the rehabilitation of their mutual friend. Micheal admitted that he felt good. Not for anything that he did. He felt great for Tommy and his family. In the event he helped in any small way so be it. He did say that he would not have been able to make it happen without the help and guidance of Father O'Rourke.

The next couple months everyone went about their affairs. Michael kept involved with the Australia project. CC worked closely with the afterschool art project and her own art efforts in both Folkestone and London. Working closely with her friend and mentor, Annie Ackley. Jimmy was managing affairs of their boat yard in Folkestone. Michael made a trip to Mallorca and his friend Eddie Boyle. Delanie spent time between London and Folkestone on her fashion business. While in Folkestone, with the help of CC, she was planning the building of a new home for Jimmy and herself. Molly was working with the Maryknoll Nuns as a Spiritual Director and her writing efforts. She purchased a home in Visby-an island nation in the middle of the Baltic Sea.

In a word they were all busy with life. It seemed that life was going in the right direction. Every member of the family was engaged in positive activity. Life is good and seemed to be getting better.

Michael and Father O'Rourke continued their efforts with Tommy and the prison program. They were scheduled for their regular visit and a business issue came up. He called to let his friend know that he would be unable to go the next day due to the issue that developed. Father O'Rourke told Michael not to be concerned. He was anxious to go. They both thought that the issue of a pardon should be coming up any day. He did not want to cancel any visits.

Early the next morning Father O'Rourke conducted 7:00 am mass, had a quick breakfast, and was on the road for the 50 kilometer trip. He checked in with the desk officer to get his pass. This was always a routine matter. Both the priest and Michael were well known at the prison.

The officer told Father O'Rourke he needed to go to the warden's office. He asked if there anything wrong. Then his next thought-Oh, great maybe the warden has news about the parole. He expressed that thought to the desk officer who evaded answering other than to say you need to see the warden.

He became a bit anxious. Why all the mystery. The few minute walk to the warden's office seemed to take an eternity. His instincts suggested something was not right.

The warden greeted him with a somber expression, shook his hands, and told him to sit down.

"What is going on. Why all the mystery," the priest asked.

The warden began the conversation with, "I do not know how to begin. This is extremely difficult. There is no easy way to tell you."

Father O'Rourke was clearly upset and told the warden to please get on with whatever there is to tell me.

The warden took a deep breath and did in fact begin. During the late-night routine check the officer responsible for the section where Tommy is housed was shocked. He flashed his light into the cells as he passed them. When he reached Tommy's, he saw what appeared to be Tommy hanging from the bars on his window facing the prison yard.

He had difficulty comprehending what he was seeing. He instantly pulled out his keys and opened the cell. Yelling for help from the other officers on duty.

In an instant he cut Tommy down from the bar. Apparently, he had torn his pants and created a rope of sorts, tied it around the bar, pulled it over his neck, and jumped off his bed.

It was difficult to tell how long he was hanging. They patrol the corridor a minimum of once an hour. The officer radioed for immediate help. Several officers were there in an instant. The medical doctor on duty was there also. It was too late. The doctor pronounced him dead and documented the time and completed a medical finding form.

Father O'Rourke was shocked. During his years as a priest he witnessed some tragic events. But nothing that even approached something like this. He came this morning hoping to hear something about a parole. He just could not comprehend what he was hearing.

The warden went on trying to make some sense or understanding of this. He did say that Tommy left a suicide note. He handed the note to the priest. He began to read the brief message:

> I have tried to fight the demons that have been in my mind ever since the trial. I have prayed with my friend Father O'Rourke.
>
> In a compassionate manner of understanding he told me that God has forgiven me. That may be true and at some level I do believe. But I am not God. I just have not been able to forgive what I did.
>
> I destroyed my family and almost destroyed my dear friend, Michael, and his family. I just do not feel worthy of living. Peace and love to all.

Father O'Rourke read the letter through tears streaming down his cheeks. What a tragic end. Tommy, Michael, and the priest grew up together. Tommy Doyle did an awful thing by stealing that money. But he was not a thief or a bad person. He believed Tommy was a good person who did a bad thing. A really bad thing.

What to do next

The warden told Father O'Rourke that the authorities would notify his wife and make the arrangements to be buried in the prison cemetery. He went on to explain that procedure is standard. There is a cemetery on the prison grounds. Many prisoners die and no one claims their remains. Rarely, but it does happen that a prisoner will commit suicide. Tragic. But it happens.

Father O'Rourke jumped to his feet and said you simply cannot do that in this case. I will go and visit his wife and explain what happened. He is not going to be buried in a prison cemetery. You can arrange to have his remains sent to the parish. Tommy was an outstanding member of the community and the parish until he committed his crime. But that does not mitigate the life he lived.

The warden was somewhat surprised to hear from a priest in the manner that he spoke. He was totally in support and agreement with the proposal. The arrangements would be made.

Father O'Rourke thanked the warden and took the suicide note with him. The two hour drive back to Folkestone was a difficult time. How would he tell Brigid, Tommy's wife, and Michael and CC. He prayed for guidance.

Back in Little Dublin he decided to visit Michael and CC first. Of course an emotional scene. Both Michael and CC were shocked. How could something like this happen. Father O'Rourke told them that the guards patrol constantly. But they were not able to stand watch 24 hours a day. To commit such a thing would really only take minutes.

Michael was devastated and felt in some convoluted way that he was responsible. He did press the charges against Tommy that resulted in his going to prison. Of course his friend told him that thinking was absurd. You need to get that idea out of your mind. The priest then went on to say that they all need to rally together to face Brigid and help however possible. Both Michael and CC said that they wanted to go with Father O'Rourke when he met with Brigid. A phone call to make certain that she was home. She was. They gathered themselves and drove to her home.

Brigid met them at the door. Seeing all three of her friends she immediately thought-this is not good. The priest told her that she was right. It is not good. He told her to sit down. Then he sat beside her and took her hands. The news sent her into a hysterical state. CC came over and stroked her back. Michael stood in a paralyzed state. He was unable to talk.

The next hour was spent trying to make sense of it all. Father O'Rourke then told her that arrangements were being made to have Tommy sent to the parish. From there they would make plans for a Christian funeral mass and burial.

Brigid looked confused and spoke up saying the church considers suicide a mortal sin and prohibits a Christian mass and burial. The Bishop will never permit it.

The priest told her not to worry. I will take care of that. I have had more than one run in with the Bishop. He will not know anything about it until it is over. The Bishop realizes that our parish is the strongest in the Diocese in many ways. Strength. Financial. School. This is definitely not something that you have to worry about. And then with his big Irish smile (Ah, that smile of his would melt anyone) he used on of his favorite lines whenever he was going to accomplish a difficult challenge-"It is easier to ask for forgiveness than to ask for permission. It always worked for him.

CC then spoke up and told the two men to leave. She would stay with Brigid a little longer. The two mothers were friends since school days. The two men agreed and left.

The two women had tea and reminisced over a lifetime of memories. CC holding and stroking Brigid's hand. It was comforting to both of them.

The next several days were difficult for everyone in Little Dublin. Tommy was a major factor in the community. He personally made it possible for most people to purchase a home and get a mortgage. He was always proud to say that every loan that he made was paid promptly and on time. More than once he went beyond standard banking procedures. He always said that he had complete faith and trust in his friends. Active in the Holy Name Society and many other church activities. Whenever Father O'Rourke needed someone at the last minute Tommy was the one person he could call and know he would get a positive-"Sure, happy to help."

The church was packed for the mass and the same at the parish cemetery.

Michael continued to struggle. Ancestors of Little Dublin, including the ancestors of Tommy Doyle, were a part of the celebration of his life.

A BIT MORE OF THIS SPECIAL PARISH

The building of Stella Maris School and the new church. In December 1925, plans for a new school on a two acre site near Radnor Park took shape. It was intended to provide accommodations for 200 children. In October 1933, work began on the site to plans drawn by Mr. E.J. Walters, and little more than six months later as was complete. On April 18, 1934, his Eminence Cardinal Francis Bourne formally opened the school dedicating it to Our Lady under the title of STELLA MARIS-The words

"Star of the Sea" are a translation of the Latin title STELLA MARIS. Obviously, a reference to the coastal sea of Folkestone.

The Golden Jubilee and Consecration of the Church (including the school) took place on January 1, 1939. Father Walters announced that as the church was free of debt consecration of the building could now take place on St. Aloysius Day. The solemn consecration of the church took place on June 21, 1939. Relics of Saints Jucundina and Verecunda were sealed into the altar table Research has failed to reveal what the relics were or details of these female saints. The singing of the Magnificat brought the four hour service of dedication to a close. A luncheon was provided at the Royal Pavilion Hotel at which many dignitaries, and parishioners were in attendance.

✍

CC THE FOLKESTONE ART SCHOOL AND PICCADILLY CIRCUS

The entire Magee family continued to be busy and active in many directions. CC was travelling to London and the Picadilly Circus art gallery of her friend, Annie Ackley.

Her usual travel plans included a weekly train to London and the Charing Station followed by a tube to Picadilly Station. She always enjoyed the commute. She found the energy of London and the subway a totally different world from the quiet and relaxing atmosphere in her quaint small town of Folkestone.

Under the tutelage and talented eye of her friend, Annie Ackley, CC had become an excellent artist in several mediums. Sculpting was her favorite. As the result of the outstanding reputation of her tutor and the location of her art gallery being in one of a favorite stop of tourists as well as patrons of art in the city the gallery was always busy.

She was always surprised when a patron entered the small space in the gallery that displayed her art. And even more surprised when someone bought a piece of her work. Annie told her that CC should not be surprised. Annie was quite convincing when she described the quality of work. Nevertheless, CC found the praise from her friend difficult to accept. However, she was always pleasantly surprised and extremely grateful. This part of her life was far different from her role as a wife and mother in quiet Folkestone.

Her activities in the Folkestone Art School took a great deal of time as well. The art school was continuing to grow. Thanks in large part due to the commitment Annie Ackley made. Her normal routine was to come to the seaside location on a regular basis. She would spend a few days at her cottage and work with the young artists in an effort to pay it forward for the help she received as a young artist.

CC was in the administrative offices of the school one day and was approached by the young woman who managed the business and administrative responsibilities for the school. She told CC that she was getting married shortly and moving to London. Her husband worked in London and they would be moving there shortly.

The first reaction that CC had was one of excitement for the young woman. She is a professional young person and committed to her work. They would certainly miss her. Then her thoughts turned to where would they find someone to replace her. Almost instantly she thought of her friend-Brigid Doyle.

Brigid was a talented business woman. As a matter of fact, that is where she met her husband, Tommy Doyle. They both worked at the bank. She served in a management position when they married. Once they began a family, she left the bank to become a full time mother.

CC thought to herself that Bridgid had all the qualifications for the job. Business skills. Professional appearance. Pleasant personality. Well respected and well known in the community. In addition, the position would provide Bridgid with some much needed income.

Hopefully she would accept the position. In addition, the job could be just what she needs to help her move on through the terrible tragedy of recent events.

CC telephoned her friend and told Bridgid that she would like to stop by and discuss an opportunity that could help both Brigid and her family as well as the art school. They agreed to meet for breakfast in the morning.

Later that night she shared her thoughts with Michael and asked his reaction. He believed it was a fantastic idea on many levels. This could be the very opportunity to help Brigid move on. She will never get over the tragedy. But this could help her in the process of getting through it. A tragedy of this type one never gets "over it." Indeed, meeting with her in the morning might just be the first step in moving on with her life. CC and Brigid were school friends and have a solid relationship.

As CC was leaving to meet for breakfast Michael gave her a hug and wished her the best. Surely talking about the past events will be difficult for both CC and Brigid. But talk they must.

Brigid greeted her at the door and they walked to the nice bright breakfast nook in the rear of the house. A bay window overlooked Bridgid's flower garden. She loved flowers of all types and got a great deal of pleasure nursing them. The sunshine coming into the area provided a delightful setting.

After a few minutes of small talk. Talk about their children. Getting updates on how they were doing. Both of Brigid's children were still single. Her daughter living in London. Her son in Canterbury. CC talked about Jimmy and Delanie. How grateful she was to have such a nice daughter-in-law in Delanie. Molly was living an interesting, albeit, somewhat different life. CC said that Molly was a wonderful young woman totally committed to the marginalized people of the world. She has been that way since she was a little kid. Always wanting to help someone less fortunate than herself.

CC suggested that they talk about the position in the school. Brigid agreed. CC spelled out the duties. All of which Brigid was more than qualified to handle. They discussed the compensation and benefits. Of course one of the great benefits being the fact that the school was but a couple blocks from home. The position is one of helping the young kids of Little Dublin. Something that is extremely important to both of them.

After more than an hour of discussion they both agreed the position would be an excellent opportunity for Brigid. Time to go. They stood up, gave each other a big hug, and when CC was ready to leave Brigid started to tear up. Thanking CC for all of her help and being a good friend in this time of need. CC smiled, and choking up said, we have been lifelong friends Brigid. That's what friends do. I love you."

CC decided to stop at the boatyard and let Michael know how things went. Of course, Michael was delighted to get the report. They both agreed that this might just be the beginning of recovery for Brigid and moving on with her life.

Just as CC was leaving, she told Michael she had another thought. Maybe she should stop by the rectory and let Father O'Rourke know of these developments He has been involved since the trial of Tommy and the ensuing tragedy. Not to mention that he was also lifetime friends of all parties.

As she approached the church Father O'Rourke was just leaving the church. She asked if they could visit for a few minutes. She explained that she had some big news. He nodded-yes of course. They sat on one of the benches in the park across from the church. Had a great visit and he told CC how proud he was of her and the manner in which she handled everything. They talked for about an hour. Father O'Rourke gave her a kiss on the cheek and he left with his signature comment of "Peace."

CC headed for home and thought to herself that it was a great day. She also had the thought how great God is. How kind he has been to the people of Little Dublin. The people of this small community, are good people. Family, friends, and loyalty are what makes it such a great place to live. She felt truly grateful to be a member of this special place and how God watches over them. Occasionally it appears that some situations will never work out. But with God all things are possible. Not in our time. In His time. CC was grateful for her strong catholic faith.

MOLLY MARIE MAGEE-WRITER AUTHOR SPIRITUAL DIRECTOR

In addition to the many hats that Molly wears as indicated above she is a Lecturer at the University of Stockholm on a monthly basis. Her programs cover a number of topics. But her speciality is social justice. Social justice has always been her driving force. She works closely with people living on the margin of society.

She has travelled all over the world to some of the forgotten places and people simply struggling to stay alive. She developed a close relationship with the Maryknoll Sisters of the catholic church. Their roots date back to the early part of the 20th Century. They have Sisters spread all over the world. Earlier in her life Molly went through discernment for the possibility of a religious life. Their mission is to serve the marginalized people of the world. A mission that Molly committed herself to many years ago. While that did not happen her thoughts and efforts are always along those lines.

While her brother, Jimmy Magee, was never much of a student Molly loves the classroom. Believing that knowledge is power. Jimmy Magee was a homebody and not much of a wanderer. Molly has continued to travel to the four corners of the world. On a spiritual retreat she was attending in Visby, a self-governing island nation in the middle of the Baltic sea, she fell in love with the place.

Now several years later she has settled there. Molly purchased a three-story stone house that was built in the last years of the 19th century. It was built to survive the harsh winters and the strong winds coming off the Baltic Sea. A difficult time to survive. Molly spent the major part of the winter travelling to distant parts of the gathering information for her novels and working with the poor.

But nine months of the year she could be found in Visby. Early morning she would be sitting by the window of her third floor studio in her favorite old wooden rocking chair. Busy arranging for retreats and conferences on a variety of subjects from Europe and the Scandinavian countries. Her retreats were well known in the academic world as well as faith based organizations.

Of course one of the major attractions to her retreats and conferences was this beautiful setting. Visby was right in the middle of the Baltic Sea some 90 kilometers from the mainland of Sweden. It is one of the most heavily visited cities in what is a part of Sweden. It is a place with a ringwall around the entire island. Molly's home sits right along the wall.

In addition to the natural beauty and tree lined streets with red roses (red roses everywhere) was the fact that women occupied a place of importance. The City of Roses. Women were held in high esteem and of true value as part of their history and culture. A bit unusual at this time in history. Partly due to the fact that the men were always at sea.

The geography of the island is about 50 kilometers wide and 176 kilometers in length. Some 90 kilometers from the mainland of Sweden. A year round population of 57,200 people. Most of them lived there for generations. They would not think of living anywhere else. Truly a small, and different, slice of paradise.

DELANIE AND JIMMY MAGEE SETTLE IN FOLKESTONE

The honeymoon over they both settled down to their careers. Michael was spending less time in Australia as that operation seemed to be going well. As a result, he was more involved in the affairs of their local ship building business. Occasionally he would visit Mallorca and his friend Eddie Boyle.

Jimmy and Delanie built a home on a piece of land that had been in the family for several generations. High atop the White Cliffs. CC was delighted that they decided to settle in Folkestone. She had concern that they might move to London. After all Delanie was involved for several years in the fashion district and had her own apartment in the Belgrade section of the city.

One day when CC and Delanie were alone the topic came up. CC explained what her feelings were. Delanie gave her a big smile and responded with, "No way. Not a chance. I love living here and I love being a part of this family. I have no desire to ever leave."

With that said CC gave her a big hug.

Delanie then continued with, "This might be a good time to tell you some good news. At least Jimmy and I think it is good news. You are going to become a grandmother.

Delanie and Jimmy agreed that is the way they wanted to handle the announcement. CC and Delanie alone. Just the two of them.

CC began to cry. Really cry. A lot. She could not stop. Delanie gave her a hug and said we hope you are happy.

Happy. What an understatement. She felt blessed beyond words.

Later that day when Michael came home arrangements were made for Jimmy to be there also. Delanie and Jimmy at one end of the dinner table and CC and Michael at the other end. Delanie and Jimmy held hands and they made the announcement together. Quite an evening.

CC and Michael went off to bed at the end of the evening. CC told Michael that she wanted to talk for a while. She was excited and not ready for sleep. Michael could clearly see that and said okay you start the conversation.

With that CC went on to say they were blessed with two wonderful children. They were two very different people-as it should be.

Molly loves to travel the world. Always wanting to help the marginalized people of the world. Believing the government should do more. A lot more. Definitely a dreamer. Has a hard time staying in one place for very long. She is an academic. Likes being in scholastic setting.

Jimmy Magee loves Folkestone. Little if any desire to go globetrotting. Feels that the government should stay out of lives of the citizens. He is rooted in hard work and does not want a handout. He never liked school and academics. He only went to University to please Michael.

She continued by saying this is just a short list of their differences. Then she went on to say on the important issues of life they are in complete agreement. Things such as morals. Integrity. Kind and generous. Loyalty. Dependability. Faith. Spirituality.

Then with a smile she said, "I could go on and on. They are children that we can be extremely proud of. And now we have Delanie as a part of our family. She is definitely like our children and I am very grateful that we have her. And just think we will soon be grandparents. God has truly blessed us."

Michael then offered the comment that the two kids are really the same. They simply have different views on how to accomplish the same goals.

CC rolled over and nestled into Michael's arms and the two drifted off for a good night of sleep.

The following months seemed to go by quickly. But not quick enough for CC. She had a difficult time controlling her excitement and anticipation of the coming blessed event. Of course, she was always talking about the baby. Then one night she got the much-awaited phone call. Jimmy Magee called to tell her that he was taking Delanie to the hospital. The time has arrived.

CC got dressed in a hurry and hustled off to the hospital. Michael was out of the country in Mallorca. He had not been there for quite a while. Dealing with the developments in Australia prohibited his checking in with his good friend, Eddie Boyle. They stayed in contact through the telephone and telegrams.

CC arrived at the hospital in minutes and went directly to the maternity ward. Jimmy met her and brought her up to date. Things were progressing in a normal manner. The nurse advised them to try and relax. It could take some time before the baby was ready to make an entrance into the world.

The two of them sat nervously, drinking tea, making small talk, and walking up and down the hallways. Several other expectant fathers and grandparents were anxiously awaiting the big event.

Jimmy looked up and saw their doctor heading over to them. He suggested they sit down. He had some big news. Delanie just delivered twins! Really. How could that be.

The doctor explained that it was highly unusual. Especially in this time with modern medicine the way it is. However, it can and does happen. Normally the doctor would detect two heartbeats. Not so in Delanie's case. There was only one, very strong, heartbeat detected.

Jimmy interrupted with the question, "Are both babies alright."

The doctor said, "They seem to be fine, but it is too early. The little girl weighs 5 pounds 8 ounces and the little boy weighs barely 3 pounds."

He went on to say the girl has a strong heartbeat and the little boy a weak heartbeat. That was probably the reason the twins were not detected. The little boy is now in an incubator and is being treated with the most sophisticated equipment the hospital has.

Fear struck both CC and Jimmy Magee. Endless questions came to their mind. Is Delanie going to be okay? What about the babies. Is there something to fear.

The doctor told them that Delanie is fine. She handled the entire ordeal in a superb manner. You will be able to see her shortly. The nurses are tending to her now. Also, the little girl is doing just fine. We need to stay close to the little boy. Hopefully, with expert attention he will be okay. It will take a few days to see if he will get out of the woods. In a very caring way the doctor went on to say the situation is touch and go.

He suggested that they have a short visit with Delanie and then they both go home and get some sleep. Delanie had been through a difficult ordeal and really needs some rest. The plan was to give her a sedative that will help her sleep.

With that the doctor escorted them into Delanie's room. The little girl was in her arms. CC teared up as she saw her absolutely beautiful grandbaby for the first time. Jimmy leaned over and gave his wife a kiss on the forehead. In everyone's mind was the fate of their baby son. A highly emotional time. A few minutes later the nurse came in and quietly let them know it was time to leave.

Jimmy drove CC home and they agreed to meet in the morning and go over to the hospital by noon. A great deal of anxiety about the little boy. A highly emotional time. Especially due to the fact that no one knew twins would be arriving-including the doctors and nurses. A rare, but totally possible happening even in this day of such advanced medical technology.

CC was up early and made a long-distance phone call to Michael in Mallorca. She furnished all of the details that she had. Needless to say, he was stunned by the news of twins. And even more concerned when he learned of the situation involving the baby boy. He told CC that he would leave immediately and be there as quickly as possible. CC did not try to talk him out of his plan. If anything, she was even more anxious than when she left the hospital last night. Clearly the entire family was on edge. She was on the front porch as Jimmy drove up. Of course they wanted to get back to the hospital as quickly as possible.

They went directly to Delanie's room. The nurse gave them an update. Delanie and the baby girl were doing fine. The baby boy struggled some during the night.

Delanie began the conversation by saying that she wanted to discuss the naming of the babies. The fact that they now had two babies they would have to rethink the naming. She went on to say that she would like to name the boy Jimmy McGettigan Magee. The name would be in honor of not only Jimmy Magee, her husband, but her father, Jimmy McGettigan. Yes, she realized that she and her father struggled. But he was a good man. An alcoholic who got sober and committed his life to helping others. She went on to say one of her few regrets was the struggles that they had.

She would like to name the baby girl Quinn Maureen Magee. Quinn was the most influential and supportive woman that was ever a part of her life. Through Quinn's efforts Delanie is the woman that she is today-no question about that in her mind. Maureen, her mother, is a good woman. But they simply were not able to connect and develop a relationship. This is not to be critical or blame anyone for their somewhat less than strong relationship. Maybe it was a sign of the times. Maybe Delanie's rebellious attitude. Perhaps her father leaving. Maureen was quite content to stay in Galway and had no interest in traveling the country. Delanie wanted to travel the world. She loved her mother.

Jimmy Magee was satisfied with the choice of names.

The nurse came in with the paperwork to complete for the babies. She also brought with her the baby girl wrapped tightly in a pink blanket. Delanie surprised CC by suggesting that she hold the baby while Delanie completed the paperwork. Of course CC was both startled and absolutely delighted. A warm smile crossed her face as she looked at what she considered the most beautiful baby ever born. What else would a new grandmother think about her first grandchild. Her expressions and thoughts were quite transparent to everyone in the room and they all had a good laugh.

Jimmy Magee went searching for the doctor and was able to corner him for a few questions about his new son. He told the doctor to be honest and not give them false hope. With that said the doctor expressed serious concern. As a matter of fact, the little fella lost a couple ounces and is really struggling with breathing. He also went on to say that he is in intensive care unit and his progress monitored constantly. But the situation is very serious.

Jimmy took this information back to Delanie and his mother. He tried to be honest and at the same time a tad with holding of information. Delanie went through a major physical and mental ordeal. He was trying to be sensitive to those facts and of course was greatly concerned. The last 48 hours have been highly stressful and exhilarating at the same time.

After Delanie had breakfast and some time with the baby the nurse suggested that CC and Jimmy leave and let her have some rest. That they did. Jimmy went off to work and CC to the Folkestone Art School.

Michael was not home yet. Air travel following World War II was not that simple. Point to point direct nonstop flights were not that common. He took a flight from Barcelona to Paris. Required an overnight stay. Followed by a flight to Heathrow Airport by way of Berlin. Arriving late in London he would spend a night in a hotel and get the first train from Charing Station to Folkestone early in the morning.

In the mean-time the medical staff informed everyone that Delanie would remain in the hospital until the situation was more stable. Jimmy would take care of the affairs of their business.

CC would develop a routine of her own. She would be up early, attend 7:00 am mass, light a candle, and go directly to the hospital. This routine gave her a feeling of some control over events. The reality is that she had little, if any, control but in some way felt that she was being of help.

On the morning of the fourth day as she walked to Our Lady an unusual feeling overcame her. Something definitely felt different. Not sure what, but her emotions were different. She left church following mass and hurried to the hospital and her normal routine of stopping in the intensive care unit to check on little Jimmy. His little crib was empty.

Her first reaction was panic. Then the thought-maybe, just maybe he is doing better. She went immediately to Delanie's room. Jimmy Magee was already there. They both looked very somber. Not good news. Jimmy McGettigan Magee's little heart stopped beating during the night.

CC went to Delanie and they both began to cry uncontrollably. Jimmy Magee stroked their back and tried vainly to console them to no avail. The nurse arrived and tried to be of help. There was definitely nothing that could be said or done to ease the pain. Finally, CC realized that she would have to regain her composure for Delanie's sake.

The next two hours were a blur. Medical staff coming and going. The doctor trying to explain the medical problems. Father O'Rourke arrived and offered his support-to no avail.

The facts were Delanie delivered twins on December 10. The baby girl is healthy and alive. The baby boy, Jimmy McGettigan Magee, is dead. His short life lasted all of four days. Born December 10. Died December 14.

CC was now visibly upset and angry. Father O'Rourke suggested that the two of them make a visit to the hospital chapel. She did not want to do that; however, Jimmy convinced her to do just that. She was becoming a bit of a problem.

Father O'Rourke led the way and they sat in the rear of the small chapel. CC was still a bit hysterical but calming down some. Father O'Rourke offered prayers, words of condolence, gentle wisdom. He then took her hand and began to speak softly, "Catherine Colleen (he was the only person to call her by her full name-everyone called her CC, including Michael) we have been friends for our entire life. Grade school at Our Lady."

He went on to say that they have shared some extreme highs and lows. Without question nothing compares to what you are experiencing right now. I realize that. I also know that there are no words to ease the pain. I can only say that you will not get over it. What you will be able to do is get through it. I am here to help you, my dear friend, in any way possible. It is extremely difficult for me to see you in such pain. Please try to talk to me and open up, even just a little.

CC with a quivering voice told him okay. I will speak. And with that she began. Yes, I am angry. Very angry. Heartbroken. Not just for me, but my family. What kind of God takes the life of a four day old little boy? No apparent reason. No explanation. I don't want anything to do with that kind of a God. Why would He do that. Whenever we look at the girl, we will have a reminder-her baby brother died four days after his birth. And with that said she began sobbing again.

Father O'Rourke then responded. Yes, right now there is no explanation and certainly no logical reason. And yes, it is impossible to understand right now. We do need remember "With God all things are possible." Maybe in this lifetime we will have a better understanding. Maybe not. The only answer I can come up with is Faith and Trust God.

He then gave her the example of Michael almost going into bankruptcy. Through a series of unexplainable events he was led to Mr. Wilkinson and the successful conclusion. How their lives were changed in such a positive way.

Tommy Doyle going to prison. A terrible event for his family and the Little Dublin community. How he impacted the lives of so many young men in prison. Making it possible for many of them to have their first real chance at a decent life. Tragically he took his own life. But now Michael and I are continuing the program. The young people we are now helping would have never received such a second chance in life without Tommy.

I am simply trying to say that the events that happen and seem tragic beyond words may one day work out in a different fashion.

With that said he leaned over kissed her cheek and suggested that they return to the hospital.

After they arrived in the hospital, she told Jimmy to take her home. He agreed. Maybe she needed a little rest. Once they got home, she went directly to bed. Whereupon she sank into a deep depression that concerned everyone.

Michael finally arrived in Folkestone and took a taxi home. He had no idea what he was walking into. He entered the house minutes after Jimmy and CC. He sensed the heaviness of the situation. Jimmy filled him in with all of the details. Including the fact that CC was in bed. The doctor gave her a sedative. Michael was like the rest of the family-somewhat in shock and disbelief. Little did he know at that moment just how difficult the following year would be.

Over the next year the family and friends tried to get through to CC. Annie Ackley, her close friend, tried unsuccessfully. Brigid reminded CC of the comfort she offered Brigid following Tommy's suicide. Whenever Michael tried to talk to her, she reacted in an ugly manner. Even Delanie could not get through to her. CC loved Delanie like a daughter but she simply did not want to hear anything from anyone.

She went through the motions of living day to day. Most of the time she could be found sitting on the front porch rocking away on one of the squeaky rockers. The entire family was gravely concerned. Somewhat fearful that she would do something drastic. Even to the point of taking her own life. An extremely dark time in the Magee family.

⤳

MICHAEL REFLECTING ON WORLD CONDITIONS

In a moment of reflection Michael paused during one of his visits to his friend, Eddie Boyle, on the growth of his boating enterprises. He reflected on his time in the Navy during World War II and how different the world is today.

Peace existed in most of the world. Of course there always is, and always will be, some maniacal dictator trying to bully a smaller country. They decide to start a war and then send young boys to fight the war. The result being natural resources, historical buildings, and incredible treasures devastated. But no loss compares to the horrific loss of young lives and the ruination of families.

But most of the world is at peace. The powerful Soviet Union is being relatively quiet. The United States and the Soviet Union are engaged in what is being referred to as a Cold War. The one thing positive that can be said about that. A Cold War is better than a Hot War.

While the three big allies during World War II were Russia, United Kingdom, and United States combined to defeat Hitler and the Nazi regime there was not any doubt. Russian was not a true ally.

During a speech Winston Churchill, the great orator, crafted the term "Iron Curtain." In a speech that he made in the state of Missouri he used the phrase, "Russian dropped across all of Eastern Europe the likes of an iron curtain." There was no question after they conquered all of Eastern Europe and created the Soviet Union they would try to spread Communism throughout the world.

The United States was committed to not let that happen. It will take more than one generation but hopefully one day communism will be destroyed.

Michael said to himself, "Okay, enough of your thought provoking reflections what does it have to do with your life." Good question.

He was convinced if the world continued in turmoil there most definitely would not be the business enterprise that he has today. It took a great deal of effort by a number of individuals from different parts of the world to create the boating operations that he has. Folkestone. Mallorca. Australia. Hopefully the French Riviera.

Through all of this help he was able to create jobs for a large number of people. This can be accomplished in time of peace. Not so in time of war.

His family, and the families of his employees, have an opportunity to grow together, have a home, decent income, and be able to educate their children.

He concluded his thoughts with a simple statement-Thank you God for all of your countless blessings. I pray that I will always be grateful and help those less fortunate than myself.

～∦～

MICHAEL BEGINS EFFORTS ON THE WAR MEMORIAL PARK

Michael was becoming increasingly more concerned with CC each passing day. Whatever he said to her did not seem to make any impact. The more he tried the more she withdrew. He made several suggestions. Maybe she should see their doctor. Go away on a spiritual retreat (she loved going on retreats.) Spend more time at the gallery in London. Talking to their dear friend Father O'Rourke. That suggestion sent her into a rage. Through gritted teeth she nearly screamed that he was the last person she wanted to talk to.

One morning as he was walking to the shipyard the thought came to his mind that he would talk to their friend, Franny. He always found the twenty minute walk to work to be a productive time. This morning the weather was clear and brisk. He reversed his direction and headed for the church. The 7:00 am was just ending so Father O'Rourke would be in the rectory. Hopefully, he would be able to spend a few minutes.

Walking up the steps to the rectory Father O'Rourke approached Michael from the sacristy of the church. They exchanged a few words of greeting and then Michael asked if they could spend a few minutes together. As always, with the good friend and priest, the answer was of course they could.

They entered the small room off the main dining room and settled in comfortable chairs. Michael had been here countless times over the year. The room was small, comfortable, and intimate. He had shared many trials and tribulations with his good friend here. The housekeeper brought tea and biscuits. Franny smiled and asked, "What do we need to talk about my friend." In a word Michael responded, "CC."

And with that said Michael went on to explain just how concerned he was about the most important person in the world and the person he loved more than anyone in the world.

He said not only CC has no direction or seemingly no purpose or direction in life, he felt the same way. He was simply going through the motions at work. Unable to concentrate on much of anything. Physically not feeling well. Afraid to approach CC for fear that she woudl react in anger. Franny, I feel lost and do not know where to turn.

Father O'Rourke responded by saying that he realized everything that was just shared. He told Michael that he was praying and hoped they would get together. The situation was obvious to most people who knew Michael. The usual upbeat, optimistic, "can do" Michael was a shell of his former self.

He told Michael that an idea was on his mind. He went on to say that the two of them had talked some ago about developing a Memorial Park to the young men and women of Little Dublin who paid the ultimate sacrifice during World War II. Several young women had served in various capacities. Nurses, motor pool, duties in the field.

Father O'Rourke went on to say that whenever Michael got involved in any project-work, the parish, community, or volunteer activity-he did it 100 percent. He asked the obvious question-are you ready to take on the challenge. It would be a major endeavor. Fund raising. Committees. Planning. The list goes on. So, what do you think?

Michael responded, "Absolutely. That is exactly what I need to do." He went on to say that he was wrapped up with a variety of projects and the Memorial Park kind of got put on the back burner. Now it needs to become a top priority. Yes, he would become the Chairman for the project.

He then said to his good friend that is why he always come to him. Whatever Michael is struggling with Franny O'Rourke seems to have the answer.

He then asked if they could include something else in the project. Would they be able to include a small area for a memorial garden for the grandson they just lost? And perhaps any future tragedies and the loss of a child in Little Dublin.

Father O'Rourke smiled, and replied, "Absolutely. And we will name the memorial garden-Jimmy McGettigan Magee Memorial Garden. Maybe when CC hears this, she might be willing to become involved and maybe, just maybe, it will have a positive impact on her.

Father O'Rourke baptized both of the babies the day that they were born. Plans were now in place for a mass of Christian burial shortly. That will occur in a few days.

They arranged to take a tour of the five acres that the parish has owned since the late 1800's. The decision was made to keep the planned event between the two of them until they could develop a framework of how to pull the whole thing off.

Early the next morning they met at the rectory and began the tour. First, the acreage was situated on a gorgeous piece of land. Some five acres located directly across the road from the Church of Our Lady, Help of Christians. The land remained as it was in the nineteenth century. Raw. Undeveloped. Trees that are indigenous to this part of the country. Silver Birch. Elm. Pine. Big weeping willow. A variety of wild flowers. Bluebell. Flowering heather. Wild red roses.

The two of them walked the entire woods on the foot trails that residents had created down through the years. As they approached the eastern end of the property, they approached The Leas-the wide promenade that stretched along the White Cliffs. Approximately 100 feet below the sea came to rest on the beaches. A beautiful sight. Indeed, created by nature and a place all residents could come and relax, enjoy, pray, and meditate.

After two hours of walking through the woods Michael became genuinely excited about the prospects of being a part of the process. The two agreed that Michael would be the point man in making the plans and Father O'Rourke would be the salesman in the community. For sure no one would be better at that job. His energy was boundless and he had contacts all over the region.

Back in the rectory they sat and began the blueprint in broad terms. Simply a rough plan. One corner on the east end would be the memorial gardens. In the center would be the memorial structure. They would seek a great deal of input from the community on what this should look like. Playgrounds for the young people. Quiet space for prayer and meditation. A labyrinth-maze-that is spiritually connected. Picnic tables. They were both getting very excited.

Father O'Rourke planned to make an announcement from the pulpit on Sunday during each mass. Committees to be formed. Volunteers solicited. Michael was hoping that CC would become part of the project. She loved her community and was involved in any number of organizations and activities.

Walking home his mind was racing with ideas. He said to himself this is exactly what I need to be doing. Something that the entire community can be a part of and clearly will improve the quality of life for everyone. The thought occurred to him that their ancestors would be pleased with their efforts. They had the foresight to purchase the land almost 100 years ago and it will continue forever to be part of the parish they created.

Michael entered the house and began to call CC. She was coming down the steps and quickly saw how excited he was. Taking her by the hand he escorted her to their favorite part of the home-the squeaky rocking chairs on the front porch. For the next hour he explained in detail, including the memorial garden, the plan that he and Franny had put together.

She seemed mildly, but not overly, excited by the plan. The idea of the memorial garden held her attention the most. Yes, she told him that she would be willing to be the chairwoman for that part of the project. Michael was quite pleased with her reaction.

The next several months were indeed busy ones. Committees were formed. Ideas developed. Everyone in Little Dublin was more than willing to volunteer. Committees would meet in the parish hall one night a week to plan the workload for the weekend. Every weekend volunteers would be in the field implementing the work. Trees to be cut. Bushes planted. The overall plan was to create a beautiful botanical garden. The one overriding decision was that all flowers, bushes, shrubs, and trees must be native to this part of the country. There was unanimous agreement that there were more than enough species in the area. There was absolutely no need to import anything. The community wanted this park to be a reflection of their hometown.

Almost to the day one year later the park was completed. A wonderful open space. The little niche for the memorial garden was peaceful and serene on the precipice of the white cliffs that overlooked the sea below. CC had worked feverishly attending to the details of every aspect. Still not the person she was before the loss of the baby; however, it appeared that she might be on her way back. As you entered the memorial garden there was an English Hedge around the perimeter perfectly manicured. The entrance was an old English iron gate with the words-Jimmy McGettigan Magee Memorial Garden-scrolled across the top. After entering off to the left was a small headstone with the following:

Jimmy McGettigan Magee

Born December 10 1949
Died December 14 1949
It broke our heart to lose you
But you did not go alone
For part of us went with you
The day God called you home

Plans were made for a big celebration of the grand opening of the park. Father O'Rourke announced the date for the big event several Sundays in advance during mass. Finally, the day arrived.

Michael came downstairs to find CC sitting at the breakfast table having her tea and biscuit. She appeared to be dressed for church. He was not sure how to react. She had stopped going to church for almost the entire year.

He smiled and said, "You look like you're going to go to church."

"That is my plan. I feel as though my faith has returned," was her response."

Michael gave her a big hug and kiss. And just like that CC was indeed back. Back to her old self. Yes, once again God works his wonders in mysterious ways. Just that simple. Faith.

God in all his glory blessed the event with perfect weather. Plenty of sun. Mild temperatures. And a gentle breeze. Anything but normal weather for this seaside community. To be sure gratitude was felt by everyone.

Following mass everyone left the church and walked directly across the street. It was indeed a packed event with an overflow crowd of Little Dublin citizens. They were the people that made it happen. Michael was extremely proud of this hard working, blue collar, faithful, and generous group.

It was a glorious day. Games of all kinds. Food and desserts that were delicious. Father O'Rourke blessed the event and thanked everyone. He went on to say how proud he was of this humble community. He also mentioned that over the years the Bishop approached him about being transferred to bigger parishes in London and other big cities. His response was always the same-These are my people and my flock. There is not any other place I want to go. I will spend all of my days right here in Little Dublin. The remarks were met with loud cheers and hand clapping. They loved him and he truly loved all of them.

The day came to a close and the sense of a job well done was felt by all. Michael and CC walked home, holding hands, and did not speak the entire way. Once in the house CC put the tea kettle on and Michael walked out to the porch. Their favorite place.

CC AND HER PLAN FOR A PEDIATRIC WING TO THE HOSPITAL

CC brought out a cup of tea and a few of their favorite homemade biscuits from the neighborhood bakery. They settled in and CC told Michael that she had a rather ambitious idea that she has been thinking about. Michael looked at her with a big smile. This is the CC that he knows. Someone who was always thinking of ways to help.

"Great, let's hear about."

With that she began to tell the plan. The idea was to build a pediatric wing to the hospital. While reflecting on the loss of her own grandson she realized that other babies in the area also did not survive. Perhaps with a wing of the hospital that focused exclusively on newborns and little children their could be more success in survival rates.

The doctors of the hospital are now required to treat all types of medical needs and all ages. They are good doctors, but simply have too many demands and are spread too thin.

CC went on to say that working on the memorial gardens and World War II Memorial gave her the idea. Yes, she realized that it would be difficult and a major time commitment but she was ready to do just that. She realized that they have been blessed in many ways. At the top of the list was the gift of, Quinn, their beautiful granddaughter.

The idea of such a wing dedicated to their grandson, Jimmy McGettigan Magee, would mean that he would never be forgotten. Maybe his death and the pediatric wing would be a way of understanding their loss a little better. The wing would be staffed with pediatric doctors who specialized in issues of children only. Research would definitely be a major part of the facility. Nothing but the latest new technical equipment. They would recruit newly graduated female doctors.

Michael was stunned. What a fantastic idea. He could not be more supportive. He reminded her of what a wonderful job she did in getting the Folkestone Art School established. Recruiting Annie Ackley, an internationally respected, artist to commit to the program. Cap'n Fitz and the boat building program for girls as well as boys.

He had no doubt that she would make this happen. It may be a couple of years in the making, but she would achieve the goal. She always does. Hard work and big challenges never stopped her. Michael always said, "Just tell CC she won't be able to accomplish some project. Then you better get out of her way."

Big hugs and a few tears. The close of a big day. Time for bed. Tomorrow she will begin her latest challenge.

Early the next day she went to the hospital and a visit to the hospital administrator. Dr Bruce Ryan, a doctor that she has known for many years. His specialty was cancer. Research was a matter near and dear to this good man. Cancer research was part of another community project involving individuals from various parts of the business community.

He listened attentively for more than an hour. He got up from his chair, with tears in his eyes, and hugged CC. What an amazing idea. How can the hospital help. We will do anything we can to advance the project.

When Michael heard the results of the meeting, he made one positive and confirming comment. With you and Doctor Ryan at the helm this will happen. No doubt. That was it. The project was off and running.

m

MORE ON OUR LADY, HELP OF CHRISTIANS PARISH

The Second World War began on Sunday 3, 1939. Father Walters announced the news from the sanctuary steps. In anticipation of the bombing of London schoolchildren were sent to the less populated areas and Stella Maris School and parish hall were taxed to the limit in accommodating children from the Downham district of South East London.

After the landing at Dunkirk in 1940, the children from Stella Maris School were evacuated to Wales. Folkestone emptied even more as the government ordered the evacuation of all non-essential persons. Houses were empty and shops closed down. There was no school and no hospital.

In June 1940 it was proposed to the diocese that the two Folkestone Parishs of Our Lady and St. Joseph should be amalgamated for the duration of the war. A fortnight later His Grace the Archbishop made his periodic visitation and appraised the situation at first hand.

His Grace closed St. Joseph's Church. He noted that seventy children were evacuated to Merthyr Tydfil and the school was occupied by the Army.

War Time difficulties and problems

The air offensive declined to some extent, apart from the nightly bombing. Shelling from the French coast increased however, most of it directed against convoys that hugged the coast but some against the town or harbor area. The two priests maintained two Sunday Masses. And one weekday Mass at both churches.

The New Year of 1942 found the parish barely solvent. The United States had been drawn into the war a month earlier. This led to the redeployment of German air power and the reduction of air raids led to some relaxation of the evacuation regulations. A trickle of citizens began to return to the town.

The year 1943 opened with the feeling that the invasion was not likely, but the civilian population was weary and debilitated. Archbishop Amigo visited the parish in May and was well pleased with the work being done. News of the final expulsion of Axis forces from Africa coincided with the Archbishop's visit and he led the thanksgiving for those good tidings.

In addition to his priestly duties Canon Walters participated in the life of the community and maintained a lively correspondence with the parishioners who had been evacuated or called to the Army. Sporadic air raids and shelling still occurred as activity increased prior to the anticipated Allied landing in Europe. A member of the congregation remembers, an altar boy, the special Mass said by Father Walmsley for the paratroopers as the day drew near. The church was packed. Weapons and accoutrements were stacked at the rear of the church as the service proceeded. In winter 1944, Midnight Mass was restored at Christmas and the year ended with gratitude for survival and growing hope for the future.

As the year 1945 opened more and more people returned to the town and Father Walmsley set about establishing the school and parish. Stella Maris reopened on 159 March with Sister St. John as the headmistress.

PART FOUR

HIS ELECTION TO PARLIAMENT

MICHAEL MAKES THE DECISION TO RUN FOR THE PARLIAMENT

While sitting and rocking on the front porch following a pleasant dinner Michael announced to CC that he wanted to share a thought that he has had for several months.

Nervously, and with a smile she said, "Okay let's hear it. Things have been calm far too long."

Before he got to his point he talked about CC and her dedication to making the pediatric wing closer to a reality. He reminded her that he offered to help when she announced her intentions. She responded to his offer with a grateful thank you. She went on to say that she wanted to do it on her own and the help of Doctor Ryan. He understood. The project was closing in on one year. Michael was extremely proud of the job and results she accomplished in that relatively short period of time.

"Okay, okay, enough about me. What is this new thought that you have?."

With that he looked at her with a big smile and announced, "I want to run for Parliament! This community has been so wonderful to our entire family I feel I need to give back. Yes, we are involved in several community efforts but I want to do more. I am so proud of our neighbors. We need to give them a larger voice in their government. Hopefully, I could make that happen. What do you think of that idea?

CC was stunned. Michael a member of Parliament. Their family came from such humble beginnings the thought of an Irish immigrant family member being a part of Parliament was something she would have never even think of as a possibility.

As always, she was supportive. She was more than willing to help in any way possible. Admitting that she knew little or next to nothing of how the system worked or how realistic the idea would be. After a bit of thought she asked him to explain how he would go about running for the British Parliament.

Michael went on to tell he had talked to a few of his close church friends, a couple business associates, his mentor Mr. Wilkinson, and last, but certainly not least, Franny O'Rourke. To a man they were all excited about the prospect of having a Little Dublin resident a member of the Parliament.

The next step in the process was to file an "application of intent to run for Parliament" with the appropriate authorities in Election Headquarters located in the County seat.

Next organize a Committee to Elect Michael Matthew Magee to British Parliament. There would be several subcommittees. Finance. Strategy. Advertising. Position Papers on various topics. Voter Registration... And more.

CC was overwhelmed. She had no idea that it was so complicated. And the fact that Michael had done so much research. He explained that the whole process just unfolded as he talked to a few people. He told her that he did not want to bring up the topic unless there was a possibility of it happening. He knew that she was totally committed to the hospital project and this might be a distraction.

CC was not upset that he had not discussed it with her. To the contrary she was totally committed and extremely excited. She definitely wanted to be a part of the process. Then she asked the obvious question, "What are your chances to win."

Michael informed her that William Hillary would be his opponent. MP Hillary (Member of Parliament) would be a formidable opponent to say the least. He was first elected 16 years ago and has grown in power and influence ever since. His wife is Victoria Wilkes Hillary, and she is a member of the wealthy Wilkes family in Dover. The family is in a position to finance his campaigns very easily.

He is a Tory, Conservative, and they have a strong political base in the three county district. There have been some difficult elections for him, but he always seems to survive. He, and his close knit group of advisors, play rough and tough politics. I do not know how he will attack me, but be assured attack he will.

Michael went on to say that he would run as a member of the Labor Party (Liberal). His platform would be built around the idea of "A hand up-not a hand out. Fortunately, the district has both Liberal and Conservative voters. The district covers three counties. Kent-strongly conservative. East Sussex-a mixture of both liberal and conservative voters. Surrey-a blue collar area that tends to be somewhat independent. It is difficult to determine how they will vote. Overall the district tends to be conservative.

They both agreed with his plan. The next day with the support of his friend Father O'Rourke, he filed the necessary documents and filing fees-the race was on and a political career was about to begin.

The two men went to lunch in Canterbury following their visit to the Election Board. Father O'Rourke began the conversation by telling Michael that he will do everything he can do to see that victory happens. There is one line that they both must be careful not to cross-separation of church and state. You can be sure if there is any evidence that remotely resembles such an act his opponent will jump on it immediately.

Michael asked the obvious question, "How do we avoid that happening."

Father O'Rourke responded with his thoughts, "Well, the first thing I will never appear on any platform when you are making a political speech. I certainly will not say anything from the pulpit. Nothing about your campaign will ever appear in the church bulletin. In the event that we have any question we will run it past your campaign staff."

"Okay, Franny then tell me how you will be able to help," Michael said with a smile.

The good priest went on to say that there would be many opportunities. When you are receiving some type of business recognition at a dinner. I will be on the dais, sitting right next to you. Holy Name dinners. We will make sure that you are interviewed with CC and her efforts for the pediatric wing. There will be countless times that we can be seen in public without making reference to your campaign

Michael chuckled, "You should be running for office. Truth be told I believe you were born a politician." No one realized more than Michael the powerful influence that his friend Father O'Rourke brought to the campaign. His mere presence was enough. Simply standing shoulder to shoulder with Michael spoke volumes. There was not any need for dialogue.

During his brief time in politics he learned the cardinal rule-Have one person that you are able to trust 100 percent. The one person who will always have your back. No question about who that would be. His lifelong dear friend-Franny O'Rourke.

The hard work began in earnest. He told Jimmy Magee that he would have to manage the boat business. Running for Parliament was more than a full time job. His son reassured Michael that he was up to the task and he will definitely be on the campaign trail as well. He told his father how excited he was and that he could not wait to tell the citizens what a great man his father is.

Committees were formed. A stump speech was developed. And he was off and running. He found out that he was good at delivering a speech. Maybe because what he was saying he believed with a passion-people do not want government "handout" a hand up yes, when needed.

Before long his opponent, MP William Hillary, was paying attention Polls indicated that Michael Matthew Magee would be a formidable candidate.

Word was getting back to Michael that the incumbent expressed some concern that his reelection might be in trouble.

Almost immediately Michael found out how rough and tumble and dirty politics could get. He was shocked to open the morning paper and see a headline accusing Michael of financial problems. That he almost filed for bankruptcy. The article went on to say that Michael placed the financial mismanagement on his longtime friend, Tommy Doyle. Continuing on the paper told the story of the trial, Tommy going to prison, and then committing suicide.

Michael was stunned. CC was furious.-How could the paper print such a story. Nothing could be further from the truth. What are you going to do about it? If this is politics then you need to get out. Right now.

The article was clearly a bombshell. His advisors told him –

Welcome to the big leagues of politics. They pointed out that MP Hillary was careful in his comments not to say that he believed any of this. He was simply repeating stories that he had heard about the whole affair.

His advisors told him that if he dropped out of the campaign then MP Hillary would have won the argument, and most likely the election. Michael would certainly appear to be guilty. Michael needed to make one brief statement stating that none of the story was true. To the contrary Michael tried to help his friend as much as possible. Then continue by saying that you have no intention of dropping out of the race and that you will not dignify this tragic event involving my lifelong friend with a single word.

Weeks passed and the subject eventually ended. But his advisors told Michael be prepared. This man and his advisors are ruthless. They will continue to search for some kind of dirt.

The campaign grind was difficult. Two or three events every day. Seven days a week. The months wore on. The polls indicated that he had a good chance to pull off an upset. It was exhausting and at times exhilarating. Breakfasts. Lunches. Dinners. Delivering pretty much the same speech. Adlib here and there to put some punch in the speech. Michael did not like the constant travel, but he did like interacting with the people. Occasionally to break up the dull routine he would get on the platform and simply ask for questions. To which he would respond. He liked that. He liked it a lot more than speechmaking.

His advisors told him that he was good at that. He agreed. He felt confident and comfortable.

One night he arrived home late after a particularly long and grinding day. He walked into the kitchen calling for CC. No response. Breakfast dishes were still in the sink. He opened the refrigerator door and poked around for something to eat. He found a couple pieces of cold chicken and some leftover salad. That was dinner. Thinking to himself he thought politicians had an exciting and glamorous career. Cold chicken and leftover salad at 10 pm, is anything but glamorous.

Obviously, CC was not home from her meeting regarding the pediatric wing project. He decided to rest on the bed until she arrived. Minutes later, still fully clothed, he was sound asleep. Somewhere around midnight CC shook him and they both collapsed and fell fast asleep.

He was the first one up the next morning and began to get breakfast together (last night's dishes still in the sink) when CC walked into the kitchen.

Michael told her to sit down that they had to have a talk.

As CC wiped the sleepers from her eyes she nodded okay. Then followed up with, "What are we going to talk about."

"You need help. We need help. We are in over our head," he replied.

With that he went on to talk about their situation. Our family has more than we can handle. CC you need a personal assistant to help you with the hospital project. Certainly we need help here at home. Cooking. Grocery shopping. Keeping the house in order. It is overwhelming.

CC interrupted, "I agree that I could use some help with the hospital project. There are so many planning, fundraising, lunch and dinner committee functions. I have found myself over scheduling and committing to events that I cannot possibly meet. Yes, I will agree I need some help.

She continued, "It sounds like you want me to hire a housekeeper. The answer to that is absolutely no. I am the descendant of Irish immigrants. They were poor people struggling for a better life when they arrived here. I grew up in that environment and so did you. The idea of someone coming into my home and cooking meals for my family is absurd. I will not let that happen."

Michael began talking again and told her that they should at least give it a try. Not on a full time basis. Maybe a couple of days a week.

The conversation (or more accurately the debate) went on for another hour. They came to a mutual agreement. CC would hire a personal assistant to help her with the hospital project. She knew a young mother at the Art School who would be perfect for the job-Diane Cleary. Pleasant personality. Upbeat. Friendly. Intelligent. Hopefully, Diane would respond favorably to the offer.

Short and sweet about the housekeeper. CC would be willing to have someone come in two days a week.

Michael, smiled, kissed her on the forehead, and replied, "Okay."

The campaign moved on. The atmosphere growing more intense every day.

Coverage in the newspaper, radio, and telly was ratcheted up a bit, if that was possible. Michael continued to take the high road. His advisors wanted him to be more negative in his remarks about MP Hillary. They tried to convince him (what was a fact in all campaigns) that negative advertisement did bring results. He was not buying that theory.

CC contacted Diane Cleary regarding the position of Personal Assistant. She was flattered and immediately agreed for a couple of reasons. First and foremost was the hospital. Diane agreed that the community with all of the young families in Little Dublin should have a children's hospital or a least a pediatric wing. Secondly, she respected CC a great deal for all of her efforts with the Folkestone Art School for the children.

CC had no problem with finding a housekeeper. A neighbor, Sharon Cook, lived on the same street, two houses down, offered to fill that role.

With the addition of these two individuals the situation was definitely improved. Not nearly the chaos of the recent past. Diane kept CC on schedule and Sharon maintained the household. Reluctantly, CC agreed that she did in fact need some help.

Michael came downstairs one morning and Sharon was already there preparing his favorite breakfast-a heaping bowl of porridge with fruit and nuts, a strong cup of tea, orange juice, and toast. He had a full day of campaigning ahead and a healthy breakfast would help.

Sharon handed him the, London Times, morning newspaper. The headline banner in big bold type-MP HILLARY HIS MISTRESS AND RUSSIAN CONNECTION.

The article went on to disclose in great deal all the unpleasant facts about a mistress that lives in Paris and that the affair has been going on for several years.

It then went on to talk about Yuri Gorsky. An extremely wealthy Russian member of the Soviet oligarchy. Gorsky is the owner of vast oil fields in Siberia. Also, steel and iron factories throughout the Eastern European Communist countries. The article infers that MP Hillary and Mr. Gorsky are well connected to each other.

The news was a bombshell to say the least. The London Times, a liberal newspaper, was at odds with MP Hillary for years. They did not approve of his arrogance and strong arms methods. They tried for years to find some real dirt with little to no success. Every lead they chased down came to no avail. Whenever they got close the answer was always the same. MP Hillary would not cross the line. He would go right up to the edge of legality and stop.

This time was different. They assigned an enterprising young reporter, James Collins, unlimited access to the files and the funds to take the search to a proper conclusion. The editorial board was convinced MP Hillary was guilty of misdeeds. They simply gave up in the past when the task became to taxing and too difficult to follow through. Not so this time. They had the facts. Dates. Times. Locations. The list went on.

Michael's phone began to ring off the hook. Advisors. Staff members. Newspapers. The local television Station. He answered every request the same way-"No comment. I will have a comment later in the day."

CC walked into the kitchen and in a confused voice asked, "What is going on. The phone is ringing constantly. Who are you talking to."

Michael brought her up to speed. He told her that he was going to campaign headquarters located in the South Cliff Hotel.

A beautiful, stately hotel dating back to the mid-1800's and with a long connection to much of the history of the area. One such connection was the building of the LCD-London Chatham Dover-Railway. The railroad that Michael's and CC's ancestors help to build. During that time some of the management lived there and supervised the final stages of completion. Also, some of the workers were housed there for short periods of times. While those workers were hoping that they were building a better future for their descendants the idea that one day the possibility of a MP-Member of parliament would be beyond their wildest dreams.

During World War I the hotel served as headquarters for The Red Cross. During World War II the Army used the location for strategic purposes regarding activities along the English Channel.

Winston Churchill was a frequent resident during World War II for both military and personal visits

Now the hotel served as headquarters for Michael's campaign for Parliament. The hotel was indeed an imposing and gracious building sitting how above the sea on the edge of the White Cliffs of Dover.

When he arrived most of his senior staff were already there. They were engaged in developing a strategy when Michael walked into the conference room. The consensus was a plan to capitalize on the news. Go on the offensive. Be relentless in the attack. Release position papers. They all felt that the news was a golden opportunity to take advantage of MP Hillary's serious issues and problems. Several of the staff were almost giddy.

Michael sat at the conference table and remained silent. Finally, one of the Staff asked him for his thoughts. He looked at the assembled group and at that moment thought how committed they all were to his winning. What he was about to say would not be welcomed by them. He knew that-but he also believed in his heart it was the right thing to do.

With that he began to state what his position would be on the subject. He would make a statement at 2 pm. He wrote his brief remarks while the staff was busy talking. He then read aloud-I have no comment to make on the London Times article regarding MP Hillary and the issues contained in the article. I will leave that to MP Hillary himself.

I have said from day one of the campaign the election will be about issues and how to solve them. I have not changed that position. I have instructed all of my advisors and staff members to respond to questions in the same manner-do not engage in personal issues. Refer them to MP Hillary for his answers to those questions.

That was it. The end of his remarks.

Everyone in the room was stunned. How could he pass up this golden opportunity? What about all of the ugly comments MP Hillary said about Michael? None of them were true.

Michael responded, "That was his decision. That will not be my decision. We will leave it to the voters to make their own decision. I do not want to be a part of a sleazy campaign and will do my part to stay above the fray. Case closed.

Reluctantly, they all agreed to follow Michael's strategy. But clearly none of them thought it was the right decision. That is all except one-Father O'Rourke. He emphatically did agree with Michael. He told Michael that he was proud of him and his decision. With that reassurance from his friend Michael knew that he had made the right decision.

The decision was made and the announcement was ready to be made. Most of the representatives from the press, radio, and latest form of communication-television-with their cameras were gathering in the lobby.

Michael, alone, walked to the conference table in the main hall, took his seat and told his advisors to let them in. There was a mad scramble by the press to be in the first row of temporary seating.

Following a few minutes of confusion and disorder Michael told all the members to settle down and he was ready to make his comments. Silence followed. Michael went on to say that he wanted to make a few comments about the article in the London Times concerning MP Hillary. He began with the remarks that his words would be few and that he would not be taking questions regarding the article.

He then said that he had seen the article, however; he did not read it in its entirety and had no plans to do so. Any questions regarding the article should be asked of MP Hillary. Further, he did not intend to answer any questions or attempts to solicit opinions on the subject. This campaign is about issues and how to solve them. He went on to say that he was ready for questions and he would be willing to respond as long as they have questions. Please ask away.

Typical of the press they all began yelling out loud trying to be heard above the others. Total chaos. All of the questions concerned the article and MP Hillary. Michael remained calm and restated his position. He would respond to issue questions only. The press finally got the message-he was not going to engage in ugly tactics.

Within fifteen minutes the session ended and the press left the hotel. They were still stunned. A golden opportunity to take advantage of a real scandal. Michael's behavior was a strange one for politicians.

Michael and his advisors retreated to the conference room. To a man they agreed that Michael handled the press conference flawlessly. Father O'Rourke, almost in tears, was beaming and told Michael he was magnificent.

Michael had truly risen above the fray. CC agreed with his handling of the situation. She wanted no parts of the ugly side of politics. Now time alone will tell if his strategy was the right one.

Michael and his staff continued down the same path the next several days. Travelling the district. Making stump speeches and answering questions. For several days he would receive questions about the scandal and he always answered the same way-Ask MP Hillary. Eventually the voters came to believe that he would not engage in the topic.

The polls did not change that much. Maybe a slight uptick in his favorable rating. Then another bombshell dropped. The press certainly was not about to drop such a great political scandal. They conducted more investigative reporting. Several things began to surface.

Apparently, MP Hillary had more political enemies than anyone realized. Stories about his marriage and how and why it happened. The press presented the marriage as one of convenience on behalf of both MP Hillary and Victoria Wilkes Hillary. It seems that she wanted power and he wanted money. Their marriage would accomplish this nasty plan.

The marriage took place more than 20 years ago. They were always seen together. Holding hands. Smiling. Attending all the correct political and social events in society London and the aristocratic Dover scene. The perfect young power couple. The truth was anything but that.

With the help of his wife he moved up quickly as a power broker in Parliament. One of the most important position came his way. Chairman of the influential International Trade Committee. It was through her connections that she got to meet Yuri Gorsky.

Gorsky and Hillary became close friends. MP Hillary was able to move favorable legislation through Parliament. Legislation that would prove extremely profitable to Gorsky. In all of their dealings they were always certain not to do anything illegal. Questionable certainly. Not illegal.

In return for his help Gorsky arranged for some perks for the politician.

Hillary had access to Gorsky's private airplanes. He was able to travel not only to Russia but all over Communist Eastern Europe. It was while on one of these excursions that he met what would become his mistress. A beautiful Parisian woman. Their secret romance continued for several years.

Gorsky owned a huge villa in Dubrovnik high on a cliff overlooking the Adriatic Sea. This secluded part of Eastern Europe was indeed a safe place for Hillary to travel. The communist world was isolated. The citizens were not free to travel outside the communist bloc of countries. While MP Hillary was well known in the UK, he was not an internationally recognized figure. So, he had a fair amount of freedom to move around in Dubrovnik. The city was one of the more popular tourist cities for the people confined to Communist countries of the east. He, and his mistress did little to attract attention. Dressing casually, walking and shopping in the centuries old walled city so typical of the ancient eastern European cities they looked like any other tourists.

All of this was uncovered during the ensuing weeks. The voters were definitely becoming shocked and disappointed in what was being exposed. In the meantime, Michael stayed his course. Hillary tried, unsuccessfully, to refute all of these allegations. The evidence that was being revealed every day was far too strong and well documented. It seems that there was a significant part of his own party that did not approve of his ruthless and strong armed politics. Indeed, there were many that wanted him to fail.

They would find out in eleven days. Election day. Michael campaigned longer hours with the passing of the final few days. The staff and advisors, including Father O'Rourke, sensed the real possibility of victory. A victory of this magnitude would never have been imagined just one year ago. It definitely seemed that this was his time. Much like catching lightning in a bottle. CC and her high profile exposure with the hospital project was of huge benefit. They definitely presented a united front and a couple that was easy to like. Humble beginnings. Faith and commitment to Our Lady Parish. Very active in their community. Jimmy Magee and Delanie, along with their daughter Molly. The presence of their children on the stage and their civic and professional activities completed the picture.

Finally-election day. The entire family was up early and had cast their vote at 7:01 am. They had a family breakfast at home following their voting. Their friend, and housekeeper, Sharon Cook had it ready. Eggs. Sausage. Bacon. Potatoes. An assortment of fresh fruit. Several different juices. Certainly, a breakfast fit for a king-or at least a member of Parliament.

CC looked at the feast and jokingly kidded, "Are you expecting the king."

Everyone had a good laugh. Sharon responded, "Well you never know who will show up. People were in and out of the house half of the night. I wanted to make certain we were ready."

Sure enough she was right on the money. Within minutes neighbors, friends, and well wishers were streaming in and out for the next couple of hours. CC gave Sharon a huge hug and a hearty thank you.

Next on the agenda was the short ride to campaign headquarters. They arrived at the White Cliff Hotel shortly after noon. The long wait was about to begin. Reporters wandered in and out. They were all asking questions that Michael felt nervous answering. Waiting for election results was yet another new experience for him.

Shortly after the polls closed results began trickling in. The first ones were from Dover, the northern part of the district. As always, especially in the Dover area, the results were trending in the favor of MP Hillary.

Michael got quite nervous. His advisors told him not to worry. Hillary always wins that part of the district by a big margin. They then pointed out that his lead was much smaller than normal. That could be a good sign.

As the night went on more of the outlying results were coming in. Good news. Actually, great news. Michael had taken the lead. Albeit a slim one, but nonetheless a lead. Finally, Little Dublin results were reporting. More than 90 percent of the vote was in favor of Michael.

Into the wee hours of the morning the final tally was made. Michael would be the new MP for the district. Final results-Magee 54 percent Hillary 46. Based on the margin of victory for Hillary in past elections these results would have to be considered a landslide. In past elections Hillary would have what would be thought of as "token opposition." That was certainly not the case in this election. Michael proved to be a formidable opponent. The room went crazy. Michael hugged each member of his family and thanked them for all of their hard work and sacrifice. The campaign was the hardest work he had ever done. It was a rough and tough experience.

At 3:31 am he received a concession phone call from MP Hillary. He wished Michael good luck and he knew that Michael would represent the district with dignity and honor. That made it official.

Michael Matthew Magee, son and grandson of Irish immigrants, was the new member of Parliament from his home district.

The big question and big gamble regarding the strategy of the high road or the normal road of dirty politics was answered loud and clear. Michael was clearly right and his decision the proper one. It is the road he always followed during his entire political career.

He would be inaugurated in six weeks. The third week in January. He had not told the family but win or lose he wanted to take all of them for a two week vacation on the French Riviera.

MICHAEL AND THE FAMILY VISIT THE FRENCH RIVIERA

Following a day or two of relaxing and unwinding the family was ready and looking to this very special vacation. Without question this would be the most elaborate vacation they ever had as a family. Maybe a few days in London or a visit to another part of England would define as a vacation in past seasons.

Flying to Paris was like a dream. Reservations were made. Bags packed. The train to London and Heathrow Airport. The flight was of the type that most passengers like-on time and uneventful. A taxi to the hotel, The Hotel de Ville, on the Champs Elysees and three days of sightseeing. The Louvre. The Cathedral of Notre Dame. Arc de Triomphe. The Eiffel Tower. Strolling on the south bank of the River Seine. The joke among the family was that they would pinch each other to make certain they were not dreaming. Then it was time to leave this beautiful City of Lights.

Early the following morning they gathered in the lobby and off to the Lars train station for the two hour train ride through Provence, the wine country, and the south of France. They would arrive in Auribeau at noon. Settling back in their seats they gazed out the windows and enjoyed the beautiful scenery.

The train pulled into the station right on time. They were amazed at the efficiency of the rail system in Europe. A convenient and dependable mode of transportation. Efficient and reasonable fares. They all gathered their luggage and as they got off the train Delanie spotted her old friend-Michel. She had written him a letter a week ago telling him of their plans. She was confident that he would meet them as planned. And indeed, he did.

Introductions and hugs went all around to the group. Luggage was gathered and placed into a small truck Michel hired. Both a truck and a driver were waiting. Between the two vehicles everyone had a seat and their luggage cared for. That was just the type of person Michel was-always thinking.

The ride was a short trip through the village square. A charming place covered with beautiful flowers all over the small park. Michael,

CC, and Delanie, rode with Michel. Delanie took a great deal of pride in giving a "guided tour" to her in-laws. Delanie spoke to Michel in more than passable French. They were both impressed and please to hear her and the knowledge she had of the area. Jimmy Magee and Molly were in the small truck with Michel's helper. Minutes later they arrived at Serenity Patch.

Luggage was taken into the main house and everyone retreated to the kitchen. Michel had some fruit, lunch meat and cheese, cold drinks and hot tea. Everyone spent the next hour becoming better acquainted. Delanie spoke up and offered to take everyone on a tour of the property. She spent a great deal of the tour showing them Quinn's studio and the part of the barn where her father did his writing.

The vegetable and flower garden, was at its best. The flowers were in full bloom. Vegetables were also. Off in the distance there was a spectacular view of the mountains.

Before they left Folkestone there was some question about bringing baby Quinn on such a long trip. Everyone agreed that bringing her was the absolute right decision. At one point, Delanie told CC she was delighted that they did and she would love to see Quinn, but doubted if that would ever happen. CC gave her a hug and said, "You never know what life will bring."

Back in the house everyone settled down for a restful night. The plan was to go to the Riviera in the morning and catch up with Jean-Claude. Michel had already made the arrangements while everyone was touring the property.

The Magee family soon found that in addition to all of his other talents Michel was indeed a French gourmet. He demonstrated his culinary skill that evening:

Nouvelle Cuisine

Slices of roast beef served with asparagus and his own cream sauce
Small portions of rice pilaf
Garnished with cherry tomatoes from his garden
Dessert
Creme Brulee

Wine
French Bordeaux from the South of France-Provence

They all agreed it would not be possible to have a better meal in a five star restaurant in Paris. Following dinner, they all gathered in the living room. Michel did not want to join in with the family. He felt it was a special occasion and should be shared with only the family.

Michael spoke up, "Michel, yes this is a special time and a time for family. My friend you are as much a part of this family as any of us. Pour yourself a brandy and come join the conversation." Everyone agreed. Michel did pour a brandy and felt quite comfortable with the decision.

The following morning, they gathered for breakfast and the short trip into Cannes. It was quite early so most likely Jean-Claude would still be on his boat. Just to make certain Michel telephoned ahead. Sure enough, he was standing on the bow of the ODAT and waved a big welcome.

They spent the next couple hours walking on the harborside. The sea was a gorgeous azure purplish blue color. Much different than the English Channel back home. Jean-Claude served as a tour guide explaining the many different activities in the area. Michael went on to say that he had been to the Adriatic, North Atlantic, Mallorca, Sydney Harbor and a few others, but nothing was as beautiful as the French Riviera. Jean-Claude smiled and admitted to maybe being a bit prejudice but he agreed.

They strolled the small cobble streets and shops in Cannes. Michael and Jimmy Magee did talk a bit of business about the possibility of acquiring a shipyard in the area. Jean-Claude thought that would be an excellent decision. That he would be more than happy to help in any way that he could.

CC became quite nervous of the thought. Their lives were changing so fast. She still saw herself as coming from several generations of Irish immigrants. The French Riviera. Mallorca. Australia. Her own gallery in London. A pediatric wing of a hospital. A Memorial park in Folkestone. Michael a member of Parliament. Her head was spinning.

Michael began laughing and told her to take a deep breath. He assured her that nothing will happen on this trip. He and Jimmy Magee were just exploring possibilities. Before he did anything, he would talk to his good friend and advisor, Mr Wilkinson. Jean-Claude did confirm many of the wealthiest people in the world have homes on the French Riviera and many of them had boats-sailboats are definitely their boat of choice. Chances are that Mr. Wilkinson would know some of them. Michael told CC that it could be a great potential opportunity. In addition to Mr. Wilkinson and his connections Jean-Claude has lived all of his life locally and he is a master sailboat builder.

Michel saw that CC was still a mite uncomfortable. He changed the subject and suggested that they have some French pastry from the bakery they were approaching. Everyone thought that to be a great idea. They sat outside on the harbor and enjoyed some goodies. Indeed, they were good goodies. The type you would find only in a genuine French pastry shop.

Jean-Claude offered the ODAT for their use over the next few days. He explained how he built the boat for Jimmy McGettigan, Delanie's father, and how he became the owner through the generosity of Quinn. He loved the boat, the original owner, Quinn and Delanie. Michael felt a bit reluctant to accept his offer for the use of boat. Jean-Claude replied by saying he would be honored to have sailors of such skill as Michael and Jimmy Magee sail her for a few days.

They finally agreed and the family spent the next few days sailing the beautiful waters off the coast. They sailed up to Monte Carlo and tried their luck in the world famous casino. Unfortunately, their luck was not as good as the time spent on the ODAT. The days went by far too fast. Departure day arrived. Lots of hugs exchanged. All agreed that they would meet again. Jimmy Magee assured Jean-Claude he would need his help in finding the right boat yard to purchase. Delanie promised Michel and Jean-Claude that she would be back and baby Quinn would be with her.

Early the next morning they all gathered at the Auribeau station for the train to the airport in Paris. They spent the night in the airport and were up early for a nonstop one hour twenty minute flight to the Heathrow Airport in London. Once again the flight was the type that travelers like-uneventful.

Operating on an adrenaline rush they decided to keep moving so they took the train to Folkestone and home. It was indeed a long day but they were home and everyone would be sleeping in their own bed that night.

Everyone agreed that the vacation celebration was a fantastic trip. But it was time to move on with their busy lives.

Michael had to get ready for his new career as a member of Parliament.

CC needed to complete final details for the pediatric wing of the hospital and her career as an artist and sculptor with Annie Ackley. She finally admitted that she needed help. And was grateful that Diane Cleary agreed to stay working with her while they were gone.

Jimmy Magee finalizing details for a business enterprise on the riviera. He would need to be in contact with Michel and Jean-Claude.

Molly Magee back to Visby and her position as Spiritual Director and Lecturer at the University of Stockholm.

Delanie and her decision to leave her fashion career and focus on being a fulltime mother and to help the family with their many business and charity endeavors.

They were a growing family in many ways. Community. Church. Politics. Business. Charity. International affairs.

$\sim$

THE LIVES OF THE MAGEE FAMILY MOVE ON

The time was fast approaching for Michael to become an official MP-Member of Parliament. He was a bit overwhelmed by the prospect of serving in such a high position. He told CC the past year was like a dream. How could he coming from such humble beginnings actually be one of the lawmakers that provided the course of direction for the entire United Kingdom.

The House of Commons had a total of 650 members representing the millions of citizens throughout the entire United Kingdom. He told CC and his good friend Father O'Rourke that he was not at all confident that he was up to the task. Father O'Rourke told him that he had a strong moral compass. Follow that compass. It served you well during the campaign and it will serve you well making your decisions. Be true your God and yourself and you will not go wrong. CC wholeheartedly agreed.

Finally the day for the swearing in ceremonies arrived. The entire family was with him. They went to London the day before and spent the night in their newly leased apartment in the Belgrade section of Westminster. Parliament convenes in the Palace of Westminster. The palace was originally built in the year 1016 and was destroyed by fire in 1834 and rebuilt 1840-76. So much history. And now Michael Matthew Magee would become a part of the history.

The family sat in the spectator's gallery as the MP's-all 670 were sworn in one at a time. Michael stood at attention and with the oath in his left hand and right hand upraised to God recited:

I Michael Matthew Magee swear by Almighty God that I will be faithful and bear true allegiance to Her Majesty Queen Elizabeth, her heirs, and successors, according to law. So Help me God.

That was it. Short. Simple. Direct. Michael was now an official member of Parliament. CC was in tears. The family beamed with pride. Father O'Rourke said a short prayer-"Please protect Michael and guide him in all of his decisions." The ceremony was over.

Michael did not want a large gathering for a dinner celebration. His preference was an intimate meal with the immediate family and then back to their apartment, spend the night, and get on with the business of governing the country in the morning. He was a long way from being comfortable in this new role.

They had dinner in the Victoria Station at the foot of the London Tower Bridge. Westminster Abbey nearby. Thames River. Hyde Park. 10 Downing Street. History that dates back centuries all around. It was intimidating and overwhelming. He told himself that it would take some time to adjust.

Following dinner Michael and CC retired to the apartment and were ready for bed. (The rest of the family decided to do a bit of celebrating.) Indeed, they did go directly to bed. CC snuggled into his arms and told Michael she wanted to share a decision that she had been thinking about ever since the election was over.

Michael said, "Okay, let's hear it. I am ready. You never cease to amaze me. What is your latest plan?"

With that CC began. She was extremely grateful for the life God has given them. Yes, there has been some very difficult and painful experiences. But she realized that everyone has to deal with setbacks and tragic events. The blessing have been too many to list.

Her plan was to give up her art and sculpting career and devote all of her energy and talents to charitable endeavors. Michael was startled to say the least. He went on to say how hard she had worked at her artistic endeavors. With the help of Annie Ackley she was a successful artist-both financial and creative. And now she was willing to walk away from everything.

Not really. Her plan was to continue her artistic activities. But not for financial gain. She thoroughly enjoyed creating art and has become validated by individuals purchasing her efforts. She always felt the praise she received from family and friends was just that-praise from the family. But perfect strangers purchasing her work in a gallery in London was different. Now it is time for her to give back.

The hospital offered a position on the Board of Governors. The Folkestone Art School offered her a similar position. Father O'Rourke wants her to serve on the Parish Council and to manage the affairs of the War Memorial Park and the Jimmy McGettigan Magee Park.

She went on to say that she felt this would be one small way to say thank you to our ancestors. The risk that they took several generations ago made the life we now have possible.

Michael kissed her and told her how proud he was of her. Not surprised at all. But proud. He offered to help her in any way that he could. They would put the plan into action when they returned home tomorrow.

Time passed and the pediatric wing was completed. The necessary funding that was raised far exceeded the cost. The building was completed and the hospital scheduled a grand opening to the public.

Doctor Bruce Ryan, President of the hospital, requested that CC be seated on the platform next to him. He told her that he wanted to publicly thank her for all of the hard work she did in accomplishing the cause. CC was reluctant to receive the credit for something that she felt so passionate about.

Following words of encouragement from family and friends she approached Dr. Ryan and agreed to do whatever he asked. But with one proviso. She wanted Diane Cleary, her personal assistant seated right next to her. CC went on to tell the good doctor just how much behind the scene work, sacrifice, and dedication Diane made over the entire project. Dr. Ryan responded with an immediate and positive reply-yes by all means.

The ceremony took place and was a huge success. Business people, church leaders, politicians, and residents of Little Dublin were in attendance. It was a "standing room only." Michael was extremely proud of CC.

CC made her brief comments and introduced Diane Cleary to all in attendance. Before sitting down the press wanted to take pictures of CC standing under the archway with the words engraved in the stone over the entrance-Jimmy McGettigan Magee Pediatric Wing. With tears in her eyes she agreed. A very emotional scene. Not only for CC, but the entire family. Delanie and Jimmy Magee teared up also.

The ceremony concluded.

Several months passed and CC stayed very busy with all of her activities. The pediatric wing became a beehive of activity. Babies and young children were being helped with health issue very day. New young doctors, male and female, were recruited to serve. An extensive research department was established. The entire operation was quite impressive. The leading press and media from London came to town and did stories on the successes that were occurring in diseases and research. CC was very pleased. Life had a purpose.

While bathing one night and getting ready to attend another fund raising function for the hospital CC noticed a small lump on her left breast. She did not think much of it. But thought to herself that she would keep an eye to see if anything develops. There was not any pain or discomfort. She thought to herself-Oh well maybe just part of the aging process.

Several weeks went by and the lump was still there. One day she decided to share the information with Delanie and see what she thought. Delanie responded immediately with her thoughts. You need to see our family doctor. CC was a bit reluctant. She was not one to run to a doctor every time she had an ache or pain. Delanie pressed forward. You need to go to our doctor and I will go with you. CC agreed and an appointment was set. Delanie then asked if she intended to tell Michael about the lump. She responded that it was a "female issue" and did not want to worry him. CC went on to say that it was still the Victorian Age and women did not discuss these type matters with men. Delanie responded, "CC this is the 20th Century!" They finally came to the agreement that they would not tell him until they hear what the doctor had to say

The day of the appointment arrived and Delanie made sure that she was early meeting CC. They drove the few kilometers to the doctor's office and took their place in the waiting room. It was quite apparent to Delanie that CC was anxious-very anxious. Delanie took CC's hand and stroked it gently. With a smile she looked at CC and said, "Don't worry. You are going to be fine." Minutes later her name was called and they entered the doctor's examining room.

In addition to being the family physician, Doctor William MacNeill, was a family friend for many years. He detected immediately that CC was stressed. In an attempt to put her at ease he began several minutes of small talk. How is Michael. You should be proud of your efforts with the pediatric wing. How is baby Quinn. Then he asked the big question-So what brings you here today.

With that said the examination began. The doctor explained that the treatment can vary with every patient. The most important factor is early detection. CC absolutely did the right thing coming in as soon as she did. The tumor is very small. And there are several options. Mammography is low dose x-ray imaging. The big breakthrough in anti-cancer made their entrance in the past few years. He went on to explain the history of one such drug. In a grim paradox the first was nitrogen mustard. This was a poison gas used to slaughter soldiers in the trenches of World War I. Soldiers who survived exposure to it suffered the destruction of white blood cells and needed regular blood transfusions. This suggested nitrogen mustard might be used to treat lymphoma tumors. It worked and nitrogen mustard was rechristened mustine. The first licensed chemotherapy agent.

Delanie listened intently as he went on about mustard gas. How amazing science is. This terrible poisonous gas that killed thousands of men and created millions of casualties on all sides of a horrible war could somehow be used to save the lives of untold numbers of women suffering with breast cancer. Sometime life is so difficult to comprehend. But there truly seems to be an order to the universe. And God is the creator of it all.

The doctor went on to say that based on all of the recent developments and treatments three of four women will survive breast cancer and live normal and productive lives. The sooner the issue is found and treated the percentages are increased.

CC tried to mentally process all of this technical information and was overwhelmed. The one fact that she heard was that she will most likely be diagnosed with breast cancer. A frightening thought. The various procedures were completed and a follow up appointment was scheduled for the following week.

It was a very quiet drive home. Michael was there when they arrived. CC asked Delanie to give the report to him. She simply was too distraught. Delanie then told Michael what the doctor explained to them. She did her best to be accurate and factual, and at the same time be positive and upbeat. Yes, CC most likely has breast cancer. But it is treatable. Fortunately, they found the cancer at a very early stage. New treatments are being discovered all the time.

Michael got up from his chair, went over to CC, and gave her a big kiss and hug. He said we have had some rough times over our married life and with God's help we are all standing, healthy, and a happy family. We will fight cancer and continue on our journey. He thanked Delanie for all of her help and support.

Delanie thought to herself this is what family is all about. Something she sadly missed through her growing up years. She did not blame anyone. Not her mother. Not her father. That was a different time and everyone involved did the best that they could do. She truly felt blessed to be a part of this family and the love they shower on her and her daughter-baby Quinn.

They returned to the doctor the following week. The diagnosis was complete. Indeed, it was a tumor-lymphoma cancer of the breast. Very early detection. Treatment would begin immediately with anti-cancer drug. Chemotherapy. Regular monitoring will take place. The doctor instructed her to continue her lifestyle on a normal basis. You may feel a bit more tired than usual from time to time. That can be expected. Especially, after a treatment session. It is important to stay upbeat and positive.

They had a family meeting to disclose the issue and the treatment methodology. All agreed that they would remain optimistic.

Prayers were offered and closed with-God's will not theirs.

✦

MOLLY IS A GUEST LECTURER AT CATHOLIC UNIVERSITY

When Molly returned to her home in Visby, she was more than delighted to find a letter from her friends, The Maryknoll Sisters, in Washington, D.C. Part of their ministry involved the Catholic University where Molly was an undergraduate student. They were extending an invitation to Molly to be a guest Lecturer for the fall semester. Molly was astounded and very humbled. She knew from her experiences at the university that this was a prestigious position. While she was attending the university prominent educators from all over the world were lecturers on a variety of topics.

She immediately put in a transatlantic phone call to Sister Therese Kelly, the ranking member of the Sisters that were part of the university. Molly told her that she would of course accept the invitation and then went on to say that she was stunned and flattered. But why me. I certainly do not feel that I have the credentials to measure up some of the past educators. Sister Therese replied, "Indeed you do. We have watched your work over the years. Your commitment and experience around the world in social justice is unmatched. We are delighted that you are accepting our invitation and that we will be seeing you in the fall." Sister Therese closed by telling her that all of the details would be coming in the mail. Molly hung up the phone still in a state of shock.

Her next thought was that she would call her family immediately. That she did. Obviously, the entire family was more than happy to hear the news. Ecstatic to put it mildly. They were all proud of Molly and her total dedication to the marginalized people of the world. She had published numerous magazine articles about millions of people existing without clean water and other basic necessities of life. Her book on environmental issues was a part of the curriculum in many universities in both the United States, UK, and Europe.

The excitement of the opportunity to visit the United States and Catholic University made it difficult for Molly to concentrate on anything else. Fortunately, the events over the next few months made it possible to focus elsewhere. The trip would not happen until fall and it was now just the beginning of a new year.

Her responsibilities as a Lecturer at the University of Stockholm would begin in a few weeks. Her lectures took place over a period of eight weeks. The subjects that she delivered were on a variety of topics. Environment. Social justice and the lack thereof. Economic inequality. Political freedom. Interacting with young college students was always invigorating and brought back so much of her own undergraduate days. She truly loved being in a college classroom as either a student or teacher.

She continued her writing of books. Both nonfiction and spiritual. Writing on both topics at the same time was definitely challenging and rewarding. Something Molly liked to do. Changing gears from one subject to the other was something she seemed to be able to do rather easily. Sitting in her wooden rocker on the third floor of her stone home, looking out the window and the Baltic Sea below was without question her favorite spot in the world. It mattered not what the season was-winter spring summer or fall. She thoroughly enjoyed travelling the world and working with the disadvantaged, but she always felt most comfortable in Visby.

The quarterly spiritual retreats were the other highlight of her busy life. They have grown over the last few years. Women from the Scandinavian Countries, Europe, and the UK usually attended. They have become so successful through word of mouth it was not necessary to do a great deal of promotion.

Several of the women returned every year (frequently bringing a new friend.) A time to relax, recharge their battery, and enjoy spiritual growth. The fact that Visby, situated right in the middle of the Baltic Sea, was absolutely beautiful in Spring and early Summer and a great place to spend a week. The village is gorgeous with huge red rose bushes everywhere. In yards, lining the streets, and the public square. Truly a sight to see. The sea was usually gentle this time of the year. Peaceful and serene.

～

JIMMY MAGEE AND DELANIE ATTEMPT TO LOCATE QUINN

Jimmy began to realize more and more with the passing of time just how important and influential Quinn was in her earlier life. This was never brought out more powerfully than when Delanie told him that she wanted to name their baby Quinn. Rarely a day went by that she did not bring up her name.

One day CC was having a conversation with Delanie and the subject of Delanie attending the Sorbonne in Paris came up. CC asked how that came about. Delanie explained that was made possible by Quinn. The career that she has in fashion was as the results of Quinn's efforts. The woman that she became was without question the result of guidance and coaching of Quinn.

The thought came to him. Maybe he could track Quinn down. Delanie had talked about the man who owned a pub in Galway. The man was a big influence in the lives of Quinn and her father, Jimmy McGettigan. He decided to do some research. He would not say anything until if and when he found him. The only thing he really knew was that the pub was in Galway and the man's name was Matty. He did not know his last name.

Needless to say, there are plenty of pubs in Galway. Over the next few weeks he began making long distance information phone calls to Galway. He did not know the name of the pub. He tried Matty's Pub. That seemed to be an obvious choice. No luck. Finally, he got lucky- The Galway Bay Pub. That was it. Indeed, during one of his telephone calls a waitress at one of the local pubs knew Matty and while the pub was listed as The Galway Bay Pub for years everyone in the area knew the place simply as-Matty's Pub.

Bingo! He placed the long distance telephone call and a few minutes later he made contact. The phone was answered by a waitress. She told him that yes it was Matty's Pub and he was there. Actually, he was kind of busy. Jimmy explained that he was calling long distance from Folkestone, England. He suggested if they could talk for just a minute maybe they could arrange to talk at a later time. The waitress managed to get Matty to the phone and they had a brief conversation and set up a phone appointment for early the next morning before the pub opened.

Jimmy was excited. Matty was very friendly and anxious to talk. He went on to say the pub was crazy at this time of day. Too noisy. After work crowds. Music playing in the background. Jimmy began to believe that the reunion just might happen. Couple of weeks of dead end phone calls, but it has finally paid off. He could not help but to think how excited Delanie will be. Then he told himself that he just might be getting way ahead. Slow down. Do not say anything until you have a conversation at some length. He leaned back in his chair and had a big smile.

With all the restraint that he could muster he managed not to tell Delanie what he was up to. He thought to himself will this night ever end. Will morning ever get here? A restless night to put it mildly, but morning did arrive. Then it dawned on him. There was no way he could place the call from home. A quick breakfast and then the short walk to work. The agreement was that he would call 9:00 am Galway Ireland time. He talked to the long distance operator at precisely nine. A few minutes later he heard the response, "Matty's Pub."

Jimmy once again introduced himself and they proceeded to have a wonderful conversation for more than one hour. Jimmy found Matty easy to talk to. They covered every topic possible. Delanie. Their marriage. The baby. Quinn. The death of Jimmy McGettigan. Maureen. And the fact that she still lived in the same flat and worked at the Rectory.

Jimmy discussed the possibility of coming to Galway and tracking down Quinn. Matty was delighted with that idea. He told Jimmy that he could definitely help to make that happen. The Connemara Region was not that far from Galway. Fishermen and farmers came to Galway on a regular basis. For shopping and purchasing farm supplies. And of course, to stop into Matty's Pub. It would not be difficult to find Quinn. Matty told Jimmy that he was sure she was well known in the area. Quinn was simply that kind of woman. Lot of personality. Attractive. Always helping someone or some cause.

Matty said that the pub was starting to get crowded and noisy. Lunch hour was fast approaching. The agreement was that when Matty had some specific information he would call Jimmy. He would begin asking today. Hopefully, in a couple weeks he would be in touch. Jimmy thanked him and the phone conversation ended. He relaxed back in his chair and thought to himself-this is going to happen. I just know that it will.

He called home and Delanie answered the phone. Giving a vague and mysterious excuse he told her that he was coming home to tell her some exciting news. Tried as she may he would not tell her what he wanted to talk about. They were giggling like two young teenagers. Finally, Delanie told him if he was not going to tell her that he needed to hang up the phone and get right home. He went on to say that he was really excited. Delanie replied that she was more than a little excited and please hurry home.

Jimmy came out of his office and told the staff that he needed to leave the office for a while. No explanation. He was a bit mysterious with the staff. This was a bit unusual. Whenever he left the office, he always gave details where he was going and how long he would be gone. With that said he was out of the office and on the way home.

He walked in the front door and was greeted by Delanie with a big smile. "Okay, what is going on. You said this is something special and I will be overwhelmed in a positive way. You know that I can't stand not knowing something. Especially if it is a nice surprise and you said it is a nice surprise and that I will love it. Well Jimmy Magee start talking."

That he did. He told her to sit down. This is big news. You are going to be thrilled. She interrupted, "Okay, okay tell me."

With that behind him he began. Tracking down Matty. The effort underway to locate Quinn. The possibility of visiting her mother.

Hopefully, a trip to Galway and the Connemara Region. Reuniting with Quinn. Everyone getting to meet baby Quinn.

Delanie began crying uncontrollably. He was right. She was overwhelmed to put it mildly. Jimmy went over to her with a big hug and kiss. Matty promised to let them know the minute he was able to get some details. A few weeks passed. The waiting was almost unbearable.

The long anticipated, phone call finally arrived. What seemed like forever was only three weeks. The phone rang and their new friend, Matty, was on the other end. Yes, he was able to locate exactly where Quinn was living and directions on how to get there. One of his regulars came into Galway for his farm supplies and always visited Matty. The two have been friends for years.

Matty asked if he knew the whereabouts of Quinn. His friend not only knew her "whereabouts" he had her phone number. The farmer had regular contact with her. He would let her know whenever he was going up to Galway and asked if she needed anything from town. He knew that Quinn did not like going into Galway. It was too crowded and busy for her.

Matty gave Jimmy the address and phone number and then gave him some more detailed information about where she was living. Quinn was actually living on a small island off the coast of Connemara about 150 kilometers from Galway.

He assured Jimmy that he would not have any problem finding his way. Connemara is a small village and home to the world famous Kylemore Abbey. He went on to explain that the abbey is a Benedictine monastery founded in 1920. The abbey was founded for Benedictine Nuns who fled Belgium during World War I. Construction began in 1867 and took four years to build. Matty told him that they will be impressed with the size and beauty of the abbey. Truly one of the beautiful treasures of Ireland with a long and fascinating history.

After Matty gave Jimmy the details on Quinn he suggested that he talk to Delanie for a few minutes. She was hovering over Jimmy's shoulders and obviously wanted to say thank you and assure him that they will absolutely be coming over. The only question was she did not know how Quinn would feel about their coming.

The conversation came to a close with Jimmy telling him that they would call Quinn in the morning. He went on to say that they have to figure out who should make the call and the strategy about the trip assuming that Quinn is agreeable. They would then have to make contact with Maureen. Delanie felt that her mother would be anxious to see her. She also felt that the visit could be a bit uncomfortable and stressful. But she reassured Jimmy that she definitely wanted to see her mother. She was anxious to show off her new husband, and of course her daughter.

Delanie felt that she should be the obvious one to call her mother. But not so sure about her making the call to Quinn. Jimmy disagreed. He felt strongly that Delanie should make both calls. He believed that if Quinn is the kind of person that Delanie described she will not only accept the call she will embrace Delanie and the idea of a visit. Delanie finally agreed-reluctantly. She just was not certain about the condition of their relationship when they last saw one another. Okay, the plan was a call to Quinn first. If that works out. A call to her mother. Big day. Time for bed.

Kinda restless night for both of them. Up early. Quick breakfast. Jimmy looked at her with a smile as if to say-okay, let's get on the phone. It is the right time of day in Connemara. Delanie took a deep breath, picked up the phone, and placed the call with the long distance operator. Almost immediately she heard the phone ringing on the other end.

"Hello, good morning," was the greeting.

"Quinn, this is Delanie. Remember me."

"Delanie! Oh my god. I can't believe it."

The next minute or so was confusing. Both talking at the same time. Interrupting. Asking questions. Crying. They finally settled down and were able to have a normal conversation. Delanie brought her up to date. She was married to an Irishman. His name was Jimmy-just like her father and Quinn's soulmate. Quinn asked the obvious question-how did you ever find me. Delanie told her about tracking down Matty and their conversation with him.

Then she took a deep breath, closed her eyes and asked the big question, "Would you like to see us?"

Quinn almost jumped through the phone, "Are you serious. I would give anything to see you." They then made the plans. Again, through the help of Matty and the farmer in Connemara they had directions and were assured that finding the location would not be a problem.

The conversation ended with Delanie telling her once they have a travel plan finalized, they would let her know. Jimmy asked what he thought to be an obvious question, "Why did you not tell her about baby Quinn."

Delanie responded, "I want that to be a big surprise. I want to be with her when she meets baby Quinn for the first time. I really think she will be pleased a great deal with that news." Jimmy agreed and thought that would be a great gift and surprise. Both of them were relieved and delighted with the reaction from Quinn. Certainly, no indication of anything negative. To the contrary Quinn sounded extremely happy.

Jimmy looked at her with a sober face and suggested that she call her mother immediately. Delanie took a deep breath and repeated the same process with the telephone operator. She decided to place the call to St. Peter Rectory. The seven o'clock mass would have just ended. Her mother went to mass every morning and then over to the rectory for her daily chores. She did not expect the phone conversation to be as animated as the one with Quinn. She was right.

The phone rang several times. Delanie's anxiety began to rise. Then she heard, "Good morning, St. Peter's Rectory."

"Mom, hi Delanie here. Are you okay?"

"Delanie, is that you. Oh, my. Are you okay? Is there a problem. Why are you calling."

Delanie, "Responded. Yes, it is me. Yes, I am okay. There is not a problem. I wanted to talk to you. I have what I hope you will feel is good news."

Maureen relaxed a bit. Just a little. And went on to say that it was great to hear from her daughter. Good news is always welcome. Please share it with me.

She told her mother to sit back and relax. Then the details were offered. Delanie explained that she was married and living in Folkestone. Her fashion career was going great. They were thinking of making a trip to Ireland and of course would like to come visit her. Would that be okay. They would probably make it a short visit. Her husband, Jimmy, is Irish and he wanted to visit the homeland of his ancestors. Would that be okay.

Maureen replied, "Yes. Of course. You remember that the apartment is not very big. There is not a lot of room. I have not seen you for a long time. When do you think you would arrive? I am not certain I could take time off from my duties. The Bishop is coming soon."

The conversation went much differently from the conversation with Quinn. This was indeed uncomfortable for both of them. Brief sentences. Stunted. Anything but a free conversation between a mother and a daughter.

Delanie assured her that they would stay in a hotel in town. She certainly understood the fact that Maureen probably would not be able to take time away from her duties.

She told her mother that they would arrange their travel plans and share them with her. In the event that they were acceptable they would proceed and come. Maureen thought that sounded like a good idea. Then she explained that she had to make breakfast for Monsignor Lyons and two visiting priests from the Diocese in Dublin.

"Okay, I will let you go and I will keep you abreast of our plans. I love you Mom."

"Me too," replied Maureen. That was the best she could say. She was never very emotional.

Delanie looked at Jimmy, "Well that was short and sweet. Pretty much the way I thought it would go."

"Wow, it sure was" Jimmy responded. He knew that the two had a strained relationship. But he had no idea it was that tense.

Jimmy decided to talk to his father about taking two weeks to go on their trip. He realized that his father would be busy with Parliament and their business. They usually talked about plans after Sunday night dinner. Following dinner, they went out to the porch and had their business meeting for the upcoming week. When they concluded the meeting, Jimmy brought up the subject of the two week trip and its purpose.

Michael was pleased with the efforts Jimmy and Delanie were arranging to make the reconciliation with Delanie's mother and Quinn. Family was the most important relationship in life. Michael was extremely grateful for the family that they had and would support in any way he could help Delanie. He loved her like a daughter. He went on to say the two weeks would be fine. Make your plans. The sooner the better.

Jimmy went back to the kitchen to help with cleaning up after dinner. He thought that he would bring CC up to date. Too late. Delanie was way ahead of him. She had already discussed in detail the entire plan. They all had a good laugh. Delanie was not exactly a shrinking violet.

The visit would involve the people that were a part of her young life. First and foremost, Maureen, her mother. Matty. Quinn. And the couple in Dublin, Mary and Jimmy Cavanaugh, owners of The Evergreen Hotel. Delanie stayed there on her journey to find her father. They were wonderful people and gave her some excellent advice and guidance. Mary had a bad experience with her father. Much like Delanie's. He was alcoholic and walked out on the family. Mary spent the rest of her life regretting that she never tried to find him. Countless questions unanswered.

Delanie reflected on a conversation she had with Jimmy Cavanaugh during her stay. He told her that over your lifetime many people pass through your life. Friendships at different levels. But only a very few make a lifelong impact. Some for the good some not so good. Definitely your parents are two of those people.

She recalled the conversation and thought to herself Mary and Jimmy Cavanaugh are certainly two of those people who have profoundly affected her life. They provided the support that she needed to continue the search to find her father. Yes, her relationship with her father was up and down. But she knew him. They had a life together. Quinn became a huge part of that life.

The people that they planned to visit were special people. Now that she is part of the Magee family, she truly realizes how important relationships and family truly are. Both Michael and CC told her many times that she is their "daughter" and not an "in-law." And, of course they could not imagine life without baby Quinn. Those two comments always made her smile. And on several occasions a tear. She felt that she was one blessed woman. The loss of her son, James McGettigan Magee, was a pain she would never get over. But as CC told her one day, "Grief like that we do not get over. With God's help somehow, we get through it."

With such positive enthusiasm from both Michael and CC they moved forward and began to make plans. Flight reservations were made on Aer Lingus flight #361 from Heathrow Airport and arriving in Dublin one hour and twenty three minutes later. They scheduled a return flight for two weeks later.

Hotel reservations were made at the Park House Hotel on Foster Street and Eyre Square in Center city Galway minutes from Galway Bay. Booking a car hire was the final piece of their travel plans.

Delanie made the necessary phone calls to her mother, Matty, and Quinn. She decided to hold off on the call to Mary and Jimmy Cavanaugh until they arrived in Dublin. Their plan was to visit them as part of the return trip. That way they could tell them how the trip went. Jimmy was fine with that plan.

The next few days were filled with anticipation. Suitcases were packed and ready to go The day of departure arrived. Michael and CC drove them the short distance to the Folkestone train station. While they had taken the train into London many times this trip seemed to take forever. But they finally arrived at Heathrow, checked their luggage, and went to the gate number assigned for their flight. The flight left right on schedule and arrived on time. They picked up their luggage and took the shuttle to the car hire station. Minutes later they were on their way for the two hour drive to Galway.

Delanie offered to do the driving. Jimmy could sit back, relax, and enjoy the scenery of the Irish countryside. After all this was his first visit to the country of his ancestors. He liked the idea. Driving in Ireland for the first time is a bit of a challenge. The roads are narrow and confusing with roundabouts and flyovers. As they drove along Jimmy said to himself Delanie had a great idea. Yes, driving here for the first time would indeed be a bit intimidating. After all they are going to be here for two weeks. Plenty of time for driving.

Jimmy agreed the countryside was beautiful. About one hour into the drive they approached a lake with mountains as a backdrop. They decided to stop for lunch, take in the sights, and let baby Quinn walk for a bit. A wise decision. She was getting impatient being restrained since they left home. The weather was uncommonly beautiful. Lot of sunshine and gentle breezes. They took a few pictures of the area including the small village of Kilkenny.

Time to move and with less than an hour to Galway Jimmy suggested that he finish the drive. He would need some directions as they arrived in Galway and Delanie would be a big help with that. As they approached Galway Delanie recalled her early life there. Pointing out different places. Her school. St Peter's Church. The Shopping District. The parks that she played in as a kid. A real trip down memory lane.

Delanie gave directions to her mother's home on Hancock Street, one block from St. Peter's Church. They parked the automobile and climbed the outside stairs to the rear of the second floor apartment. The closer they got the more nervous she became. As she began to knock Jimmy squeezed her hand and kissed her on the cheek. The door opened and there stood her mother, Maureen McGettigan. They had not seen each for several years. A few phone calls and letters represented their token connection.

They embraced, kissed, and tried to enjoy the moment. It was not easy for either of them. Once in the kitchen Delanie introduced her husband, Jimmy Magee. He was not sure how to react as he leaned over took her hand and kissed her on the cheek. Jimmy was holding baby Quinn and he offered her to Maureen. Delanie said, "Say hello to your grandaughter."

Maureen held her tight to her breast and kissed her several times. Grandmothers instinctively know how to react to their grandaughters. Baby Quinn was special. She could have been on the cover of an Irish national magazine-Bright red curly hair, Irish green eyes, big smile, and freckles sprinkled all over her face. The fact that this was the first meeting of the two mattered not. They seemed to bond immediately.

The first question was asked, "Delanie she is absolutely beautiful. What is her name."

Silence. For a brief moment.

"Quinn."

Again silence.

Followed by a brief bio of her daughter. She is three years old. Well, almost four. Born in Folkestone, England. She had a twin brother. Unfortunately, he died days after his birth.

Jimmy could sense some tense moments. Delanie and Jimmy had discussed how this scene would probably play out. It played out exactly how Delanie anticipated. The plan was that Jimmy would leave following the opening several minutes. That would give the two of them some time alone and hopefully they could do some bonding-the three of them.

He spoke up and commented that he would take a walk and visit the center of Galway and walk down to the famous Galway Bay. The trip and driving, was long, and he wanted to stretch his legs a bit. He told them he would be back in an hour or so.

Everyone agreed and thought that was a good idea. Yes, they would like to be alone for a while. There was a great deal of territory to cover. Maureen wanted to get to know baby Quinn and reacquaint with Delanie.

Jimmy gave Delanie and the baby a kiss and walked the few blocks to Foster Street and Eyre Square. He asked for directions to the Galway Bay Pub, Matty's Pub as it is known to the locals. He followed directions and was standing in front of the pub in a matter of minutes. The sign above the entrance read-THE GALWAY PUB... EST. 1824.

He entered the pub to a full house. Irish music in the background. Lots of laughter and conviviality. Jimmy looked down to the corner of the bar and spotted a huge man behind the bar. No question. It was Matty. He introduced himself and was immediately the recipient of a big hug. Yes, it was Matty and he was obviously happy to meet Jimmy.

Matty waved over to an open table off in the corner. Sort of an "office" and an area where Matty conducted business. Jimmy mentioned the sign over the entrance-THE GALWAY PUB... EST. 1824. And went on to say that it must be the oldest pub in Ireland.

"Not even close," Matty responded. He went on to talk about the pub known as DURTY NELLY'S a pub in Bunratty that was established in the year 1620. There is a great deal of fact, fiction, and legend about the Pub. The place has been in the same location all these years. The owner was a woman. No one seemed to know the origin of her name- Durty Nelly. But that part of the legend seemed to be a fact. Indeed- that was her name. The stories were all quite colorful and exciting.

The two men had a great visit that went on for two hours plus. Jimmy found Matty to be an interesting character in his own right. A lover of the arts. History. Ireland. Music. He had a great voice and would break into a song at a simple request from one of the patrons. Singing all the great Irish folk songs.

Jimmy hated to bring the visit to a close, but he told Delanie he would be back in an hour. He was well past that time. They hugged and Matty told him to hug Quinn-she was a special person in his life. They agreed to stay in touch. A promise they both committed to keeping. Matty was the one who told Quinn to get out of the pub and waitress job. She had a great deal of talent and should develop it to the fullest.

Back to the apartment he found Delanie and Maureen still talking. Baby Quinn was napping. That was a good thing. It gave the two of them time for a nice visit. Maybe it was going better than Delanie thought it would.

Jimmy suggested that they have dinner on Eyre Square near the hotel. A pleasant meal and overall a good visit. Delanie told her mother that they were going to stay in the hotel overnight and drive down to the Connemara region in the morning. She explained that would work best. Delanie remembered that the Bishop was coming and there was a lot to do in preparation. Maureen thought that was a good plan.

They finished the meal, exchanged goodbyes, and walked back to the hotel. Not any real emotion. Pretty much all very matter of fact. This part of the visit made Jimmy feel uncomfortable. Once back in their hotel room he expressed those feelings. Delanie smiled and said that is just the way it is with her mother. I have not seen her in forever and we talk like we were together yesterday. He shook his head in a disbelief manner.

They were up early and on the road for the what Delanie was hoping to be an exciting visit on several different levels. Jimmy was behind the wheel for this part of the drive. A beautiful stretch of road following route 9, parallel to the sea some 150 kilometers south, to Connemara. The view and scenery was beautiful. About an hour or so into the drive they spotted a "scenic overview" with a parking area. They decided to stop, stretch their legs, and enjoy the view.

Obviously, a popular rest stop area. The sea was some 100 meters below with waves crashing on the rocks, the sea a beautiful green, and the sun shining. The park was filled with visitors taking in the sights and having a light fare for lunch. A small playground just perfect for baby Quinn. She enjoyed running and riding on the swing. Delanie and Jimmy shared a sandwich and a cup of tea. A great break and now it was time to move on.

Not long after they were back on the road, they spotted signs advising that the Kylemore Abbey was only 15 kilometers down the highway. They were both getting quite excited. Delanie looked over and told Jimmy she could not believe what was about to happen. With a tear in her eye she looked over and thanked him. She knew it would have never happened if he had not done the research. The trip would turn out to be a life changing experience for not only her, but the entire family.

They drove past the Kylemore Abbey, a magnificent structure, and almost immediately saw a crudely homemade sign indicating "Ashton Island" was off to the left. A dirt road with plenty of potholes. Following a two kilometer bumpy ride they arrived at the end of the road. Certainly not an impressive sight. A small dock for the hand barge that carried passengers across the narrow bay. Off to the left a structure that served as a parking garage for travelers. Bicycle rack for visitors to the island. Public telephone. Water closet for men and women. Inside the garage a tin can receptacle with the words- "Donations greatly accepted. All contributions are used to maintain the facilities." Primitive "facilities" to put it mildly. They both laughed as they talked about the comparison to the beautiful park and scenic overlook they took their rest on an hour or so ago.

The plan was to call Quinn when they arrived and she would drive her pickup truck down to the dock on the other side of the inlet. Quinn instructed them to park their car in the garage. Not to worry. It would be safe. There has never been a problem in all the years she lived on the island. Outdoor lovers come. The beaches are beautiful. Never crowded. A great family place. Little, to no expense, to enjoy a weekend and camping out. An absolute paradise for naturalists.

Delanie took some change from her purse and approached the telephone. To say that she was filled with emotions ranging all over would be putting it mildly. Anticipation. Fear. Hope. But most importantly excitement. The possibility of reuniting with Quinn was overwhelming. Quinn was such a powerful influence in so many aspects of her life. Nervously she dropped a coin in the phone and ringing began. Moments later, "Hello." It was Quinn!

Delanie responded, "Quinn, Quinn, it's me-Delanie."

"Oh, Delanie it is so wonderful to hear your voice. I have been waiting all day for your call. Are you at the dock? I cannot wait to see you. I will be there in five minutes."

With that she hung up the phone. Delanie turned to Jimmy and said, "She is on her way she is anxious to see me-us. I am so anxious for you to meet her. And of course, for her to meet her namesake-our Quinn."

Minutes later Quinn pulled up to the dock and jumped from her pickup truck and waving, "I will be over in a minute. With that she jumped onto the barge, unhooked the rope pulley, and feverishly began to pull herself the 100 meters to the other side. It sure seemed like an old time form of transportation in this modern era halfway through the 20th Century.

Delanie waited anxiously waving and tearing up. In a few minutes Quinn was across. She secured the pulley rope and jumped to shore. They embraced and both began to sob.

Delanie stepped back, "Quinn you are so beautiful. You do not look a day older. This island obviously agrees with you. I am so grateful that we are together again."

"Talk about beautiful. Delanie you have grown into a gorgeous woman and mother, I am so proud of you."

Jimmy was standing off to the side holding baby Quinn with a big smile on his face. With that Delanie started laughing and began, "Quinn, I am so sorry. This is Jimmy Magee and our little girl-Quinn, named after you of course. There was never any doubt what her name would be once we knew she was a girl."

Quinn became quite emotional and gave Delanie another big hug. She began thinking of their days at Serenity Patch. Delanie's father-Jimmy. The three of them. The good times together and not so good times. Jimmy and his heart attack and death. Such powerful memories and emotions. She thought how proud Jimmy would be of his daughter and now his granddaughter and son-in-law.

An extremely emotional reunion. Quinn collected herself and they all agreed it was time to move on. They climbed onto the barge and Quinn pulled them the short distance across the inlet. Securely on the other side they climbed into Quinn's beat up pickup truck for the couple kilometer ride to her farm. Quinn explained that the truck was part of the farm. It had a long history and when she purchased the farm the truck was part of the deal. She was not certain but she believed the model year was 1932 and she would never think of replacing it with a newer model. The truck was used to haul vegetables from the fields up to the main house-and she always did the driving. Both Jimmy and Delanie had the same thought. With all of her success in the fashion world and name recognition Quinn was not one bit pretentious.

A short drive up the main road of the island and a right turn off to one of the few side roads and three kilometers later they entered the driveway to her farm. A dirt road that twisted a few hundred meters and they arrived at the main house. They were met by a couple-John and Nelly Kelly.

The couple have been with Quinn since she bought the property. They were married for several years and had three children. Quinn had taken them in and treated them like they were her own children. All these years later they were her family and indeed her children. When they first met John was a struggling artist and Nelly a struggling writer. The arrangement was that the couple would help Quinn operate the farm. In return they would receive room and board plus a modest stipend. An arrangement that worked out fantastically well for all concerned.

Both had become successful in their artistic efforts. They now had three children of school age. Everyone, including Quinn, worked hard on the farm and cared for the several horses. Riding the horses and exploring the island was exciting. Fishing the streams and bathing in the Irish Sea was both refreshing and healthy. Both John and Nelly could not imagine a better life-anywhere. The notion of leaving Quinn and this special place never entered their mind.

John took the luggage to their room and they all settled in on the front porch to relax and begin the process of getting to know each other better. Quinn said that they would take a tour of the farm after tea and some lunch. Delanie could not help but notice that there were several structures on the farm. Similar to the property on Serenity Patch. She thought for sure one was for Quinn as a studio.

Quinn thought that this might be a good time to tell the history of this special island known as Ashton Island. She began by explaining that the island was ten kilometers east to west and fifteen kilometers north to south. And the Ashton family owned virtually all of the island. Full time residents were very few. Mostly members and descendants of the Ashton family. Weekends and summer holiday season nature lovers populated the island through the generosity of the Ashton family. The few other property owners had to buy from the Ashton family. And they were quite persnickety about potential owners. Thus, ownership pretty much remained in their hands.

However, they were more than generous letting people enjoy the island providing they were careful with the natural resources. Any abuse and you were instructed to leave-now. Most visitors felt the same way about the island. Thus, it was a rare occasion when someone was told to leave.

Quinn decided that this would be a good time to take a little tour and for everyone to stretch their legs. Lunch was finished and the sun would be setting shortly.

First a tour of the stable and horses. Quinn loved to ride through the unspoiled wooded areas off to the east of the island. She routinely would be riding just as the sun was rising. The trails that she rode led to the white beaches of the Irish Sea. A ride that took about two hours. She described the outing as a true spiritual experience.

The tour continued with a visit to her art studio. A rambling structure with just the right exposure for sunlight. Probably her favorite spot on the farm.

Next was a weathered building in need of paint. Something they talked about doing-but never happened. The building housed various farm equipment. Tractors-big and small. Backhoe. Hay wagon. Both John and Nelly liked to say that the weather beaten structure had a great deal of character. Quinn agreed. Painting would not be happening anytime soon.

Then to the open fields of vegetables. Vegetables of every type-corn tomatoes, peas. Beans. You name it and they grow it. Another staple of the farm is peat moss. Used as a heating fuel in rural Ireland. The farm produced several acres every heating season.

They had circled the entire farm and were back to the main family house. Delanie and Jimmy were quite impressed with what Quinn described as her "little slice of heaven." The only thing missing was Jimmy McGettigan, Delanie's father. That is why she had a sign at the entrance of the farm-Serenity Patch II. There were many similarities to the original Serenity Patch. You could enjoy the peace and quiet of the island and yet in a matter of minutes you could be on the mainland and the Connemara Region with Galway a short drive on the highway north.

Delanie then took the moment to bring Quinn up to date about the original Serenity Patch and its keeper-Michel. Tears flowed from both of the women. Jimmy and Delanie assured Quinn that the arrangement she made with Michel regarding the property would stay exactly as she had left it.

As they sat around the kitchen table following the evening meal Jimmy asked if Quinn would tell the history of Ashton Island. Laughingly, Quinn said, "I thought you would never ask."

She began by saying that the country of Ireland is famous for its many islands that cover the entire coastline of this beautiful country. With a smile she said in her opinion (perhaps a bit a prejudiced) that this small island was the most beautiful of all. Still pristine. Almost totally isolated from the rest of the world. No commercial development of any kind. A dream place for nature lovers. All are welcome. Quinn's remarks to all visitors-"You are welcome. Stay as long as you wish. Take all the photos that you want. But leave behind only your footprints-no litter."

The history of Robert Ashton and his family dates back to the 1800's. He was a prosperous businessman involved in several different enterprises. He lived on a large parcel of land next to Mitchell Henry, owner of the castle that in 1920 became home to the Benedictine Nuns and the Kylemore Abbey.

Both were members of Parliament (MP) and loved the region. Mr. Ashton visited the island regularly and would bring members of the family for outings. He was approached by Mr. Henry on one of their sessions when Parliament was meeting. He told Mr. Ashton that rumors had it that the Irish government wanted to relinquish ownership of the island.

The national government was under financial stress and owning this island was a financial drag. It generated no income to the government-only expense. A situation that existed with many large tracts of land the government owned throughout the country.

Mr. Ashton was more than excited about the possibility of taking ownership. A win-win situation. The government would receive a sizeable bit of income and Mr. Ashton would take ownership of this special place. After some protracted negotiations a price was agreed upon-$250,000 pounds-the deal was concluded. Mr. Ashton, the naturalist, created a legal document that carefully stipulated what could and what could not happen on the island. All these years later the document is still in effect and no one is tried to contest it.

The island has basic services of electricity, telephone, and maintenance of a few roads. The dock where the barge carries passengers across the narrow inlet and a crude bridge approximately one kilometer south are the only means of getting on the island. The barge being the choice for almost everyone. Definitely a romantic and nostalgic means of transportation. The bridge is accessed by a dirt road that is overgrown with weeds and rarely used.

Jimmy asked how did Quinn ever get the Ashton family to sell her the farm. Quinn told of the scholarship program that she established at Trinity University in Dublin known as the Jimmy McGettigan literary award. He was a well known Irish writer and well respected by the government. The Ashton family knew her and respected her views and how she would use the farm. A simple agreement was drawn up and both parties signed. There has never been even a hint of a problem.

Both Jimmy and Delanie were amazed at the history of the island and the way Quinn has conducted herself. Truly a woman of high principle and moral character. She indeed was a story in herself. As well as John and Nelly Kelly and their commitment to her. They truly met any definition of family. All of them. There for each other-always.

The next several days were busy ones. Horseback riding. Hiking through the trails off to the west. The most densely parts of the island were to the west. The winds that blew and storms came off from the Irish Sea to the west. With the forest so thick, it was nature's way of protecting the part of the island that was populated.

Picnics on the beach. Swimming in the ocean. Camp fires after dark. Quinn and Delanie taking long walks on the beach. Jimmy Magee getting to know John and Nelly Kelly. Baby Quinn building sand castles.

Sitting around the kitchen table following dinner and visiting late into the night. Quinn and Delanie reminisced the times on the French Riviera and Serenity Patch. They talked at length about Jimmy McGettigan. Delanie said that any failures or troubles in their relationship was her fault.

Quinn offered her thoughts-She explained it was more complicated than that. Her father struggled mightily with the fact that he abandoned her. The fact that Maureen was not able to discuss much of anything certainly did not help. The fact that Quinn continued having an affair even though she knew that he was married did not help. Yes, Delanie your behavior was not the best, but you did the best you could. Life is always much more complicated-always. It is never simply black and white. Almost always it is various shades of gray. If I would offer you any advice it would be to love your mother and be good to her. Stay in touch with her. Share your daughter with her grandmother. I have no doubt that is the advice your father would give you.

The days flew by and it was time to start the journey back to Folkestone. They all agreed that it was a great visit. They prayed that the bond would grow stronger. Quinn, with tears in her eyes, told Delanie the fact that she named their daughter Quinn, was the most beautiful gift anyone ever gave her.

Early the next morning they packed the car and were ready to drive to Dublin, a distance of 267 kilometers. Delanie placed a telephone call to Jimmy and Mary Canavan. They were ecstatic to hear from her. Yes, they would have a room waiting for her. How often they thought of her. Jimmy just went on and on. He was so happy to hear from her. Delanie replied by saying she had a great deal to share. That she did not want to do it over a telephone. Jimmy agreed. Then he followed up with, "Get in that car and get cracking over here."

Hugs and kisses were exchanged and they were off. Quinn took them down to the barge and Jimmy pulled them across the inlet and they were on their way. Some five hours later, with only a quick stop for petrol, they arrived at The Evergreen Pub and Hotel, owned by one of Delanie's early supporters of the time she began the journey searching for her father. Hugs were exchanged and it was as though they were never apart.

Some relationships are just like that. You meet and bond. Long periods of time pass with little to no contact. Then you are reunited and pick up like you were together yesterday. Hard to explain. But the relationship between Delanie and Mary and Jimmy Cavanaugh was one such relationship.

They all talked late into the wee hours. A reunion. Introduction of her husband, Jimmy Magee, and their little girl, Quinn. How Delanie found her father, Jimmy McGettigan, and their up and down relationship, his heart attack and passing. A few laughs and a few tears. Lots of hugs.

They spent two days sightseeing Dublin. Walking across the Ha'Penny Bridge. Trinity University and the papers and books of her father, Jimmy McGettigan. At one point, Mary Cavanaugh joked about all of the "Jimmy's" in Delanie's life. They all had a big laugh.

It was time to go to the airport for the short flight to London. Delanie promised that they would be back. They had several reasons to keep that promise. Her mother, Maureen. Dear friend, Matty. Jimmy and Mary Cavanaugh. And of course, Quinn.

The short ride to the airport. Baggage checked. Seats assigned and boarding. Jimmy looked over to Delanie and held her hand. Tears began and he could see that she was lost in her thoughts. He said nothing, just squeezed her hand, and gave her a kiss on the cheek. Baby Quinn was sound asleep in her arms. She thought how truly blessed she was, they were. A powerful and highly emotional couple of weeks. They were all more than a little exhausted and drifted off to sleep as the engines droned on. The next voice they heard was that of the captain instructing passengers to fasten their seat belts and prepare for landing.

The landing was the type that passengers always liked-uneventful. They gathered their luggage, took the shuttle to the train platform, and after a short wait the train arrived, and they were on their way for last leg of the trip. The Folkestone Station would be next.

Michael and CC met them at the station and of course were anxious to hear about the whole trip. CC had dinner prepared and they all sat at the dinner table for a couple of hours. Questions were asked. Both Jimmy Magee and Delanie provided the answers. Lots of questions, lots of answers, lots of laughs, a few heavy moments, and a few tears. Indeed, the trip was a huge success. CC could not have been happier than when Delanie announced that she was definitely going to stay in touch with her mother and include baby Quinn in their lives.

Finally, exhausted both physically and mentally the day came to a close and everyone headed off to bed.

MOLLY LEAVES FOR CATHOLIC UNIVERSITY

To say that Molly was excited about returning to Catholic University and the United States would be a huge understatement. Summer was coming to a close and fall would soon follow. A beautiful time of the year in the Washington, DC area. The temperature was pleasant and the leaves of the various type of trees would be bright and brilliant in colors of every type.

Her living quarters would be on the campus of this historical university. She had remained in contact with a few of the staff and professors. It was very rewarding to Molly that a couple of the professors were proud of her writings and publications on topics that they had helped her with.

The university was minutes from all of the history of this great nation. The White House, home to the President of the United State. The Capitol, which is the nerve center of the country. Home to the United State Senate and House of Representatives. The Supreme Court. Countless federal buildings performing the work to make this great country function.

She could hardly wait. Before flying across The Pond (Atlantic Ocean) as it was called during World War II, she spent a few days with the family in Folkestone. Of course, the family was excited about this opportunity for Molly.

While most of the family was content to stay at home and close to their roots everyone knew that Molly was a world traveler and as the expression goes-"had sand in her shoes." Always looking for the next great adventure.

What she was about to set out on certainly met the definition of "great adventure." Living in another country. Teaching at a prestigious university. Exposure to the United States Congress.

The day arrived and goodbyes to everyone and she was on a flight out of Heathrow headed for Washington, DC. Sister Therese met her on arrival and they drove the short distance to the home of The Maryknoll Sisters. The apartment where she would be residing was directly across from the academic buildings. Sister Therese told Molly to relax, take a nap, and settle in a bit. She would be back in a couple hours and they would have dinner with the other Sisters in their quarters. With that she left. Molly looked around and wanted to pinch herself. Could this really be happening. She felt too excited to take a nap, but she stretched out on the bed and immediately drifted off into a deep sleep.

The next few days were exhilarating to say the least. Molly began to settle into her teaching schedule. Meeting the new students. Most were eager to learn. Especially from Molly. Many students that were interested in the topics of social justice and the environment knew of her. Of course, this pleased her. Not so much for ego reasons (But she did admit to herself there was a bit of ego) but more importantly there were young people very much interested and committed to these issues. Academics and the classroom were going well.

The area of Washington was so alive and full of energy. Some group was always protesting some issue. Politics provided a great deal of theater. Museums of all types seemed to be on every corner. Indeed, a major metropolitan area and all that it presents. A much different setting than the quiet and peaceful setting of her home in Visby. Lecturing at the University of Stockholm was exciting. The city was filled with energy. But the cultural and diversification did not compare to Washington, DC. She thought to herself that she loved both places. They were simply different.

Several weeks into the semester she received a phone call from Sister Therese. She invited Molly to a combination social and political dinner to be held at the home of the Maryknoll Sisters. Sister Therese went on to explain that the causes that Molly was interested in (the same causes that the Maryknolls were interested in) would be at the top of the agenda. She went on say that there would be a wide variety of guests. People from the business world, politics, philanthropists, socially conscious citizens, and regular citizens who simply support the efforts of the Maryknolls.

Molly looked forward to attending the event. The night arrived and Molly arrived early. The anticipation was a bit more than she could handle. What an opportunity. The attendees began to arrive and you could feel the energy in the room. Probably a group of twenty-five or so. Most knew one another. Sister Therese began to introduce her around. As though saving the best for last, she finally introduced her to a young man. Molly thought to herself-wow, he is one good lookin' guy. And that he was. Six feet tall. Pleasant smile. Blue eyes. Easy to look at and easy to talk to. They were around the same age. Both single. His name a good Irish one – Liam Callahan.

Sister Therese suggested that they sit, have a drink and get to know one another. Molly thought that was a great idea. So did Liam. They found a quiet corner and began to visit. Liam was a member of the US House of Representatives. He represented the residents of the Rittenhouse Square section of Philadelphia. His family was in the construction business with more than a three generation history. A well known construction company in the Philadelphia area focusing on high rise commercial buildings and center city apartments. The family believed in the concept of helping those less fortunate than themselves. Being in the construction business they were also committed to conservation of resources. Resources both natural and man made.

Molly thought to herself I like this man on several levels. They appeared to have similarities in many areas. He was definitely easy to talk to and definitely easy to be with. Friendly. Irish heritage. A strong family history that is supportive and important to all members. Molly then talked about her family, their history, and the areas of common interests. And there were many. However, they would discover that there was definitely one area where there was a huge difference. That would not be discovered until several weeks later.

They both agreed that they should join the rest of the group. Unaware of the time they suddenly realized that they had been talking for more than an hour. Sister Therese smiled as they approached her, "Well it is obvious the two of you had no problem talking. I am sure you will be seeing each other again. Soon, I suppose."

They all had a good laugh. Shortly after the evening came to a close. The two exchanged telephone numbers and promised to stay in touch. Liam offered to walk Molly home. Explaining that she lived only a block away and that would not be necessary. He did not argue, simply thanked her for a pleasant evening and they left. The short walk home found Molly reliving the hour or so that they were together. A really pleasant evening and she hoped that he would indeed call her.

He did. Several times. They spent the next several weeks getting to know each other on a more personal basis. They found that they enjoyed each other and had a great deal in common. At this time it was purely a platonic relationship. Dinner. Movies. He invited her to spend a weekend in Philadelphia at the home of his family. Molly agreed. She had never been to Philadelphia and looked forward to the visit.

Liam picked her up early on a Saturday morning for the two hour drive through some beautiful rural country. They arrived at his family home, 1823 Delancey Street, in Rittenhouse Square in the heart of center city Philadelphia. A beautiful, upscale neighborhood to say the least. Townhouses dating back more than 100 years. Four story homes on tree lined streets. Molly was quite impressed. It was here that she began to realize how wealthy the Callahan family must be. One would never realize that fact the way her friend conducted himself.

A member of the United States House of Representatives. A successful family business. It was during this visit she discovered just how committed the Callahan family was to helping the less fortunate residents of the City of Brotherly Love. They were the epitome of the designation.

They provided all of the funding for a facility that carried the name-The Manger. A home for unwed mothers. An alternative to abortion. The young women could stay there for one year. They received first class medical treatment. Taught skills for caring for a baby. Attended class to learn how to earn a living.

The construction company recruited young men from the ghettos and enrolled them as an apprentice in a skills training program. Plumbers. Welders. Electricians. Carpenters.

When Molly heard this, she was speechless. At one point she suggested that they take a walk. Liam said fine and off they went for a walk thru Rittenhouse Square. An absolutely beautiful park located right in the heart of the city. It was during the walk that Molly discovered the family political views.

They were politically conservative. Boom. Was this going to be a problem in their relationship. Liam gave a confusing look and asked, "Why. Why would this present a problem?" Molly replied that she was a leftist and liberal.

Bill replied, "I think we want the same thing for society. A better life and opportunity for all citizens. It seems to me the conservative view is to accomplish this goal through private citizens. People on the left believe that it can be best accomplished through government and taxes. We all want the same result. Two different methods of accomplishing same goal."

They managed to enjoy the rest of the weekend. But there was not any question the conversation put a damper on the weekend. Late in the afternoon they drove back to Washington. The trip was a bit on the quiet side.

The next several weeks were busy ones for both of them. Congress was in session and hearings were being held on a variety of subjects. Liam's committee was discussing the topic of clean water. He decided to call Molly and ask her to testify on the subject. She was surprised to say the least. He went on to say that he had read a paper that she had written on the topic about conditions in Appalachia and the text that she was teaching at the University.

This pleased her on several levels. First, the respect he had for her professional credentials. And on a personal basis. She was beginning to think that the brief political conversation they had in Philadelphia had scared him away. When she told him this he laughed! Not at all was his response. The hearings were totally consuming. He suggested that she testify toward the end of the week prior to the committee adjourning for several days. When the hearings ended, they could drive to the Jersey Shore for the weekend. The family owned a vacation home on the small island community of Ocean City.

Molly agreed to the plan. Her testimony went well. This was of course an entirely new experience for her. An extremely exciting experience. Testifying before the Congress of the United States. Maybe someone believed that her credentials were worthy of being heard. Liam reassured her that was the case. Congress wanted to hear from people that were experts on a variety of topics. Wow! Someone believes that I am an expert.

The hearings ended and shortly after they began the drive to Ocean City, New Jersey. During the three hour plus drive he told her the history of the Jersey Shore. All along the eastern coast of the Atlantic Ocean the towns are referred as the "beach." Not so in New Jersey. The New Jersey coastline is referred to as the "Jersey Shore." A truly special place.

The Callahan family owned a vacation home in the small community of Ocean City. An island seven miles long and one mile wide. The home was on the corner of Wesley Avenue and Seventh Street. A large, three story Victorian home, with twelve bedrooms, built in the late 1800's. The house was three blocks from the beach and a boardwalk some two and half miles long.

He gave her a history of this special slice of the Jersey Shore. It began as a religious town for summer retreats in 1879. The house on Wesley Avenue was built not long after. The town began, and remains, a "dry" town. Meaning you cannot buy alcoholic beverages anywhere on the island. The town began with the slogan "America's Family Resort." The island just north was Atlantic City. A much different place.

They had a wonderful weekend together. Their conversations covered a wide range of topics-including politics. Very enlightening. Yes, her family was liberal. Her father was a member of parliament-MP and a member of the Labour Party. The more they talked the better she understood that both families wanted to help people have a better life. Driving back to Washington she closed her eyes for a bit of sleep and thought maybe we can still be close. Who knows where the relationship will go? Maybe they will just let time answer the question.

Monday morning arrived and it was back to the classroom. The semester was coming to a close and the experience was wonderful. The university had extended an invitation for her to return next fall. Sister Therese had seen to it that possibility would happen. The two were in regular contact the entire fall and early winter. Sister Therese was well aware of how the relationship between Molly and Liam was developing. And she was quite pleased. She suggested to Molly to simply let the relationship unfold as it will. She told Molly that they were both good people. Stay in touch by mail and telephone. Continue to work for the causes that you believe in. Molly valued Sister Therese's input. They were friends before Molly came to Washington and the relationship was now at another whole level.

The fall semester was drawing to a close. She thanked both Sister Therese and the Administration for inviting her and extending the invitation for the following calendar year. She assured them she was honored and would definitely be back. Later that week she spent an afternoon with Sister and discussed a variety of topics-at the top was their mutual friend-Congressman Liam Callahan.

The night before departing the two had a pleasant dinner in a downtown Washington restaurant, a long walk along the Potomac River, and passed the great monuments-Washington Monument, Lincoln, and the Mall.

They agreed to stay in touch over the winter. It was definitely difficulty to say goodbye. During an honest exchange they agreed taking the relationship to another level would be difficult. Feelings and emotions were strong by both of them.

Liam talked about his commitment to his political career was very important. He was in line to become a committee chairman. Some of his associates advised that Speaker of the House was a real possibility. Affecting the direction of the country was in the realm of possibility.

Then there was the company business and philanthropic interests were a part of who he was. The long family generational history of being connected to Philadelphia. His father getting older.

Molly said that she understood clearly what he was saying. She is strongly committed to the issues that are important in her life. The marginalized people of the world. Her travels around the world to those places that do not have clean water. The environment. Lecturing at the University of Stockholm. The spiritual retreats she conducts in Visby. The family long connection to the English Channel area. The catholic church. The family business.

They agreed to stay in touch and let life unfold the way that it will. They embraced, kissed, and said good night.

Early the next morning she left for the airport and before long was on her way to the Heathrow airport and London. The long flight gave her plenty of time to reflect on the events of the past several months-and reflect she did. On the top of the list was the name Liam Callahan. There was not any question that he was special and that something was stirred within her. Just how would it all work out. Oh well... time will tell.

Her work at Catholic University was extremely rewarding on several levels. She loved being in the classroom. The students (especially the girls) were interested and committed to the subjects that she taught. The dynamics and give and take is exciting. She looked forward to returning next fall.

Time with her friend Sister Therese Kelly was enjoyable. Their time together and intimate conversations deepened the relationship and strengthened the bond between the two women. Molly felt that she could share at all levels and not feel threatened. Sister Therese was indeed a dear friend.

The trips to Philadelphia and all the history of this great city along with spending time in Ocean City, New Jersey and learning about the "Jersey Shore" was wonderful. Molly said that she heard the term "Shoobies" the local residents used frequently. She asked, "What is "Shoobies." Liam laughed and then went on to explain the origin of the word. People that came down from Philadelphia for the day usually brought a picnic lunch in a shoebox. Slowly the term evolved into "Shoobie." In other words, a shorthand way of identifying weekend visitors from Philadelphia. The trip, with its own vocabulary was an education in itself.

There was no doubt in her mind that she would be back.

The entire family was home when she arrived in Folkestone. Hugs, kisses, and questions were in abundance. What was the best part of America? How did it feel teaching American Students? How did Ocean City compare to the English Channel? Are you going to go back?

Molly began laughing and told them to give her a minute to get settled just a bit. She promised them that she would answer all their questions. She noticed that her mother was teary eyed. Walked over gave her a big hug and kiss on the cheek and asked, "Why are you crying?"

CC said, "I am afraid we are going to lose you. Everyone wants to go to America. We really missed seeing you."

"Not to worry mother. I know where my roots are. I know where my family is. I love Little Dublin. Don't worry. Don't worry."

Michael came over and hugged the both of them and said, "We are a family and nothing will break it up. Not even the Atlantic Ocean and America."

Then he summoned everyone together-CC, Molly, Jimmy Magee, Delanie, and Quinn-and they had one of their famous group hugs.

The plan was for Molly to stay at home for several days before heading off to Visby and her world there. Later that night while lying in bed before sleep came, she thought about how blessed she was with her family. She thought her father was right-nothing could happen that would split up the family. A sound sleep followed.

PART FIVE

MICHAEL AND THE "THE CHUNNEL" PROJECT

Michael's career and sphere of influence continued to grow in Parliament. He rose to the position of Chairman of the powerful Infrastructure Committee. The committee was responsible for (but not limited to) road, bridges, and tunnels throughout the United Kingdom.

For the past several years he was laying the groundwork to be in the position to propose building a tunnel under the English Channel from Folkestone to Calais, France

The title "Chunnel Project" became a high-profile description of his vision for a tunnel under the English Channel from Folkestone, England to Calais, France. Michael was very much aware of the history of such a possibility. Over the years, politicians made feint attempts. But their efforts were always met with resistance from various sources – disagreements between the English and the French (nothing new about disagreements between the two countries). Cost and the means of raising the funds. Taxes and strong objections from citizens on both sides of the English Channel. Mostly from citizens residing in parts of their countries far from the channel. Paying taxes for such a folly (in their view) that provides no advantage to their remote part of the country. The list of reasons for failure are long and varied.

None of this discouraged Michael. He believed that the tunnel would provide huge benefits to all parts of the two countries. He was passionate whenever he discussed the project and the possibility of making it happen. Over the years, as a member of Parliament he delivered speeches throughout the entire United Kingdom, including Scotland, Wales and Northern Ireland. He worked the backrooms of the UK Parliament talking with members from both Tory and Labour Parties in an effort to build support. The harder he worked the more confident he became. Support was definitely growing. He realized that he had a long way to go and made a decision to approach the French Parliament.

During his time in Parliament he had many occasions to interact with his counterparts in the French Parliament. He developed friends and relationships with members of both the National Assembly and the Senate. France has a two chamber form of government. The same as the United Kingdom. That was a huge help to Michael. He was well acquainted with the systems of both countries. How committees work. How negotiations and compromise develop. He was excellent at the process.

As part of his presentation he always outlined the history of the many attempts:

The first attempt occurred in 1802. A French mining engineer, Albert Mathieu, presented the first ever design for a Channell Tunnel.

Followed closely in 1802 by an English design proposal by Henri Mottray.

French mining engineer, Thome de Gamond spent 30 years by mid19th century developing seven different designs.

Michael was quick to point out that the French was always on the cutting edge in technical engineering proposals. Michael always made it clear the French led the way and the United Kingdom was supportive. An example of his expert political skills at work.

He began to realize that his time was being consumed by the project. Something needed to be done regarding his boat business. He definitely felt a pull in two different directions. The conclusion that he came to was that changes needed to happen. He told CC about the conflict within himself. She smiled and replied that the situation was quite apparent. Then as a follow up she went on to say that he needed to turn day to day operations over to Jimmy Magee.

"Yes, that is the answer, why didn't I think of that!?" he shouted. CC continued, "the obvious answer is that you are so engrossed in what you are doing. Of course, the boat business is important. It is important to the entire family and the source of our living. But the chunnel would affect the entire United Kingdom and all its citizens. Not to mention France. You have a responsibility to carry the project to conclusion. Jimmy Magee is more than qualified to manage the boat business. You do agree, right?"

He went on to say that he had no question about Jimmy Magee's ability and in reality, he has been doing just that for the last several months. CC suggested that the four of them have a discussion after dinner. Michael telephoned Jimmy and asked if he and Delanie could come to dinner to be followed with a business discussion.

Jimmy Magee said of course. Delanie could see from his expression that something was going on. Something important. When she asked, he said that he had no idea. But from the tone of his father's voice it sounded serious.

During dinner they had their usual family talk about such things as Quinn, activities at the church, CC gave a report on the pediatric wing of the hospital. Typical family topics for the Magee clan.

Jimmy finally asked, "What is going on Dad?"

With that said, Michael began. The chunnel project has become more than a full time project. Completion of the chunnel would affect countless numbers of people on both sides of the English Chunnel. Untold economical impact to both countries. He did not want to screw up. I am going to turn our business ventures over to you. I am totally confident in your ability.

Jimmy was stunned. His father had poured his life into building the boat business. A business that was now located in England, the island nation of Mallorca, Australia, and prospects to expand to the French Riviera. And just like that his father was turning it over to Jimmy. He realized what the tunnel could mean to the entire region of this part of the world. A big deal. A really big deal.

Looking across the table he saw Delanie smiling and nodding yes. Tell him yes. You have to do it and you are capable of doing it.

They all stood up and gathered for one of their famous family group hugs. A new chapter was about to begin. Michael would devote all of his waking moments to the channel project. Jimmy Magee would the same regarding the boat business.

The next three years found Michael totally immersed in the project. Everything seemed to take a back seat. He worked feverishly as though he was racing against the clock. Trips to Paris to visit with politicians and businessmen. Speeches all over the United Kingdom. He was definitely making progress. His presentations and arguments were difficult to disagree with. He was a man on a mission and would not be deterred. CC and the other family members were very supportive. Interestingly, when they were talking to other people, they would invariably bring the subject up. Their good friend Father O'Rourke joined the effort. He would give a progress report from the altar. The entire Little Dublin was excited. A tunnel that brought traffic into Folkestone from the Continent would have far reaching results.

Whenever he needed a break from the pressure and exhaustion one source of recovery was always there. Quinn. His granddaughter. She was now a teenager and the two of them had developed a strong and loving relationship. Michael would take an afternoon off and search for her. She could usually be found somewhere close to the boatyard.

Quinn loved the open water as much as her grandfather. Maybe a bit more if that was possible. She grew up spending any free time at the boatyard. Together they built a 20 foot sloop that was perfect for two people to sail. Try as they may, both Jimmy Magee and Delanie could not convince her that the way to success was education. Working on boats and sailing were her life.

Michael mentioned to Jimmy that Quinn reminded him of someone else that he knew – Jimmy Magee. The discussions they had about Jimmy going to University and the struggles over the whole matter. Finally, both Jimmy and Delanie conceded. If this is her passion that would be fine. They trusted Michael and knew that he would not do anything that would jeopardize Quinn's future. More importantly they were delighted to see how Michael and Quinn had developed such a powerful relationship and bond. It was a beautiful thing to see how much they enjoyed being together. Talking. Laughing. Hugging. Michael teaching the ways of the sea.

Quinn had definitely developed into an experienced sailor. The two of them would spend an entire afternoon sailing the open waters of the English Channel. They would sail into some little private cove that they had discovered and eat the lunch that CC prepared for them. Quinn was always asking question about the history of their family. She loved listening to her grandfather's stories. He went on to tell that her ancestors were true pathfinders and people that Quinn could and should be proud of. With nothing but the desire to provide a better life for future generations of the Magee and Kelly family they left Ireland and escaped the Irish Potato Famine of the 1800's. He would tell her that she had a wonderful heritage and she had a responsibility to carry that forward. Quinn began to understand why her grandfather was so committed to the channel project.

On one occasion she asked about her twin brother and his death. Michael did the best he could to try and explain what happened. Quinn asked why would God let that happen? He always relied on his friends, Father O'Rourke's comments, "God is a loving God and we have to have faith. More will be revealed." He then talked about the commitment her grandmother made to the pediatric wing of the hospital. Countless little babies have ben saved through her efforts. And that will continue for generations to come. With that said, Quinn noticed a tear in the eyes of her grandfather. She stood up, gave him a big hug and said, "I love you and Grandmom."

PART SIX

THE AUTUMN OF THEIR YEARS

Michael continued his efforts with great passion. Progress was clearly happening. Although he was frustrated that things were not happening faster. Then to his surprise one of the key figures in the French Parliament came out publicly in support of the tunnel. This was a major movement. He now had a strong advocate in France. Momentum was developing in the UK as well. He told CC this whole thing just might happen...and sooner rather than later. Several months passed quietly and then the big moment was announced.

The Prime Minister of the United Kingdom and the President of France were going to meet and sign the proper documents to proceed with the construction of the tunnel. Michael had done all the research, campaigning, speech making, networking, and hard work. Now that the project was about to become a reality two politicians take center stage and the credit with a great deal of fanfare. They were doing this without any prior notice to Michael. The fact that both men were from the opposition party of Michael, might have played a part. That's politics. A nasty business. He understood that intellectually. On a common decency level, he struggled with the way it was handled.

When his friends and family found this out, they were furious and said so to Michael. He told everyone to relax. He confessed that when he first heard about the two heads of state meeting without including him, he too was upset. Extremely upset. He visited his friend Father O'Rourke and exploded. How dare they! Father O'Rourke reminded Michael that they are politicians, (he reminded Michael that he too was a politician.)

This tunnel is a big deal to both countries. A perfect opportunity to be center stage. It is natural to do what they did. Not very nice but understandable. You kept your eye on the prize and brought the tunnel to a successful conclusion. Is not that the most important thing? It is amazing what we can do when we do not worry who takes the credit. All of that made sense to Michael. Father O'Rourke usually does. A cool and level head. That was why he always called on his friend in moment of high anxiety. Michael told his family and friends that he was fine. Yes, there might be a small smidge of resentment. But the completion of the tunnel is the most important thing to consider. Not the ego of two politicians.

Shortly following the press conference of the two leaders the Parliament of the United Kingdom reconvened. The whispering in chamber halls was all about how Michael had been slighted. Several members (from both parties) approached Michael and expressed their indignation with the two men. By now Michael had developed a response to those who approached him. It was how he truly felt. First, he thanked them for their kind comments and support. Then he would quickly add that he was fine; adding that the singular most important fact is "The Chunnel Project" is going to become reality. For almost 200 years the issue has come and gone. Now it is going to happen. Citizens will be able to cross the English Channel in their automobile.

Nonetheless, there was frustration on behalf of members of the parliament (MP). Michael went on to further give some insight into his thoughts. He told them that one day travelers would take the tunnel for granted. Not even give a second thought about the history or when it was built. Michael compared himself to a pebble on the beach as to his part in the history of the tunnel. He believed that people like the French engineer, Albert Mathieu, who first proposed he possibility of a tunnel in 1803, French engineer, Thome de Gamond, who spent more than 30 years developing seven different designs, would be pleased that it was finally going to happen.

Continuing on he stated that he was but one more person struggling with the vision of a tunnel. He offered that years from now, the two heads of state that grabbed the headlines will be long forgotten.

All of his statements above did in fact come true.

Now that the tunnel was going to happen the mundane details followed. Technical work of engineers. Floating bonds to raise the money. Letting bids out. Governmental regulations. Reams and reams of regulations. The list seemed endless. But the fact remained that the "The Chunnel" will happen.

Life in the Magee household returned to a more normal routine. Without question Michael was around a great deal more. Those sailing outings with Quinn happened more frequently. CC was even finding time to visit with her mentor and friend, Annie Ackley, in London. She even got back into her painting and sculpting. Although everyone realized that her first commitment, as always, was the pediatric wing of the hospital. Jimmy Magee and Delanie continued to manage the various boating operations. Delanie discovered she had some talent in the area of marketing and finance, Molly was back in Visby with her varied activities. Lecturing at the University of Stockholm, writing spiritual books, conferences on the environment, and conducting her all important spiritual retreats. Even Quinn was engaged. She was doing well in her school studies (although no scholar) and working at the boatyard (her true love) with life time family friend and mentor, Cap'n Fitz.

CC decided it was time to have a celebration with family and friends. The past few years were stressful for everyone. Not just the family. They had many friends in Little Dublin and they saw how hard everyone in the Magee family was working.

The celebration was arranged for a Sunday afternoon following Mass. CC asked Father O'Rourke for his thoughts on having the affair at the park across from the church. He thought that was an excellent idea. Father O'Rourke announced the event a few weeks in advance. He told the congregation that everyone was invited. The day arrived and it was indeed a beautiful day.

All of the immediate family was there. Molly came in from Visby a few days ahead. Cap'n Fitz was not feeling well. Age was starting to catch up with the old sailor. He told CC that there was not anyway he was going to miss this tribute. Most of Little Dublin residents were there. The Magee family was held in high esteem in the community. Father O'Rourke gave a blessing and had some kind words for his childhood friend. He then introduced Michael and suggested that he say a few words.

Michael felt very uncomfortable. Over the years he had made countless remarks and speeches in Parliament and other venues with no problem. Somehow this was different. He was among his family, friends, and neighbors. Receiving all this attention simply made him feel ill at ease. Nonetheless, he did make a few comments...How grateful he was for the support and encouragement he received over the last several years in making the tunnel project a reality. He had no doubt it would not have been possible absent of the support. Wherever he went in the community someone would approach him with kind words and tell him how grateful they were. Everyone realized what a huge economic benefit the tunnel would be to Little Dublin.

His remarks were brief and he concluded that it was time for a good old fashion Irish picnic. The weather was perfect. The Irish music was perfect. Food was bountiful and delicious. All the old Irish tune s were playing – "When Irish Eyes Are Smiling" – young and hold were doing the Irish Jig. The sun began to set far too soon. But set it did and time to head home.

CC and Michael walked the short distance home and sat on the porch in their favorite old rocking chairs. Michael made some comment about how important the rocking chairs were in their life. Over the years they made many major life decisions while the two of them rocked and discussed the issues at hand. Molly went home with Jimmy Magee and Delanie and Quinn. They thought, correctly, that their mother and father might want to be alone at this time.

Looking out over the English Channel, Michael remarked, "Just think CC one day a tunnel will connect the United Kingdom with the continent of Europe and the Magee and Kelly family played a small part in making that happen. He then added that their ancestors help build the railroad that now spans England from the Irish Sea to the English Channel."

CC looked over to Michael and took his hand, "That is so true. Hopefully we can be proud of our heritage. A typical Irish citizen will be able to take a ferry boat across the Irish Sea and ride a train to Folkestone and then through The Chunnel and arrive on the European Continent. Just think Michael, our family is a part of that history and making that trip possible. We, a family of such humble roots, can include that in our genealogy." She stood up, kissed him tenderly on the head, said how proud she is of him, and went to the kitchen to make a cup of tea for them.

While preparing the tea and biscuits the telephone rang. She answered and a member of the Administration Department of the Pediatric Wing of the hospital was on the other end. It seemed as though there was a procedure question and disagreement between two employees. CC had grown in such stature whenever there was a dispute or disagreement it was referred to CC for resolution. The phone call took some 15 minutes. CC hung up the phone and gathered the teapot and biscuits and headed out to the front porch.

Still caught up in the excitement of the day she talked to Michael as she walked through the house and out to the porch. She was a bit surprised that Michael did not respond to the rapid fire barrage of questions she asked. Putting the tea on the table she looked over and had her answer. He was sound asleep. At least that was her first thought. He had a busy day. Lots of attention. Something that always made him feel uncomfortable. Once again, she called him by name. Again, no response. She began to shake him by the arm. No movement. She was beginning to panic.

She went to the pone and called their family friend and doctor, Bill MacNeill. He arrived in minutes. A quick examination and he looked up to CC and gave her the news she was terrified to hear. Michael apparently had a fatal heart attack. He embraced CC as she fell into the doctor's arms crying uncontrollably. The next several minutes were like a nightmare. A sedative was given to CC. The doctor called Jimmy Magee and Delanie, Molly, and Father O'Rourke.

Over the next several days the planning and preparation for a funeral Mass at the parish and an Irish wake were made. Somehow CC managed to deal with what had to be done. Molly, Jimmy Magee, and Delanie were at her side through the entire process. Father O'Rourke visited every day and made all the arrangements with the local funeral director for the viewing and for the Mass.

CC and Father O'Rourke were having a conversation and she went on to say that the pain is unbearable. During the day, with the help of sedatives, she managed to get through what she had to. It was difficult as she went through and dealt with the necessary events of the day. Almost in a fog. The real difficulty came at night when she climbed into an empty bed. Through tears she told her Priest and friend that they knew each other since grammar school days. Grew up and married. Raised a family. Went through good times and some not so good times.

Now she is alone in bed. No longer comforting each other. No spooning. No hugging and telling the other – "it will be okay" – whatever that meant. She went on to say that no amount of any sedative would relieve the ache and emptiness in her heart – a void that will never be filled. Father gave her a big hug and replied, "CC somehow, with the help of God we will get through this together and as a family that is filled with love."

The night of the Irish Wake the sidewalk in front of the house was filled with friends and neighbors. CC sat next to the casket surrounded with family members. Most of Little Dublin was in attendance. While it was an emotional evening tomorrow would be a great deal more emotional.

The funeral Mass was set for 11:00 AM. The crowd began filling the church well before. In addition to friends and neighbors, politicians and dignitaries from London were arriving. Father O'Rourke informed CC that several of them requested to make a few remarks following the eulogy. CC told him that Michael would not approve of the attention from politicians; however, any local Little Dublin friends who wanted to ay a word or two that would be fine. Father O'Rourke passed those comments along to the London visitors.

Mass was about to begin. The six pallbearers (all local friends from schoolboy days) began the procession into church with the choir singing one of Michael's favorite tunes from World War II-The White Cliffs of Dover. The Brits loved this song. It was a rallying song for all of England. Michael shared with CC they would play the song on the ship through the sound system at night when the war was silent. Sailors laid in their hammocks during these rare times and reminisced. Very emotional lyrics...

THE WHITE CLIFFS OF DOVER

There'll be blue birds over the White Cliffs of Dover,
Tomorrow, just you wait and see
I'll never forget the people I met braving those angry sky's
I remember well as the shadows fell
The light of hope in their eyes
And though I'm far away I still can hear them say
Sun's up for when the dawn comes up
There'll be bluebirds over the White Cliffs of Dover
Tomorrow, just you wait and see
There'll be love and laughter
And peace ever after
Tomorrow, when the world is free.

Not a dry eye was to be found in the entire church. Several friends offered their feelings about this Special neighbor. Clearly, he would be missed – greatly.

The services were moved outside to the parish cemetery just a few paces from the church. Father O'Rourke offered a final blessing. A short distance from the gravesite another former friend from grammar school played Amazing Grace on the bag pipes. Very powerful. Very moving.

Lots of tears.

Several months passed and everyone struggled to move on with life. Both CC and Father O'Rourke told the family and friends that is exactly what Michael would want to happen. Michael often talked about how proud he was to be a member of the Magee family. How fortunate and blessed that he had been. A wonderful family. Great business career. Served his country during World War II and Parliament. Hopefully, he made a contribution and the community is now better and that he made a difference. That he did.

So, move on they did. Each member of his family and circle of friends did their best. But make no mistake missed he was and missed he will be.

ᴍ

CC was busy at the hospital trying to focus on the matter of babies with health issues. This was the one activity that would divert her from thinking about Michael. The phone rang. She answered and was a bit surprised to hear the voice of a member of Parliament. One of Michael's close allies in his efforts regarding the Chunnel Project.

He told her that there was a group of five MP's who would like to meet with her and discuss something that they would like to do as a form of gratitude and a lasting memory of Michael for his efforts in bringing the tunnel to a reality.

CC agreed to meet with them at their convenience. She did say that both she and Michael would be reluctant to a "monument" (whatever that meant) of any type. The meeting was scheduled for the following week. They would be happy to come down from London and meet in her home. CC was fine with that.

They suggested that if she wanted the children to be there that would be fine. CC thanked them for the offer, but said she would prefer to meet alone until more details were available.

On the appointed day and time, the five members arrived at her home. CC knew only one personally. Interestingly, they were not all from Michaels's party, nor were they all from England. The group was a true cross section – one from Wales, one from Scotland, one from Northern Ireland, and two from England. Representation from every part of the United Kingdom. This was by design. The group wanted the message to go out to not only CC and family but to everyone that this proposal and efforts of Michael are appreciated by all of the citizens of the United Kingdom.

The committee went on to say that work on the tunnel has in fact begun. More contracts will be let out to engineering firms, steel contractors, tunnel builders, and architects. They then got to the heart of the meeting. Parliament has approved the funds to build a green space park at the entrance of the tunnel on the English side.

The park will cover some five acres. Trees, flowers, bushes, and various plants that are indigenous to the area will cover the area. A 500 foot pier that will extend out in channel will be included. Boat slips for personal watercraft will be on both sides of the pier. A covered pavilion will stand at the end of the pier. A small restaurant selling fish and chips and soft drinks will be available. A playground for young children. An area at the end of the pier will be arranged in such a way to take photographs. A Guest House with 50 rooms. The channel and the world famous White Cliffs of Dover will provide an inspiring background. There will not be any fees to access the park or any of the activities.

At the entrance to the park will be a plaque that reads:

THIS PARK IS DEDICATED TO MICHAEL MATTHEW MAGEE, A CITIZEN OF THE UNITED KINGDOM, AN INDIVIDUAL WHO GAVE A LARGE PART OF HIS LIFE TO MAKE CERTAIN THAT THIS TUNNEL WAS BUILT TO THE BENEFIT OF ALL CITIZENS OF THE UNITED KINGDOM, FRANCE, AND CITIZENS FROM AROUND THE WORLD.

The plaque brought tears to CC. She shared that Michael would love the park and marina for pleasure watercraft. He would love the "no fees" part. She asked if she could add one more sentence to the plaque. Their response was "of course".

She then went on to say that his favorite optimistic philosophical belief is "THE BEST IS YET TO COME".

The committee agreed unanimously.

Hugs were exchanged and CC thanked everyone for this high recognition. She went on to say that Michael was a modest man, but she believed that he would approve of the project. And if the plaque had to be a part of the agreement, he would be okay with that.

The first thing CC did when they left was to call the family and share what just happened. They all agreed that their father was more than worthy of the recognition. With that said it was time to move on and live life to its fullest – and that they did. Find new projects to develop and continue the legacy of the Magee history. A legacy that had its beginnings in the 1840's when the first immigrants crossed the Irish Sea on a ferry boat.

EPILOGUE

CATHERINE COLLEEN KELLY
"CC"

CC lived the rest of her life in the family home that had been in the family for generations. She continued creating art in various forms and donated the proceeds to various charities. All of the profits went to her passion-The Pediatric Wing of the hospital.

JIMMY MAGEE AND DELANIE

They continued to manage the boat business at the various locations around the world. Continuing the lessons learned from Michael, their father, they gave part ownership to the people responsible for the success of each location. They watched as Quinn, their daughter, grew and became involved in the business.

MOLLY MAGEE

Devoted her life to the various activities that were her true passion. She gained an international reputation in environmental issues – with clean water at the top of her list – for the marginalized people of the world. Molly maintained a platonic relationship with her life long friend-Liam Callan.

She made regular visits to Washington DC, the Maryknoll Sisters, and her dear friend, Liam.

LIAM CALLAN

He continued a relationship with Molly. But as her commitment was to the environment his was to politics. He rose to the powerful position of Speaker of the House in Congress. Liam never wavered from his political commitment to those less fortunate citizens.

Interestingly, the two of them accomplished their mission from entirely different political positions and beliefs.

QUINN

She grew into a beautiful young woman and immersed herself in the family business. To say that she became an excellent sailor would be an understatement. Quinn could build sailboats as well as any of the veteran employees. She made regular visits to Ireland and spent time with both her namesake, Quinn, on Ashton Island and her grandmother, Maureen.

The relationship with her grandmother grew stronger, much stronger, with the passing of time. She was able to accomplish what her mother, Delanie, could not.

FATHER O'ROURKE

After a lifetime of service to the parish Our Lady, Help of Christians he retired. Arrangements were made for him to have residence in the Rectory for the rest of his days. He loved the Parish, Little Dublin, and all of the residents. He often said how blessed and fortunate he was and could not imagine a better life – serving God and the good people of this little parish.

Made in the USA
Middletown, DE
16 August 2024